CINDY DORMINY

SAM squared

Sam Squared
Red Adept Publishing, LLC
104 Bugenfield Court
Garner, NC 27529
https://RedAdeptPublishing.com/

Cover Art by Streetlight Graphics[1]

This is a work of fiction. Names, characters, places, and incidents either are the product of the author's imagination or are used fictitiously, and any resemblance to locales, events, business establishments, or actual persons—living or dead—is entirely coincidental.

---

1.   http://StreetlightGraphics.com

Chapter One

Samantha

Sweat covers my palms and trickles down my back as I prepare to take my two shots at the free throw line. The Bulldogs' players wave their hands to distract me. The ref throws me the ball, and I twirl it around in my hands, once to calm my nerves, another time for good luck. I flick my gaze to the scoreboard. The Bulldogs lead by two points with only fifteen seconds left on the clock. The sounds of the cheering crowd and my teammates fade away. The only noise I hear is my own breath being sucked in and blown out as I calm my nerves.

Bounce, bounce. Knees bent, arms over head, release, and *swoosh*. All net. Oh yeah. One more. I can do this. The second one hits the rim and teeters on the edge before it falls into the basket.

"Sam-Man!"

Even through the cheering, I pick out that deep, silky voice. I don't have to scan the crowd to know Samuel—or as I call him, Mule—is at the top of the bleachers with all his cool friends, hands cupped around his mouth like a megaphone, cheering for me.

When I least expect it, he'll acknowledge my good game. It may only be a smile or a knuckle bump—or more likely, a snide remark—but I'll know he was watching and that he approved. He drives me crazy most of the time, but when I'm on the court, his presence is calming.

Of course, I'd never tell him that. His head is big enough as it is.

We're tied when the Bulldogs take possession out of bounds. The inbounder quickly tosses the ball to a teammate, and we pressure her into wasting most of the five seconds she has to dribble, pass, or shoot. She lobs the basketball to her guard, who zooms right past Jenny. The guard bounce passes to her teammate, but Jenny bats the basketball away. Paige reaches the loose ball first. She dribbles toward our basket while taking a quick second to glance in the coach's direction. He points to the clock, giving her the green light, then motions toward me.

The crowd yells, "Nine, eight, seven."

"Hey," I yell at Paige.

She jerks her head toward me then lobs the ball. It sails through the air, landing in my hands.

"Four, three, two."

Coach doesn't have to tell me what needs to be done. I go for the three. I jump into the air as the ball flies out of my hands, and I'm airborne. The ball swooshes through the net before my feet hit the floor as the buzzer blares through the gym, and the place goes berserk.

Paige grabs me around the neck in a congratulatory hug.

"Samantha, what a shot!" She drags me to center court, where our team lines up to slap hands with the Bulldogs before we head to our locker rooms.

The last Bulldog says, "Good game."

"You too. Y'all didn't make it easy."

She smiles and walks off the court with the rest of her team.

Amid the ruckus, one voice stands out. "Saaam-Mannn."

After my shower, I change into street clothes, reliving the game. It shouldn't have been that close. If I had been hitting throughout the game, we would have beaten them by ten points easily.

But that shot... If the Auburn scout had been here, my scholarship would have been sealed, regardless of my saggy GPA. I let out a sigh as my phone buzzes. It might be my brother, Craig, wanting to know how I did tonight. He would have been right next to Samuel cheering me on if he wasn't away at college.

I retrieve it from my bag and swipe my finger across the screen, and my heart races faster than when I was on the court. An email from the college board testing site stares at me, letting me know my latest SAT scores are available. I squeeze my eyes shut and pray the results are better than last time. They can't be worse.

Not wanting to ruin the high from the game, I shove the phone into my back pocket and yank open the locker-room door to exit into the hallway. I'll deal with the message later, in private.

Heading toward the gymnasium where the boys' team warms up, I find Samuel leaning against the wall. He's a six-foot, gorgeous, cocky player who loves nothing more than to pester the living daylights out of me. Our families have known each other so long, we fall into the taking-baths-together-as-babies category. That's an image I'm glad I don't remember.

Most of the girls at school can't believe I don't fawn all over him like they do. He's a hot slice of pizza, but yuck. Good looks aren't enough to erase the snide comments he's slung my way over the years. I don't care if he's got long blond hair that girls line up to run their fingers through. There's not a scholarship big enough to get me that close to Nashville's finest Neanderthal.

"Hello, Sam-Man."

"What's up, Sam-Mule?"

We walk side by side toward the gym. "Nice shot."

Even though he irritates the crap out of me on a daily basis, I can't keep the smile off my face. It *was* an awesome shot. "Thanks."

"Good thing you got fouled at the end because... Ooo boy, the rest of your game..." He sucks a breath in through his teeth. "Not so good."

I get nose to nose with him. "What did you say?"

He takes a step back, jerks his head to the side to flip his hair out of his eyes, then holds his hands out in a defensive position. "Hey, stats don't lie. You were like ten for twenty-three from the field."

Oh no, he didn't go there. I cock my head to the side. "How do you know my field goal percentage?"

His mouth twitches with a slight grin, then he stretches his arms over his head in his usual "I'm stalling because I'm lying" tactic. Mule's T-shirt rises to expose his abs.

He smirks. "You done gawking, Sam?"

Eye roll. "Answer the question."

"I, uh, overheard when I walked past the scorers table."

That smarty pants did the math in his head. Show-off. "So what's Paige's percentage?"

He snorts and motions with his head for me to follow. "Sucky as always. She should stick to softball."

I am not going to let him get a rise out of me, so I force my emotions down a notch. "Says Mr. 'I Think I'll Sit This Year Out' King."

We round the corner to enter the gymnasium as the boys' team begins their game. Cheerleaders shake their pom-poms, among other things, to get the crowd psyched up.

Taking two steps at a time, he climbs toward the top of the bleachers, with me right behind him.

"I don't get it. Who quits sports their senior year? Hello? Scholarships."

He runs a hand through his messy hair and stares off into space. "There are other things that need my attention more."

"How do you not need... Oh yeah, it's because your dad's a doctor and you're so—"

His body swings around so fast I teeter on the step. He reaches out to steady me, the palm of his hand splaying across my back, and it feels a little too pleasant.

Samuel grits his teeth. "Zip it."

I nudge him to sit. "Oh please. You're still keeping up this charade?"

"Yep."

"Why does it matter if you're... you know, a"—I whisper in his ear—"genius?"

Before I know what he's doing, he throws an arm around me and clamps my mouth shut with his hand, causing a giggle to erupt from my throat. "That's supposed to be our little secret, Sam-Man."

Only Samuel would be embarrassed about being smart. He's got it stuck in his brain that he needs to appear as a slacker who doesn't care about grades, while he actually gets really ticked off if he misses one point on a test. If I had his problem, I would be shouting it from the top of the bleachers.

In all honesty, I probably have something to do with his attitude because I teased him about his intelligence in gym class during middle school. The razzing he got didn't do anything for our friendship. But he called me dumb, one label that hit too close to the heart.

One finger at a time, I pry his hand from my mouth. "You're mad that I know. And you still can't get over the fact I kicked your butt in T-ball when we were five. Holding a grudge isn't very attractive."

"Pfft."

"Not to mention crushing you in tennis and volleyball."

He throws a hand up to stop my bragging. "All right, you are jockier than me, but only because you care more."

"I have to care more." My father is unemployed and has to referee basketball games, not to mention clean up the school for extra money. And I am not a genius. Far from it.

The barbed words we lob at each other don't matter on days like this because we share a common love—basketball. Throughout the first half of the boys' game, Mule and I become the best armchair quarterbacks ever. Sometimes we agree, but most of the time, we fuss over each other's opinions, irritating everyone sitting near us, not to mention the referee—otherwise known as my father.

Mule points to the court. "Did you see that? Reaching in."

I jump up and yell, "Oh, come on, ref. Are you blind?"

My dad points to me and says, "One more loud comment, and I'll eject you both."

And he would. It's a good thing he's not allowed to ref *my* games because I'm pretty sure he'd be harder on me than any opponent.

Samuel's mouth drops open. "You wouldn't do that, would you, Mr. Baughman?"

Dad shakes his head one slow time and replies, "Try me."

With a firm hand on each shoulder, Mule forces me to sit. "I'd rather not get ejected unless I'm playing ball."

"Oh please. You saw it too."

"Yell at him when you get home."

"You know I will."

One of the cheerleaders on the opposing team waves at Mule then blows him a kiss.

"Gag. Have you run through all our cheerleaders and now are working your way through the other team's?"

He flashes a movie star smile and whips his hair out of his eyes. "Jealous?"

Gross. He doesn't deserve an eye roll. "Don't flatter yourself. Maybe I should tell her how much you used to cry when you would get dropped off at day care." I rub my eyes to remove fake tears.

"She loves me."

I do a full-body shiver. "Do you even know her name?"

"Not yet."

A sarcastic laugh bursts from my mouth. "You are unbelievable."

My phone buzzes in my back pocket. I pull it out to see I have a new email from my mother, who hasn't figured out how to text. Right as I click on the one from her, Mule jostles me when he stands to cheer for his friend who made a shot, causing my thumb to hit the link that opens my SAT scores. Note to self—don't autosave passwords.

All of my focus goes to that one email. No sound from the game or even the rowdy crowd can compete with my heartbeat pounding in my ears. I stare at my phone as my head swims so much I have to blink a few times to stay steady on my feet.

"Sam, what's wrong?"

My chest tightens as I shake my head. "I have to go."

He grabs my arm. "What's wrong?"

"Nothing." I jerk my arm away and stumble down the steps, out of the gymnasium, and toward my car in the parking lot. When I get to my VW Bug, I let my backpack slide to the ground and lean over the hood, staring at the email again. Surely I misread the results.

Nope.

Only I could have worse SAT scores the second time around. The Auburn recruiter made it crystal clear that my GPA and SAT scores had to be high. Mine are borderline mediocre at best. I have to face the fact I'm not going to Auburn. I'm going to be stuck doing a dead-end job like my mom and watch as all my friends go off to the schools of their choice.

A large, warm hand touches my arm. I swing around, ready to pounce, but it's only Samuel. A furrowed brow and concerned expression replaces his usual smiley eyes.

"What are you doing here?" I stuff my phone into my pocket then glue my arms to my side so I don't hit something.

"You seemed upset and now... Yeah, you're upset."

"I'm fine." My voice screeches so high it hurts my ears. "Please, go."

He shakes his head. "I can't do that."

"Yes, you can."

I find my keys and attempt to unlock my car, but my shaking hands aren't cooperating.

Stubborn Mule snatches the keys from me. "Sam, spill it. What's going on?"

Suddenly, the asphalt is way more interesting than gazing at his piercing eyes. He tips my chin up with a finger, and I swat it away. "You wouldn't understand."

"What makes you so sure of that?"

"Because..." I stare at the sky and take a deep breath, mentally watching my future swirl down the drain. With a clenched jaw, I say, "Because you are Mr. Perfect SAT."

He lets out a deep sigh. "I guess that means you didn't do great again."

With a trembling bottom lip, I shake my head. "I did worse. I think the only points I got were for spelling my name right." My voice catches in my throat. "My GPA stinks, I'm failing Trig, Coach has already given me a warning, and..."

When he touches my arm again, I jerk away. "Don't you pity me. I take pretty much anything from you. You can make fun of me, pick on me, tell me my percentages are too low, but don't ever feel sorry for me."

He takes a step back, holding his hands up in defense. "It's not pity, Sam."

"Pfft. Pity, teasing... Whatever it is, I don't need any of that." I snap my fingers. "But if you are able to hack into the college board system, that would be appreciated."

His eyes grow big as if I outed him on yet another hidden skill of his. He gives me a warning expression not to go there.

"I'm kidding."

His stormy expression makes me want to break down. It's not happy and playful. It's... I don't know what it is, but if he is feeling sorry for me, I might smack him.

"I'm really sorry," he says.

After a few more raspy breaths, I can form words. "Thanks. Make sure you write to me from whatever Ivy League school you choose."

"Sam..."

"I'm kidding, sort of. Go. I know you don't want to miss the half-time cheer routines." I hold out my hand for my keys.

He nibbles on his bottom lip, and I focus on my shoes to avoid staring.

"If you're sure," he says.

I paint on a fake smile, the kind I've perfected over the years to congratulate the opposing team when they win a game. "Positive."

We stare at each other another second, then he lets out a groan before he hands me the keys. "Actually, I need to get home anyway before my dad calls the National Guard."

"What did you do this time?"

With a wicked chuckle, he replies, "Nothing new. Just me being me. See you later, Sam-Man."

"Bye, Mule."

This day went from the best to the worst in less than an hour, and to top it off, Samuel knows. Thank goodness Mom will still be on her shift at the hospital and Dad's still working the basketball game, so I'll have the house to myself for a while. I can't let them know what's going on. I know it would be a burden on my family to send me to college, and we were all hoping a scholarship would allow me to go to my dream school. I must figure out something. I've come this far. I'm not going to give up. Not yet, at least.

Chapter Two

Samuel

Dad starts in on me before I get one foot inside the door. At least with his surgery schedule, he's usually gone before I wake up, reducing his lecture time.

"Sit." He points to the kitchen table.

Like an obedient dog, I plop next to Mom.

"What'd I do this time?"

He runs a hand through his hair. "You know."

"I didn't pull the fire alarm Monday. I made sure Mr. Henderson saw me leave the class with everyone else." I turn to Mom. Her eyes are sunken in with dark circles underneath. "We had to stand outside in the rain, and I practically caught a cold."

She stifles a cough, and I notice she's paler than usual.

"Did you get drunk when you visited Craig a few weeks ago?" Dad asks.

Son of a...

"Let me explain."

He clenches his fist and stares at the ceiling. "And you got into a fight? How many times have I told you—"

"I had it under control."

"We allowed you to go because you promised you wouldn't drink. You're underage, remember?" He paces through the kitchen while he pinches the bridge of his nose. "You punched a guy in the face. We talked about this. What were you thinking?"

I hang my head and let out a sigh, remembering what happened when Rocky said those things about Craig's sister. Nobody talks about Sam-Man like that.

Mom puts a clammy hand over mine. My heart sinks. I clench my fists so tight, my knuckles crackle. Dad swallows hard.

I turn my focus back to Mom. "What's going on?"

She sighs and has a defeated expression on her face. "Nothing. I'm fine. The scan showed no improvement." She glances at Dad, and he collapses in the chair next to her to wrap an arm around her.

My heart sinks as I stare at the ceiling. She's been doing so well, I really hoped it would be good news this time.

"It's not progression, so that's good," Dad says. He always has his doctor hat on, even when he's talking to us.

No, it's not.

Dad covers our hands with his, like we used to do. "I really need you to please keep your shenanigans to a... minimum."

Squeezing my eyes shut, I give him a slight nod. Worrying about me isn't doing her any favors. In fact, it might be making her worse.

Worst son on the planet.

"You quit sports. You're bored in school. What's next? Juvenile detention?"

"No." I blow out a breath. "I'll try to..."

"Straighten up," Mom adds.

Dad finishes his standard saying, "And fly right."

"You want me to be more like Mason."

Mom smiles. "Nothing wrong with that."

My cousin is a great guy, but he wears his smarts for all to see like a Boy Scout badge. "You want me to hang out in the library, bragging about scoring a one forty-two on the IQ test?"

As he laces his fingers behind his head, showing off his biceps, he chuckles. For an old guy, he's still in pretty good shape. "You don't have to brag. Just stay out of trouble."

Mom taps me on the hand, bringing my focus back to her. "You're a good kid. Do this for me. Please?"

My mother, the one who sticks up for me, who lets me do things my own way, wants nothing more than for me to behave. She's my biggest supporter, the person who may not be alive to see me graduate and only asks me to stay out of trouble. Quitting sports so she didn't feel the need to be at every game isn't enough. I need to do this for her.

"All right," I whisper.

Dad pats my back. "Now that we have that out of the way, how did Samantha do?"

With a puppy-dog head tilt, I plaster a fake confused expression on my face then shrug. "She scored a three-pointer to win the game."

He beams. "She is amazing."

Yes, she is.

"Was her mom there?"

That's a mom question, for sure. "She had to work."

Mom's mouth turns down. "She works too hard. I'm glad you were there to support Samantha."

"I was there to watch the game."

Liar. I slide out of the chair and saunter over to the refrigerator to retrieve a water bottle.

Dad stands behind me and chuckles. "Whatever helps you sleep at night. I'm exhausted. Good night."

"What's that supposed to mean?"

He throws his hands up in defense as he leaves the kitchen, his footsteps getting fainter the farther down the hall he goes.

To put out the flames of my embarrassment, I gulp some water, and when I come up for air, I notice Mom smirking. "What?"

She lets out a heavy breath, stands, and gives me a kiss on the cheek. "You need to solve that problem yourself."

It is completely obvious Mom knows about my crush on Samantha. I mask it behind sarcasm and insults, but she's no dummy. Now that Dad is picking up on my feelings, I am in big trouble.

Chapter Three

Samantha

My VW Bug's engine whines as I force it to go faster than each gear can manage. I pat the dashboard and talk to it in soothing tones. "Sorry, Bug. I don't mean to take it out on you. It's been the worst day."

To add insult to injury, I hit the curb with the back tire as I turn in my driveway. When I slam her into Park, I let out a deep breath. "Thanks, Bug."

Thank goodness my parents aren't home, because I am not in the mood to talk to anyone. Upon entering my house, I slide my bag to the kitchen floor, plant my palms on the granite countertop, and stare at my distorted reflection in the stainless-steel refrigerator. I crumple onto the tile floor, covering my face with my hands as I rock.

I scrunch my knees into my chest and let out the loudest *argh* ever.

"Sam?"

With a loud screech, I yell, "What the heck, Craig? You scared me." I stand up and open the refrigerator to stuff my face inside while I try to regain control of my emotions.

"Sorry."

"I didn't know you were coming home this weekend." *Why this weekend?*

Like he's a game show host, he waves toward the kitchen window. "My car's in the garage."

"Didn't notice."

"You have obviously never tried to study in a dorm room the size of our kitchen."

And I probably won't ever get to, Mr. Full Academic Scholarship.

"What's wrong?"

To downplay my outburst, I grab an apple from the bowl on the counter. "Nothing." My voice comes out so high-pitched and fake, a stranger would know I'm lying.

"Bull." He snatches the apple from me and takes a bite. "You were ten seconds shy of throwing a tantrum like you used to do when you were three."

"I'm fine. Bad day."

He hands me the apple back, but I swat his arm away. *Ick.*

He scoops up a laundry basket and motions with his head for me to follow him to his room. "You want to help me fold my clothes?"

"No thanks."

I snatch my bag from the floor and tromp up the stairs to follow him into his bedroom. Even though he only comes home occasionally, his room still reeks of sweaty armpits. Balled-up, ratty T-shirts rest in a corner, and a pizza box peeks out from underneath his bed. I'm so glad my room is at the far end of the hall.

With my nose pinched closed, I walk past the threshold, one tentative step at a time. "Does your dorm room smell this bad?"

He grins. "Pretty much."

The image makes me grimace. "No wonder you're single."

"Hey," he says, flopping onto his bed, his long legs dangling off the edge. He pats the mattress beside him as an invitation to have a seat.

"Is it safe?"

"Sit. What's wrong? Did you have a bad game?"

I stand in front of his bed with arms wrapped tight around my stomach. The way we always bickered, I never thought I would miss him when he went away to college, but we've become closer since he left. I even confide in him things I don't dare discuss with my best friends, Paige and Rachel.

"Tell me about this bad day."

The mattress springs creak when I collapse next to him. Maybe if I focus on the Green Day poster on the wall, I won't fall apart.

He lifts his chin. "Are you and Mom fighting?"

I shake my head.

"I know it can't be Paige. You two are thick as thieves."

"We're good."

"How'd you score tonight?"

"Meh, but I did hit a three-pointer at the buzzer to win."

With sarcasm dripping from his voice, he says, "Ooo, that sounds like a really bad day." Craig quirks an eyebrow up into his hairline. "Is it a guy?"

My cheeks feel like they are on fire at his question. He's my brother, but if I had a boyfriend, there would be no way I could keep that bit of information from him. Besides, he would interrogate any poor soul who ever dared to ask me out. "I wish, but no. It is definitely not boy troubles."

He sits up, pulling me close, and I melt into him, letting out a deep breath. "My SAT scores suck. GPA sucks. Gonna lose... lose the scholarship."

My big, burly brother rubs my arm as I fight back tears. I clear my throat and sit up straight, then fix my ponytail as if that's the most important thing right now.

"Don't take this the wrong way," he says. "But how did it get this bad?"

I shrug one shoulder. "I thought I could dig my way out of the hole, but I kept getting deeper and deeper. My first SAT scores were bad. The second ones were even worse."

"Really?"

"My letter of intent to Auburn could be revoked." I scrub my face with my hands.

"That sucks."

"Tell me about it. I've only got one more chance to take the test."

"Don't jump off the cliff yet." He nudges my knee with his.

"I still have to at least get a B in Trig to bring up my GPA." After a moment, I add, "I wish I was smart."

"You are." He lets out a sigh, like he's trying to find the right words to keep me from losing it again. "No one is good at everything."

"I guess."

My phone buzzes in my bag, and I flop back on his bed. "Will you get it? It's probably Paige checking on me. I don't feel like talking."

Craig rummages through my bag until he retrieves my phone. He gets a scowl on his face as he reads something. "Hmm."

"Who is it from?"

"It's a message from King. Why is Samuel texting you?"

"Delete it."

He shakes his head. "Stay away from him. He's bad news."

With a flick of my wrist, I wave him off. "He's a jerk but all talk. Besides, isn't he supposed to be your friend?"

Craig points a finger. "And that's why I'm warning you. There are things about him you don't know."

While I appreciate my brother's protectiveness, I'm not a helpless snowflake. He forgets we all grew up together. There is nothing about Mule that I don't already know, and there may be a few items Craig isn't even privy to. "He's a cocky player, and I'm not interested, so calm down."

"Good. Focus on scoring better next time. You can do it."

I sure hope so.

Chapter Four

Samantha

Between my head spinning and my stupid phone buzzing every thirty minutes, I don't sleep a wink. I know Samuel's only checking up on me, but I can't deal with him. The boy wonder can't understand, and I'm not sure I trust him not to use this information against me. Although, with all the secrets I know about him, he better not. But it's best I steer clear of him until this all blows over.

With Craig home for the weekend, Mom makes whatever he wants for breakfast, no matter how tired she is from working the late shift, and this morning is no different. The aroma of waffles and sausages wafts throughout the house, leading me down the hall toward the goods.

Craig and Dad sit at the table, arguing about who is going to the Final Four this year. Craig thinks it will be Tennessee, but Dad sticks with his alma mater, Georgia. Usually, I would say Auburn, but I don't want to utter that school's name.

Dad's eyes light up as I slink down into my chair. "You should have seen Samantha last night. She was on fire."

As much as I want to be humble, I know his words are true.

Like the proud papa he is, Dad beams. "She was lit."

Craig groans as he stuffs another sausage link into his mouth. "Don't try to be cool."

Dad chuckles. "Well, she was great. I'm not supposed to be biased, but I am." He takes another sip of his coffee. "I did come close to ejecting her and Samuel from the boys' game."

Mom gasps, and Craig gives me the evil eye.

"They were heckling me." In a mocking-Samuel voice, Dad says, "You wouldn't really do that, would you, Mr. Baughman?"

Heat rises up my neck as I remember the altercation. I cram my mouth full of scrambled eggs. "You totally missed that guy reaching."

"I can't call what I don't see."

Mom wipes her mouth with her napkin and turns to me. "Maybe it's time he gets his eyes checked."

Craig and I high-five Mom while Dad grumbles into his coffee.

I catch her staring at me with one of those "don't you have something to tell me" faces. The next time I go to the bathroom, I need to check in the mirror to see if there is a sign on my forehead that reads Sucky SAT Score.

Craig steals the waffle off my plate and inhales it before I can even protest. Only thirty-six more hours before he goes back to college, not that I'm counting.

Mom smacks his hand and says, "I'll make more if you're hungry. Your sister has hardly touched her food."

I slide my plate in front of my brother. "It's fine. I'm full anyway."

He takes the invitation and shoves the rest of my food into his face. Between bites, he asks, "You want to play some ball before I leave?"

Dad chuckles at Craig. "Do you think that's wise after all the grub you ate?"

He lets out a belch. Mom and I cringe. Dad, of course, laughs like he doesn't care about the belch as long as Craig is home, so it's an even playing field in the house.

"I feel better already." Craig rises from the table and kisses my mother's cheek. "Thanks, Mom."

He picks up his plate and takes it to the kitchen. "Sam, let's do this, if you think you can take it."

My brother knows exactly how to motivate me, but even with a full stomach, he whips my butt on the basketball court. I usually can hold my own with my five-eleven frame, even if he is five inches taller than me, but today I am off my game. He hits the third layup in a row, ticking me off. The madder I get, the worse I play.

"You and King were at the game together? What's that all about?"

I steal the ball from him and take a shot. Total air ball. "Nothing. We were watching the game. That's all."

"Sam…" He throws the ball to me, and I bounce it to calm myself.

"It's nothing. We go to school together, in case you don't remember. We have the same friends, the same interests. We are bound to end up at the same places. Chill out."

I throw him the ball with a little more force than necessary.

"Touchy, touchy."

"Let's play."

After one more stupid round of H-O-R-S-E in silence, he clears his throat. "I thought you were going to have another freak-out at breakfast when Mom asked you about your day."

I steal the ball from him and attempt to hit a three-pointer but fail. "Was it that obvious?"

"Yep." He shoots a basket from the free throw line, making that cool *whoosh* sound.

The toe of my shoe finds a crack in the driveway, and I stumble as I chase after the ball. He blocks my next shot, sending the ball down the driveway.

"What is wrong with you? That was goaltending."

He throws his arms up in surrender. "Since when do we go by the rules out here?"

Like a petulant child, I stomp toward the ball, calling him every name I can think of under my breath. "You think you're so good at everything." With that jab, I lob the ball, hitting him square in the chest.

He lets out an *oof.* "Where did that come from?"

"Oh, shut up."

Craig shoots another basket. "I guess it's time for a change in subject. I heard we've had some break-ins in the neighborhood. With your attitude, we're safe from someone wanting to tangle with anyone in this house."

After an exasperated groan, I stomp into the house. I slam my bedroom door behind me and flop onto my bed. It's a sad day when I can't even play a stupid game of pickup basketball.

Chapter Five

Samuel

Usually, I am a beast with video games, but today, Brody beats me in three straight games of Grand Theft Auto. I slump back into my game chair in defeat.

Brody lets out a wicked *bwa ha ha* as he downs a swig from his water bottle. "King, you're out of practice."

"Shut your hole."

"Are you getting soft on me?" He accentuates his taunt by wiping fake tears from his face.

I give Brody a titty twister then grab his chin.

He smacks my hand away.

"Excuse me, ladies, it's time to kiss and make up." Craig gallops down the steps into the den.

After I throw one more playful punch at Brody, Craig holds out a fist for both of us to bump. Last night's tongue-lashing I got from my parents still echoes in my ears, so he's not exactly my favorite person right now. "'Sup? Are you here to cause more trouble?"

"Huh?" He plops on the floor between me and Brody then steals my controller. "Only for the weekend. But Sam's in a foul mood, so I had to escape that drama."

My heart skitters when he mentions his sister. I relax back in my chair, hoping to sound casual. "Brody, no offense, but I need to talk to Craig alone. Do you mind?"

He glances from me to Craig before standing. "Sure. See y'all later. I'm having Paige withdrawals anyway."

Gross.

As soon as Brody is gone, I say to Craig, "Thanks for nothing."

"What are you talking about?" He starts a new game like he doesn't have a care in the world.

I glance down the hallway to make sure no parental is overhearing this conversation then say, "I got chewed out about that little incident at the frat party. How did my parents hear about it?"

He holds up his hands in defense. "Heck if I know."

"Riiight. You let it slip. I know you."

The muscles in his jaw clench when he places the controller on the end table then stares at the ceiling. "I promise, I didn't say a word. This is not the first time your dad has caught you doing something you thought was under the dome of secrecy."

"That's not the point. Your college friend is no good, and he caused my recent troubles."

"Rocky's fine."

If Rocky is the definition of "fine," then I am a saint. "You still believe him over me."

"I have no reason not to."

"You should rethink your new friend group. You believe a wasteoid over someone you've known practically your entire life, and then you have the nerve to narc on me."

Craig's face turns red, and I practically see steam spewing from his ears. "I swear, I don't know how the good doctor found out."

I snort. "Please. Spare me the innocent Craig bit. Anything to make you appear like the angel you aren't."

"Stay away from Samantha, especially now."

"That's a nice way to pivot from the topic at hand. Besides, Sam is smart enough to take care of herself."

"I can take you any day, King. Don't make me prove it." He punches me in the arm to emphasize his words. "Leave my sister alone. She needs help but not your kind."

I throw my hands in the air in exasperation. The way his comments ping-pong around are giving me a headache. "What's that supposed to mean?"

"She needs a tutor, and we both know you can't help in that department. Maybe your nerdy cousin would work with her."

"Is that what you want?"

"I want you to find someone to help her and for you to keep your paws off. You know I'll kick your butt if you touch her. Got it?"

Slowly, I stand and give him a patronizing salute. "Yes, sir. I'll ask around. Anything for you, good buddy." I back away from him because, even though I'm usually able to hold my own in a fight, he could turn me into a soprano without breaking a sweat.

He pinches my cheek, and I swat his hand away. "I'm glad we cleared that up."

The front door to my house closes, and footsteps get louder as someone heads toward the den. Craig mumbles, "I mean it."

I reply by giving him a one-finger salute.

Dad props himself against the entrance to the den, looking more disheveled than usual.

"Hey, Dr. King," Craig says. The way he turns on the charm when adults are in the room is sickening, and it's hysterical to think *he* assumes he can pull one over on *my* dad. I've had years of experience, and I haven't been able to master that.

"Nice to see you, Craig. Would you excuse us for a minute?"

Crap. That only means one thing. Lecture time, dead ahead.

"Yeah, sure. See ya, King." Craig pats me on the back like we are buddies again, as if he didn't threaten me only a minute earlier.

As soon as Craig is out of sight, Dad says, "I wanted to talk a little more about our conversation from last night."

I shrug. "I got the picture loud and clear. No need to elaborate."

Dad chuckles and loosens his tie. "I only want what's best for you. You must know that."

Maybe he wants what is best for *him*. "I guess, but what you want and what I want aren't always the same."

He stares at the ceiling, like we've had this conversation before, which we have. "What do you want?"

That is the million-dollar question, and I don't know how to answer him, so I just sit there and pick at my fingernail. "Not sure yet."

"That's my point. You aren't being challenged, and you also need a hefty dose of discipline."

I inwardly groan. This conversation should be recorded so I could just hit Play any time we need to hash it over again.

"My schedule doesn't leave me with enough time at home to be the disciplinarian. Don't force me to transfer you to an alternative school, because I will. Then you will kiss college scholarships good-bye."

"I don't want to go to a different high school—alternative, military, religious, or whatever."

"Do you even want to go to college?"

That question makes me blink out of confusion. This has never been a topic of debate. "Of course I do."

Dad rolls his eyes, and it makes me angry. It's hard to watch him without thinking about how much we favor each other physically. It's time that I begin to think like him.

"I've been taking college courses online, and all my AP classes count toward college credit, so what's the problem? I practically have enough credits to be a sophomore already."

Before he has a chance to reply, I continue, "And I'm going to stay out of trouble. I promise. For Mom. She doesn't need any more stress." The thought of doing anything to hurt my mother when she's so vulnerable makes me want to kick my own butt.

Dad stares at me for a minute, and my heart beats so strong, it feels like it will give out. Then there won't be a need for *any* kind of school. He glances toward the door, and Mom stands in the doorway, watching us.

He stands and ruffles my hair. "Okay, for now."

She kisses him on the cheek as he leaves the den then gives me a slight wink. No matter how much stress I cause her, she's always my biggest advocate.

Chapter Six

Samuel

Teachers should be bored of meeting with me by now, because I'm tired of seeing them. Walking toward my math teacher's room, where I've been summoned—again—I frown. I promised my parents I would behave, so if this isn't a "you've been a good boy" conversation, I'm toast.

When I open the door to my math class and catch Mr. Henderson and Mrs. Connor in a powwow, I freeze. My spidey senses are telling me to run away. Fast.

"Sit," Mrs. Connor says, pointing to the desk in the front row.

"What'd I do this time?" I slump into the nearest desk and let my backpack fall to the floor.

She retrieves three pieces of paper and places one on the desk in front of me. "This is your history exam from Friday."

She's written a ninety-nine in red ink at the top. "What did you count off for?" My attention goes straight to the red X mark. "Seriously, you couldn't read that one word, and you counted off for it?"

"If I can't read it, it doesn't count. Anyway, that's not important right now."

Maybe not to her, but it is to me. That test was a walk in the park. She's still mad because I called her out on the various reasons for the fall of the Roman Empire, one of the few times I slipped up during class.

She slides the other two pages toward me. "This one is Brody Campbell's, and the other is Jared Green's. As you know, you're in my second-period class, but they both take my fourth-period class."

Crapity crap on a stick. *The next time I see Brody and Jared, I'm going to beat the snot out of them.*

I point to Brody's paper. "I guess Brody studied."

She taps her long fingernail next to question fifteen. "Read this out loud along with Brody's answer."

With as much enthusiasm as I can muster, which isn't much, I recite, "What was the reason for the French and Indian War?" And I read Brody's chicken-scratch answer. "The immediate cause of the war was a dispute over land west of the Appalachian Mountains." I peek up at her. "He got it right. And to think you could read his handwriting but not mine." I tsk her, knowing that's not the best re-action.

With a pink-painted fingernail, she drags it then taps on question sixteen. "Read."

"Who became prime minister of England in 1757? Thomas Pell-ham-Holles."

"Very good." She points to Jared's paper. "Check out his question fifteen. Read."

"Who was the—" I glance up, knowing where this is going.

"Go on. What was his answer?"

I gulp. "The immediate cause of the war was a dispute..." *Alternative school, here I come.*

"I tend to reorder the questions... a lot." Mrs. Connor looks very proud of herself.

Gulp. I may be smart, but sometimes I am so stupid.

She perches on the edge of Mr. Henderson's desk, and I hope she doesn't break it with all that mass. My usual self would say something about mass being equal to density times volume, but I don't think that's appropriate. I'm in enough trouble as it is. The best thing to do is to act cool, so I grab a pen off the desk and correct a typo on Brody's paper that she missed. I'm pretty sure I hear her growl.

Then, in rapid-fire speed, I click the pen on and off as I recline back in my chair. "I can't help it if we discuss school stuff. It's what we do. We love your class so much."

"Samuel," Mr. Henderson says, snatching the pen out of my hand mid click, "we know you're a bright kid."

Before this day is over, the enamel will be completely worn off my molars. Why did Mom insist on having my IQ tested? I should have failed that test on purpose, but my wiring won't let me fake stupidity on an exam. So the next best thing is to hide it as much as possible. Brody and Jared think I had the right answers because I stole a copy of the test. They would have a field day if they found out I have a photographic memory.

Mrs. Connor says to Mr. Henderson, "I heard his IQ is over one thirty."

I'd like to tell her she's off by twelve points, but I better not, so I stretch my legs out in front of me and let out a bored yawn. "Am I gonna get kicked out?"

They glance at each other. Mr. Henderson breaks the silence. "No."

Knowing better, I grin anyway. They have no proof I did anything. It's only a hunch that I was involved. It's a darn good one, but that's all it is. I rake a hand through my hair, relieved this situation is over. "So what is it? You want me to grade your papers?" *Smart aleck.*

"You really should skip senior year and go straight to college."

Mr. Henderson sounds like my dad. Not. Gonna. Happen. Just because I could sail through gen ed courses in my sleep, doesn't mean I'm ready to buckle down. I still want to have fun.

"And I know you're only in my trig class," Mr. Henderson continues, "because you've already taken all the advanced classes and Trig fit into your schedule."

No one really knows the real reason, and I'm not going to enlighten them.

They stare at each other for a moment, then Mrs. Connor nods. She clears her throat. "This has your name written all over it, but we can't do much about it since we can't prove you told them the answers. I'm sure you don't want me to call your parents in for yet another conference, do you?"

My whole body tenses. I clench my fists so tight, my knuckles crackle. If Dad finds out about this, I'll get another "I'm so disappointed in you" lecture, and no telling what it will do to Mom.

Mr. Henderson draws in a breath and lets it out super slow, like he's pondering his next move. "I have an idea to use your brain for good instead of evil."

"Lame." I hate it when teachers try to be cool, but I'll hear him out. This should be interesting. Does he want me to do his taxes? Help him choose some stock options?

"If that's how you want to play it, Mr. Smart Mouth, then this is how it's going to be. I am going to turn you in for cheating."

I cross my arms over my chest and scowl. "You wouldn't."

His eyes gleam with satisfaction. "Unless you do one simple thing."

If I don't cooperate, my father will jerk me out of this school so fast, I won't even get to clean out my locker. If I agree to be at Mr. Henderson's mercy, no telling what I'll have to do.

Mentally going over my options, I really have no choice but to agree to it. "I'm listening."

"I want you to offer to tutor a student who is struggling."

My body trembles with laughter. "Same thing. If I'm seen hunched over books, I might as well announce it over the intercom—Sam King scored a one forty-two on the IQ test."

"No one said you had to do the tutoring at school, and I'll let you pick who the student is, within reason."

They have got to be kidding me. I shake my head. "Nope."

Mrs. Connor crosses her arms and lets out a huff. "I told you he wouldn't do it. He lacks empathy."

Mr. Henderson sighs and says, "Fine. It's your choice, Samuel. I think I have your father's number on speed dial." Then he has the gall to hum the theme to *Jeopardy* while he waits on my answer.

He can't call my dad. This will be the last straw. I'll be sent to boarding school and have to wear a tie and khaki pants every day for the rest of my senior year, not to mention my hair. It would be buzzed on the first day.

"He's in surgery all day." That should kill his threat.

"There is a note in your school file to call him no matter how busy he might be."

My heart races faster after I lose that round. There's no way to confirm if my dad actually told the school that, but it sounds exactly like something he would do. And even if it isn't, I don't know if this is the time to test that.

Mrs. Connor smirks. "If you don't call, I will. He'll have to come in for a conference to discuss transferring you to alt—"

"I'll do it." I have no intention of tutoring some poor schmuck, but as long as they think I do, it's all good. Maybe I'll say I'm tutoring Brody. It's obvious he needs it.

Mr. Henderson hangs up the phone with a pleased smile on his smarmy face. "So nice of you to... volunteer. I'll be in touch to hear what arrangements you've made and who the lucky guy or girl is."

Clenching my fists, I say, "Can't wait."

Chapter Seven

Samantha

The buzz of conversation in the cafeteria is getting on my last nerve. My mystery-meat burger sits untouched on my tray, and the fries are nothing but a cold, greasy pile. Even if I had an appetite to stomach this mess, it wouldn't stay down for long.

Paige makes her way through the crowded cafeteria and slides into a chair beside me. For the first time in weeks, she isn't superglued to her hot model boyfriend, Brody. I hate being jealous because she's my best friend, and they make such a cute couple, but I wish somebody would gaze at me that way, like I'm his beginning and end.

"What's wrong?" she asks, stuffing fries into her mouth.

I shrug. "Nothing."

She nudges me with her shoulder. "Come on. I know you too well. You've got that look."

"What do you mean?" Rachel asks, sitting on the other side of me.

Rachel never has the *look*, the one that screams desperation or failure. She has perfect hair, perfect face, and perfect grades. She rocks a cheerleader uniform like no one else, yet she still hangs out with Paige and me. Where Paige and I prefer to be playing every sport possible, Rachel would rather be on the sidelines, making up crazy cheers about us. Everyone knows her. Every guy in our school drools over her, and to top it off, she's super sweet. No wonder she's the class president.

"I'm having a bad day. No biggie." I plaster on a sweet-as-sugar smile.

"You know you can talk to us, right?" Paige says.

Rachel nods then waves to a football player, causing him to stumble into a chair. She yawns, making us giggle.

"Not this time. I mean, I'm fine."

Paige glances at Rachel then back at her fries. "If you're worried about how you played this weekend..."

Bad game? Try having a bad brain.

I shove my tray away from me, suddenly not hungry at all. "Actually, I'm not feeling well."

Rachel puts her hand up to my forehead.

After I scoop up my backpack, I say, "See you tomorrow."

"Hope you feel better. Get some rest," she says.

"Thanks."

"And drink plenty of fluids," she yells at the back of my head.

My feet can't transport me fast enough as I racewalk through the cafeteria, chanting to myself, *breathe in, breathe out.* I push the door to exit, but at the same time, someone opens it from the other side. It opens faster than I anticipate, sending me flying through the opening. I'm about to face-plant onto the nasty floor when two strong arms catch me, saving me from humiliation.

"Whoa, where's the fire?" Samuel asks, helping me regain my balance.

I gaze up into his big blue eyes, and for once, he's not being cocky. Ever since my SAT confession, he's been creepy nice. Five texts on Saturday night and seven more on Sunday to make sure I was all right. And I didn't have the nerve to reply one time. Nice Samuel is hard to resist, and I don't need that right now.

"I'm good." I push past him, and this time, he lets me walk by.

"Want to talk about it?"

I turn around and walk backward while I stare at him. "Mule, leave me alone."

He backs away and grumbles.

As soon as I round the corner, I let out a breath. If I don't get out of here, I'm going to embarrass myself.

rig class. Ugh! I should have gone home, but that would result in my mother getting a call about me missing a class, and then I would have that to deal with.

And Mule's here. No wonder I can't ever concentrate in this class when the hottest, most annoying guy is within eye-roaming range. I don't like admitting to myself that I like gawking at him, but I do, and that ticks me off.

As usual, Mule side scoots through the aisle and sits one row over and one seat behind me. If I turn my head a teensy bit to the right, I'm able to see him out of the corner of my eye. He bends over to retrieve his notebook out of his backpack, and I'm in full-on gawk mode. His hair falls over his face, and the back of his shirt rides up, exposing a nice strip of tanned skin.

I take out my cell phone and send a quick text before class starts.

Me: *Hey, Mule. Need your opinion. In private, please.*

His chuckle resonates through the classroom, signaling to me he got my message. My phone vibrates with an incoming text.

Mule: *Is this about sec?*

Not sure what he means. Auburn is an SEC team, but there is no reason he would ask about that. I suck in a breath. Maybe he means sex. Heat rushes up my neck as I text back.

Me: *NO!! Will you meet me at the Green Hills Library after school?*

Mule: *What's it worth to you?*

Pondering my reply, I take a peek around to see him mouth, *Well?* He is infuriating, and I can't believe I'm going through with this.

Me: *I won't tell anyone you cried when Nemo's mom died.*
Mule: *You wouldn't.*

While I relive that moment, I bite my lip to keep from laughing. He was a blubbering idiot throughout that entire movie after the first scene. It's my word against his, but he knows it's all true.

Me: *Try me.*

Mr. Henderson clears his throat, our cue to stop the chatter. Samuel slumps back in his chair, sliding one leg into the aisle. He glances at me, and thank goodness my reflexes are fast enough to not get caught staring this time. My phone buzzes one more time, and I take a quick glance at the message before Mr. Henderson snatches my phone from me.

Mule: *C U soon sec.*

I force myself to listen while Mr. Henderson babbles on about the inverse function of something and tangents and co-tangents, but I need to formulate a plan to improve my GPA. That's step one to secure my scholarship. If Mule doesn't go for it, I don't know what I'm going to do.

The bell rings, and most kids rush away from our teacher's love affair with the word—*secant*.

Samuel snatches his backpack from the floor. When he scoots past me, I catch a whiff of him. His scent is clean and soapy. I hope he didn't notice.

"Daydreaming again, Sam-Man?"

"No, I was totally engrossed in the subject matter."

Samuel chuckles and shakes his head.

"I love this stuff," I yell at his back as he leaves the room. "Ugh."

Mr. Henderson stares at me until I drag myself out of my desk. I jerk my chin up and walk out the door.

The day felt like an eternity until the last bell rang. I am glad this agonizing day is over. It's time to put my plan in place.

"Hey, Samantha, you must be feeling better," Paige says, leaning against the locker next to mine. "Some of the guys are going to play softball at the park. Are you coming?"

That *would* put me in a better mood, but not today. "Uh, I'd like to, but dang it. I can't."

Paige scrunches her nose then smiles. "Oh yeah. It's Tuesday. Say hello to Grandma Wilkes for me."

No one will ever suspect anything since I do spend some Tuesdays visiting my grandmother at the retirement home. "That's right. I promised to get there early today. Maybe next time on the game?"

"I heard about the break-ins, so try to get home before dark."

"Yes, Mother."

Paige's smile brightens her face when her boyfriend slides up next to her. "Are you coming?" Brody asks me.

I shake my head. "I can't."

"Dang. I guess I'll have to pick this li'l bit to be on my team." He winks at Paige.

She gasps as if she could ever be really mad at him. "You better watch it."

He slips his arm around her waist and leads her away. "I always *watch it.*"

She groans, and so do I. "See you later. Stop by the park if you get done early."

I nod, knowing good and well I won't be going. "Sure."

If I survive my groveling session, I'm going straight home to eat a massive serving of humble pie then crawl into bed to hope this is all a big ole nightmare. After all these years, I've never asked one thing from Mule. I hope he doesn't laugh in my face.

He is one hundred percent going to laugh in my face.

Chapter Eight

Samuel

The silence kills my ears, reminding me why I don't come to the library anymore. The fluorescent lights buzz like they are about to burst. And the smell of books takes me back to when my mom used to bring me here when I was little, way back when I couldn't get enough of reading.

I still read about three books a week, but with the invention of book apps, no one knows what I'm doing. Most people think I'm scrolling through social media or checking out naked pictures of hot girls, but I'm really reading. This week, I read *The Bell Jar...* for the third time. And I still had time to spare to take a gander at a few naked pictures.

After I scan the room to see if the coast is clear, I sling myself into a chair near the entrance and focus on my phone. Five minutes late, and I'm out of here. I rock on the back two legs of my chair, hoping she doesn't show. Her message was cryptic, but I know exactly what she wants, and I can't give it to her, not if I like my teeth in their current position. I'll hear her out, and hopefully, she'll understand.

Two more minutes, tops, and I'm gone. Maybe she went to the pickup softball game instead. That's where I should be. I'll give her one more minute, then I'm leaving. My chest tightens. I rub my sweaty palms on my jeans. It's Sam, the only girl I've ever really wanted but have always been too chicken to do anything about. I don't deal with rejection well, and it would kill me if she put me in the friend zone for good.

The door creaks open, and she walks in like she's afraid of waking a sleeping baby. Her face is all blotchy, and her lips form a thin line, but it's her eyes that always clue me in on what she's thinking. Her brown eyes sparkle when she's about to make me eat my dust on the court. They turn stormy and dark when she's upset, and right now, I'm seeing a hurricane in her eyes.

"'Sup, Sam-Man."

She drags me by the arm through the periodicals to a study room in the corner. I slide into the nearest chair with her across from me. She tugs her ponytail tight. Neither one of us says a word for the longest time. Her fingers drumming on the table is the only sound in the room.

I glance at my watch and say, "This has been fun, but I'm out of here before someone sees me."

As I stand, she blurts out, "I need your help." She squeezes her eyes closed, like she's afraid of my reply.

"With what?"

She blows out her breath and stares at the floor. "Help me pass Trig, and teach me how to get a good score on the SAT."

A chuckle bursts out of my throat, and I get shushed from someone reading right outside the study room. "No."

I sling my backpack over one shoulder and head for the door. Out of the corner of my eye, I notice Sam is slack-jawed. I can't help her. I promised Craig. Before I take two steps toward the entrance, I hear a chair scraping against the floor then feel her death grip on my bicep. "Why not?"

While I continue out the front door, through the parking lot toward my truck, Sam clings to my arm. "Stop."

When I reach my truck, I plunk my backpack on the ground and focus on the sky because if we lock eyes, I'll cave. "All you need to do is study harder, and you'll do fine. It's not that difficult."

What a jerk. A knife to her heart would have been less painful. Her bottom lip trembles, and I fidget with my keys to keep from hugging her.

"I *have* been studying." She sucks in a ragged breath. "Please."

Darn you, Craig. On the verge of caving, I let out a groan. "I... can't. Try Mason."

She shakes her head. "I don't want anyone else to know. It's embarrassing. Plus... Coach is giving me another chance to improve my grade before he benches me. He didn't have to do that, and if word gets out, it could get him in trouble."

Sam's right, but I made a promise to Craig. He'll kick my butt if I spend any time alone with her, even though I would never treat her wrong. I've witnessed what his fists are capable of, and I don't ever want to go down that road.

I make the mistake of staring into those big brown eyes begging me to help her, so I bury my head and unlock my truck door. "I'm sorry, Sam, but I can't."

She scoots in between me and my truck, blocking the opening with her body. She's about the same height as me, so her hot breath falls on my neck. "Do you realize how hard it was for me to ask you for a favor?"

Because I'm a jerk, my only reply is a shrug.

She slides out of my way and holds her arm out for me to have free access to my driver's seat. "Go."

Her rapid breaths make her chest rise and fall, and I do my best not to stare. I slip into the driver's seat, and she slams the door.

"I bet if a cheerleader asked, you'd do whatever you could to... help. But me? Nooo. I'm actually glad you refused because I don't need people like you in my life. I'd rather fail than owe you anything. You're not worth it."

I drum my fingers on the steering wheel. "Are you finished?"

Her mouth falls open. "Yes, I am done. Totally done."

"Bye, Sam-Man." I crank my truck engine as she backs away.

In my rearview mirror, Sam stands as tall as a tree, arms crossed over her chest. My tires squeal as I step on the gas, needing to get out of here ASAP. Bro code stinks.

I can either join the ballgame with my friends and be in a sour mood the whole time or go home and risk twenty questions from Dad. Have you thought about Carnegie Mellon? *No, Dad.* What about Princeton? *Nope.* Vanderbilt? *Not in a million years.* And, once I decide, round two of questions will be about what major I should choose to get into the best medical schools. It never ends.

The odds of Dad still being in surgery are pretty high, and Mom only lobs soft questions, so option two wins. The house is quiet when I enter the kitchen. Mom's note on the counter reads, *Gone for a jog.*

Yes! I have the house to myself while I kick myself in the butt.

I retrieve a gallon of milk and a bag of lunch meat from the fridge and plop down onto a barstool. Between gulps of milk straight from the jug, I shove slices of turkey into my mouth. Right when I'm about to take another swig of milk, my mother stumbles into the house. Beads of sweat glide down her face.

"Hey, sweetie." She pants as she bends over the counter. She yanks the milk jug out of my grasp and guzzles the cold liquid, wiping the milk mustache away with the back of her hand.

"Ahh, that tastes good." She gives me a sweaty kiss on the cheek.

"How far did you go today?"

"Five miles." She throws a leg onto the barstool and stretches out her hamstrings. "Your father would have a fit if he knew I was training for a marathon."

"As much as it hurts me to say this, I would have to agree with him."

"Pfft. I'm fine. It gives me energy and something to focus on be-sides..."

I squeeze my eyes closed. We've made a pact not to say the C word ever again in this house.

She pats my cheeks. "Besides, my baby doesn't need me all the time anymore."

"Aw, Mom. Not true."

She stares at me, and I know she's reading my mind. Might as well get it over with. I take a deep breath. "I need advice, but I don't want Dad to know."

She sits up straight. "Did you kill anyone? Hurt anyone? Cause property damage or do anything illegal?"

With a chuckle, I reply, "Surprisingly, no. Only being stupid as usual."

"I can handle stupidity. Your father is smart, but he's a big ol' dummy about real life stuff, so spill."

"A friend asked me for help, and I said I couldn't help her. I mean him."

Mom grins as she stands. She rests one hand on the counter as she stretches her quads. "Are you the best person to help him... or her?"

"Actually, I am." I tap the side of my head.

"Ahh. School stuff?"

I swallow another slice of turkey. "Yeah, but I'm not supposed to help."

Mom switches to her other leg. "I don't understand."

"Bro code."

Mom rests on the stool and swipes a slice of turkey from my grip. "You'll have to use mom words because I'm not following you."

Before replying, I take a deep breath. "If a guy friend tells you to stay away from his sister, you do it. End of story. No questions asked. I promised I would stay away from her."

With a sly grin, she asks, "Who is it?"

I cover my face with my hands. "Samantha."

When I brave a glance at Mom, she has the brightest smile on her face. "I think you should help her anyway."

"Craig will kick my butt."

She gulps more milk. "I've seen the way you look at her. Maybe this is what you need. A sweet girlfriend instead of those... fake girls."

With a thump, I rest my head on the counter. "It's tutoring, not going out on a date. Gah."

"You've known Samantha your entire life." She focuses on the ceiling and sighs. "That girl is like a daughter to me. She gives me an excuse to shop in the pink aisle."

Suddenly, the cap of the milk jug is more interesting than this conversation. She taps my hand to get my attention. "Why does he want you to steer clear of her?"

"Let's say, I've done my fair share of crap to validate his warning."

Mom wipes sweat from her brow. "It's all in the past, right?"

I nod. "That crap got old. I'm not like that anymore, but he still sees me as the wild friend. And some of that stuff isn't even true."

"Did she come to you?"

"Yeah."

Mom pokes me in the chest. "That means Samantha trusts you. That's the important thing. And it will give Craig a chance to realize you're not a heartbreaker."

Heat radiates off my face. I should have played ball with my friends. It would have been less embarrassing than this conversation. "I'm leaving before you say any more non-mom phrases."

She takes hold of my arm. "Don't worry about Craig. If he gives you any trouble, tell him Dr. King will set him straight."

I snort. "I am *not* telling Dad."

Her grin gets even bigger. "I'm talking about me, the love doctor."

Somebody put me out of my misery. Rising from my chair, I say, "And with that, I'm going to take a shower."

She slides my hair out of my eyes and kisses me on the cheek again. "The love doctor is on call twenty-four seven."

"Mom!" My heart doubles in size knowing I have the best mother in the world, but it also pains me, wondering how long she'll be around to embarrass me.

Chapter Nine

Samantha

My VW Bug is never going to forgive me as I grind the gears like I've never driven a manual transmission a day in my life. The undercarriage scrapes on the curb as I take the turn into my driveway practically on two wheels. Craig throws a bag of laundry into his trunk and jumps out of the way, landing in the rosebushes.

"Watch it. I'm not ready to die." He crawls out of the prickly shrubbery, arms covered in scratches. I don't even acknowledge him as I exit my car.

"The least you could do is say goodbye. I won't be back for a few weeks."

"Bye!"

I stomp up the stairs toward my bedroom, not caring if Craig follows me.

"What is wrong with you?"

"Go away. Go back to college among smart people."

I slam my bedroom door in his face and crumple into a ball on my bed, but he barrels right into my room. I'm so stupid I can't even remember to lock my door.

"What's up with you?"

"I don't want to talk about it." It's bad enough that he knows about my SAT woes. I would be mortified if he knew I asked Samuel to tutor me *and* he refused. Craig would laugh his butt off.

"Any more bad news?"

The mattress sinks when he sits on the edge.

I roll over to face him and take a deep breath. "I'm sorry. I didn't mean to be so cranky. It's really embarrassing. I tried to get someone to help me, but he wouldn't."

"Who?"

"Never mind."

He cocks his head to the side. "Who is it?"

I cover my face with my hands. "I'm not saying, so drop it."

"There must be someone else to ask."

"This person is smarter than the whole senior class combined. And I can't ask Rachel. That's too embarrassing."

Craig scratches his chin like he always does when he's pondering something or when he's trying to think of a good lie. "Don't panic yet. It will work out. I have faith in you."

"That makes one of us."

I still can't wrap my head around why Mule won't help me. I know girls follow him around like he's some kind of crack dealer, and they can have his body. I only want to borrow his brain.

Craig pats me on the leg. "I gotta get back to school for my evening bio lab."

"Let me know how it feels to go to college."

He throws a pillow then runs out of the room before I whack him in the head with it. Before I can scream, my phone buzzes. I fish it out of my purse to notice that Samuel left me a message.

Mule: *Don't be mad at me.*

Delete.

I can't talk to him right now. Because of that jerk, I must find someone who's smart enough but won't go public with my entire sucky situation. I don't know if I should be hurt or angry that Mule won't help me. If things were reversed, I would have done anything within my power for him. That's what friends do. I always thought our snark fests were our little way of teasing each other. He drives me crazy, but I must admit, I look forward to our playful banter sessions. I guess all this time it was all one-sided.

My phone buzzes. This text is from Craig.

Bro: *Call me if you need to talk. I'm only an hour away.*

Me: *THX*

My phone buzzes again. Ugh. *Will this day stop dumping on me?*

Mule: *I'm not the big bad wolf.*

Me: *Since when?*

Mule: *Ouch.*

Me: *Don't talk to me.*

Mule: *I thought we were friends.*

Me: *Wrong. Go away. Jerk.*

That'll show him. He stooped lower than I thought even he could go. It doesn't matter if we've known each other our entire lives. If he can't spend five minutes with me to make my life the slightest bit better, then I don't need him around.

Mule: *I still think you're se-c.*

Argh. What does that even mean?

Me: *Are you trying to rub it in that I won't get into Auburn - SEC school? If so, that's low even for you. Jerk!*

I power down my phone and cover my face with a pillow then let out all the anguish of the day in one huge growl. I guess I am on my own. If I don't do any better on the next trig exam, I'll never get a B. Sitting for the SATs again will be a waste of time.

Chapter Ten

Samuel

By the disgusted groan she lets out, I know the exact second Samantha walks into math class. She hardly gets one foot inside before she backs out, knocking over the trash can in the process.

Mr. Henderson yells, "Hey, get back in here," but it's too late. She's gone.

A few classmates snicker. He stares a hole through me like it is my fault, and I guess it is. "Class, let's get started."

I bury my head and add another doodle in my notebook. I'm not about to waste good paper on math problems that I'm able to do in my sleep. Drawing is the only thing that keeps me from going insane in this dry-as-toast class. My photographic memory allows me to trace Samantha's stunned face, and within ten minutes, I have another drawing of my favorite subject. Tonight, I'll render it with my artist software, and I'll safely store it in the file labeled Trig.

"Mr. King, what's the answer?" Mr. Henderson's voice doesn't even make me glance up at the board. Half my brain is still paying attention even though I try to block it out.

"Cosine two."

Several people giggle as if I can't possibly have the correct answer.

"It appears somebody did their homework."

My eyes flick up to stare at him. One corner of his mouth twitches.

The bell rings, and I stuff my notebook into my backpack. I try to avoid Mr. Henderson's stares, but he pins me in place with that grumpy-old-man face.

He crosses his arms across his chest. "Have you thought any more about our agreement?"

Slinging my backpack, I attempt to scoot past him, but he blocks my exit. "I said I would."

"Yes, but I know you. I need a name by the end of the day, or I'm making the phone call to your parents." He motions with his head. "Am I clear?"

"Crystal." I salute him.

Before I exit the room, Bucky, a frail sophomore, runs smack-dab into me. My backpack makes contact with his glasses, sending them off-kilter on his head. I readjust them, and he flinches like he's afraid I'm going to punch him in the face.

"Sorry, King. I didn't mean to—"

"Relax. You need to save your energy for this invigorating lecture." I spread my fingers wide next to my head. "Mind-blowing."

"Samuel. Out," Mr. Henderson orders.

You don't have to tell me twice.

By the time Brody and I get to the cafeteria, Samantha's already there, with Paige and Rachel sitting across from her. Brody slides into the seat next to Paige. He slips an arm around her waist, and she does this wiggle-slash-happy dance I wish I could unsee. Jared is trying to make his move on Rachel again, so the only open seat at the table is next to Sam.

When I plop my tray onto the table, she glowers at me. "What do you think you're doing?"

"Eating lunch." I glide into my chair. "You see, Sam-Man, the food we eat gets metabolized, and it turns into glucose for our cells to use. And big, strapping guys like me do a lot of metabolizing."

"Ugh." She pushes my tray away from hers. "Only you could make a biological process sound dirty. Go away."

I glance around the table. Jared shrugs. Rachel mouths, "I have no idea."

To further irritate her, I add, "The dirty part is after our body has removed all the nutrients and what's left over—"

"Ew." Paige covers her ears. "Gross. Some of us are eating."

Sam points to a table full of football jocks. "Why don't you teach them about metabolism?" She flicks her wrist to shoo me away. "Nobody at this table cares."

Her face is bright red as she cuts at her lasagna until it's unrecognizable. My friends stare at me, waiting for my response. I tap Sam's tray with my fork. She stabs at my hand with her fork.

"She's still miffed that even though she scored the winning goal, her percentages sucked."

Sam slams her fork on the table. "You need to get over that. I did fine."

"Stats don't lie."

If she could shoot daggers with her eyes, I'd be a dead man. "What's it to you anyway?"

"I'm only stating facts."

Between bites of her lasagna, she says, "I don't give a flying fudge monkey about what you have to say." She scans the table.

Paige and Rachel shake their heads, probably too afraid to dispute her word.

"Jared cares, don't you?" I ask.

He freezes, like a deer caught in the headlights. "Uh, I plead the sixth."

"The fifth," I say.

"That too."

Sam wads up her napkin and tosses it onto her tray. "If you don't leave this table right now, I will."

Paige latches on to Sam's arm. "Why are you so angry at him?"

"I'm not." Her voice screeches to a level that could break glass.

"Are too," we all reply. When her livid expression falls on me, I wink. *Bad idea.*

"You. Are. A. Jerk."

"I think you need to practice more."

A collective gasp comes from the entire table, and even I know I have gone beyond my usual razzing.

Rachel tsks me. "Samuel King, that was not nice."

Brody chuckles. "You two need to get a room and make up."

"Gah!" Sam picks up her backpack and tray. When she stands, her bag whacks me on the back of the head. "Stop watching me play if my ability disgusts you so much." She stomps away, adding, "Scum bucket."

Jared shakes his head. "You better do damage control."

I groan and start to leave when Rachel grabs my arm. "Not now. I don't know what's going on between the two of you because she usually doesn't let your pestering get her panties in a twist. Let her calm down before you apologize."

My mouth drops open. "Who says I need to apologize?"

"I do," Paige says. "But not now. She's probably in her decompression chamber anyway."

"What did you say?"

"Her father's been filling in for the custodian who is on medical leave, remember? She knows the key combination to his supply room on the C hallway, so she goes there to get her head in the game. I'd bet my LEGO Millennium Falcon, which is safely stored away under my bed, she's there."

Rachel taps the table. "You stay here. We'll go."

Paige gives Brody a sloppy kiss before the two girls rise from the table to go after Sam.

Jared holds his arms out to Rachel. "Wait, don't I get one?" He wiggles his eyebrows like that would seal the deal.

"Maybe next century."

Rachel's deadpan voice and emotionless expression do not discourage him because his face lights up as he replies, "Yes! She didn't say no."

They leave, and Jared dives back into his fries while Brody shakes his head. "Dude, it's not going to happen. Ever."

"I know, but I do love to make Rachel squirm."

I steal some fries off his plate. "Are you still in fifth grade? That's not how it's done."

Brody rests his elbows on the table, and with a twinkle in his eyes, says, "Maybe he should be more like you and find something about Rachel to insult."

"Burn." Jared pops me on the back as he walks away, leaving me with Brody.

"Are you going to give me modeling advice now?" I ask.

Brody hates it when I bring up those commercials his mother roped him into doing for her company when he was in middle school.

He sneers. "You better fix this thing with Samantha because you ticked off the wrong girl."

He's right. I know it, but she's so mad, I'm not sure if she'll even listen to me. I thought a lot about what Mom said. If I'm the best person to help her, that should be more important than my promise to her brother. Plus, I've got Henderson breathing down my neck. With the way my day is going, I'll get my butt kicked by all of them before sunset.

Knowing Brody is right, I go in search of Sam. I skid to a halt when I round the corner to find Samantha at her locker. Ducking into the water fountain alcove, I take the opportunity to secretly watch her without getting her dagger-filled glare. She fidgets with her combination lock then hits the door when it doesn't open. Her forehead rests against it, and several strands of hair escape her ponytail to hide her pretty face. With a quick swipe, she slides the hair behind her ear, but it keeps falling into her eyes, and I'm tempted to help her out. She blows the hair out of her face, and for the first time in my entire life, I forget how to breathe.

Chapter Eleven

Samantha

After three attempts, I yank my locker open, and papers fly all over the floor. This day keeps getting suckier. I crouch in front of my locker, but I don't care enough to pick them up. I can't believe Mule won't help me and that he has the nerve to act like everything is fine. Nothing is fine. And that snide remark about my stats...

"Ugh." I slam the door with so much force, it opens the locker on top, whacking someone in the face with the door.

"Ow."

Samuel stands there, holding his eye, and I groan. Abandoning the papers all over the floor, I dash away toward my safe place inside the janitor's closet. Dad would flip if I ever got caught using the code to get inside. I punch seven, four, one and scoot inside, letting the door slam shut behind me. In complete darkness, I back up as far from the door as possible.

A sliver of light passes across my face as the door creaks open. I hold my breath. *Please don't come in here.* The light from the hallway fades as the door closes again.

"Sam-Man?"

Nooo. "Go away."

"Let's—oh, ack." Water sloshes, and a body hits the floor with a thud. "Sam-Man, help a guy out. I'm not going to hurt you."

Sure, he isn't.

"Please." His plea slices through the darkness.

My fingers graze over his eye, and if I were a vindictive person, I would latch on to a chunk of his long hair and give it a really good yank. He grabs my hand, and his body weight adjusts as he pulls me toward him. I let out a squeak from the surprise contact.

When we're only millimeters apart, his quick, mint-scented breaths drift across my face. Not typically this close to him, I don't realize how all our body parts are in perfect alignment. He slides his hands to rest them on my hips, and I let out a gasp.

I try to add space between us, but his firm hands hold me in place. Resigned to the situation, I slide my hands to rest them on his biceps. They flex at my touch. "How did you get in here?"

"I saw you punch in the code."

"Can you turn off that photographic memory for one day? Don't torture me anymore because I've had enough for a lifetime."

"I'm sorry for what I said at lunch. It was the only way I could get you to talk to me."

"I'm talking to you now. So you can go away." I jut out my chin, ignoring the fact that he can't see me. I straight-arm him to keep as much distance between us as possible. "Admit it, I'm too stupid to be around you."

"Never call yourself stupid again."

I cross my arms over my chest.

Light from his cell phone illuminates his face. I blink to adjust my eyes to the sudden brightness then slip a strand of hair behind my ear.

"Why are you here?" I turn my back on him.

He places his hands on my shoulders to rotate me. The cell phone light shining into the corner of the room illuminates the shelf filled with paper towels and liquid soap. "The CliffsNotes version is, I have reconsidered helping you."

"Too bad. I take back my request."

"But—"

"Did you think I would sit around waiting for you? No sir. I've got three tutors lined up, ready to go." That's a big fat lie, but he doesn't have to know that.

He growls, and that makes me as happy as hitting a three-pointer. "Who?"

"None of your business. Besides, you're probably pranking me anyway."

"I'm serious. I'm not pranking you. I will help you pass."

When I don't answer, he says in a soft voice, "Let me help you."

With all the fight burned out of me, my body sags, and I let out a sigh. "I don't know."

"I promise that you will pass Trig *and* raise your SAT scores." He takes a step closer, and his breath tickles my cheek.

I gaze up to look into his eyes.

"Do you trust me?"

For some strange reason, I do. "I think so."

He blows out his breath. "Good, but we need to keep this our little secret. Promise?"

"Pinkie promise."

"We're not in the third grade."

His strong hands on my arms make me shiver. "I promise." He walks backward, keeping his gaze on me.

"Watch it," I say but not in time before he hits the door.

We fall into an uncomfortable, lingering silence, and I'm not sure what to do or say. This is such a one-eighty from earlier today, it's hard to wrap my head around it.

He clears his throat. "So, are we good?"

What choice do I have? "I guess."

"How about I meet you at the Centennial Arts building after school?"

My gaze snaps back to his as my brain processes his words. "You go to the arts center?"

"I sometimes need to pick up my little cousin from dance class. There's a storage room in the back that I hang out in. I use the park right outside the building as an excuse in case someone sees my truck. You know. The 'jock going for a jog' excuse."

"You are really going to do this for me?"

"Yes," he says before he clears his throat then adds in a more subtle tone, "I mean, what are friends for, right?"

The door clicks open, slicing a stream of light across my face. My mouth gapes open like I'm an idiot. He holds my gaze for a moment longer then adds, "I'll see you this afternoon."

Before I say *heck yeah* or *no thanks*, he leaves.

Samuel is my tutor. He's beautiful and athletic and smart. But my friend? That's a hard one to figure out. I always thought we would be stuck in the frenemy zone forever. He's much easier to deal with when he's aggravating me. This is going to be awkward at best, but it's my best chance of keeping my scholarship.

Chapter Twelve

Samantha

Mule's already at the arts center when I arrive. He sits facing away from the door, at a table in the middle of the room amongst the props and dance costumes. His big feet rest on the table, earbuds in his ears. His wavy hair bounces as he sings to the music, and his voice is so sweet and smooth it's going to give me a cavity. I lean against the doorframe and listen for a moment then venture into the room to stand right over him.

His eyes fly open as he slams his feet onto the floor. He then smiles at me with a slight blush on his cheeks. "'Sup?"

I slide into the chair on the other side of the table. We stare at each other for only a moment, but it seems like hours. He yawns as if he's incredibly bored, then he grins.

"This is really funny to you, isn't it?" I grab my book bag and stand to leave.

He bolts out of his chair to block me from reaching the door. "Hey, now. Don't be sensitive. When a guy can't smile at a pretty girl, we've got real problems."

My bag slides out of my hand and lands on his foot. When I bend to pick it up, I bite my lip to keep the schoolgirl-crush grin from taking over my face. I pop back up and blow out a breath. Ever since our janitor room encounter, I can't stop thinking about him in a more-than-frenemies way, and that scares me. At the most, we're supposed to be buds, but that felt like something more.

He shuts the door, drowning out most of the piano from the dance classes, then takes me by the arm to settle me into the chair next to his. "If we're going to do this, you need to sit beside me so we can work through problems together."

Being alone in the same room with him is hard enough. Sitting right next to him—smelling him, feeling his breath on my skin—is going to make me pass out. I blow out a raspberry. "If you say so."

The chair screeches against the floor when he drags it so close to me that his hairy leg brushes against my not-so-hairy leg, and I regret wearing shorts today. I didn't expect skin-to-skin contact for math help. He opens his notebook and hands me a pencil. My hand trembles so much I drop the pencil on the floor, and it rolls under the table. We both bend down at the same time, bumping heads.

"Sam-Man, you need to relax." He rubs his forehead and laughs. "Boy, I've got to earn your trust, don't I?"

I snort. "Trust the bad boy. Piece of cake."

"I deserve that. I'm really trying to be a better person. Ever since Mom got sick, I..." He taps the pencil on the table.

My heart breaks into a million little pieces. I don't know what I would do if my mother had a terminal illness. Sometimes, I forget about the crap he deals with at home.

He clears his throat then continues, "I want to be a better person for her."

For a quick second, sadness washes across his face before he snaps out of it. "And Craig doesn't trust me within a mile of you, so don't mention this to him."

"Craig is an ogre, and he's not the boss of me."

Sam cocks his head to the side. "Good to know. And for the record, I *can* be sweet if I want to be."

"You're more like devil's food cake sweet. Sinful and yummy at the same time."

His laughter rumbles through the room, and I wish a hole could open up in the middle of this room and swallow me. "I'm going to stop talking now."

"Please don't. It's cute."

Cute? Holy crap. He's never used that word when talking about me.

He scoots closer as he opens his notebook, and I feel his leg hairs on my bare leg again. Why am I completely aware of his body hair all of a sudden? He's a guy, and I know he's bound to have hair, but I've never touched any of it before and… gah. So soft. I'll never be able to concentrate now.

"Before you get any ideas about me thinking you're stupid, I want to back up and go over some algebra basics. If you don't understand these concepts, you'll get frustrated later. Got it?"

"Yep."

"Let's solve this algebra problem. X plus six equals ten. What's the first rule in algebra?"

He writes out the problem, and I mull over his question. "Um, is it whatever you do to the left side, you have to do the right?"

"Pfft. And you said you were stupid. So if we subtract six from the left side, we have to subtract six from the right?"

I nod, understanding him so far.

"Samuel rule number one—'Always show your steps.' Repeat after me. Always show your steps."

With my hand held up like I'm going to pledge scout's honor, I repeat, "Always show your steps."

"Good. So what is the answer to the problem?"

Snatching the pencil from him, I subtract six from both sides. "X equals four."

Sam throws his head back and grins like a proud papa. "Samuel rule number two—'Samantha is smart.'"

Like an idiot, I blink at him as I mull over his words.

"Go on. Say it."

"You called me by my real name."

He nudges my shoulder with his. "Don't get used to it. Say it."

"Samantha is smart." My grin couldn't get any bigger.

"That's my girl. Now let's go on to the next step."

I wipe my mouth in case there's any drool spilling over. He said "my girl." If mindless, accidental touches during our session make my mind go blank, calling me his girl is going to turn off my ability to breathe. It would be so much easier if he was being his normal pesky self. At least then I wouldn't be leaning in close in hopes of getting a smooch.

He stares at me and smiles again. "Are you all right?"

"Yes," I say about three octaves higher than my regular voice.

He places the pencil on the table. "You are so wound up." He stands and motions to the door with his head. "Come on. We could both use a jog."

"Are we done with math?" *Please say we're done. I can handle one problem a day.*

He chuckles. "Not even close. We'll talk while we jog."

Well, crud. "I'm supposed to write the steps. Samuel rule number one is 'Always show your steps.'"

"You're trying too hard. Trust me on this. You and I are a lot alike. We do our best thinking when we're doing something physical. You'd be surprised how this will clear your mind, and the answers will appear out of nowhere."

Mule leads me outside, and I let him because he's still holding on to my hand and I want him to do that for a while longer. We walk the first lap around Centennial Park, hardly saying a word. Out of the blue, he asks me, "X plus six equals ten. Solve for X."

"Four."

He stops to stare at me then raises his hand for me to high-five. I slap it with too much enthusiasm.

"Samuel rule number four."

"What happened to rule number three?" I ask as we start out with a light jog.

With a shocked expression on his face, he replies, "You are paying attention. Rule number three—'Trust Samuel.'"

"That will be hard to do."

He runs ahead so he jogs backward in front of me. "Sam-Man, trust me."

"I'll try."

Three miles later, we've gone over all the properties of a circle. I surprise myself when I can carry on a conversation with him about math, and he hasn't given me one snarky retort. We work our way back to the arts center and collapse into our chairs. He takes out a piece of paper and writes. I crane my neck to get a peek at what he's doing, but he rotates his big body to block my view, his hair falling over his face.

"No peeking." He scribbles some more then hands me the paper. "Don't think. Answer the questions. Remember the Samuel rules." I stare at him, and he says, "Don't Think. Do. Exactly like you do on the court."

"You sound like Yoda, but I think they should be called Sam Squared rules. We're both Sam, and it's math. See what I did there?"

He high-fives me. "Impressive. Sam Squared rules from here on out."

I take the paper, and before I know what I'm doing, I scribble all my answers and shove the page back to him, cringing. He'll probably laugh then post my mess on Snapchat.

He scans over the page, then his eyes flick back up at me with an annoyed expression. He crumples the paper and tosses it over his head. My heart sinks, and so do my hopes. I thought I knew the answers.

"See? You know this stuff. Tomorrow, we go over triangles."

"What are you saying?" With an outstretched foot, I retrieve the balled-up paper and flatten it out. "I got them all right?"

"Uh, yeah. Do you doubt my abilities as a tutor?"

I stare at the page and shake my head in disbelief. "I guess not." My top teeth graze over my bottom lip. "Thank you."

He winks. "You're welcome."

Internal happy dance.

That night, I drift off to sleep thinking of the diameter and radius of a circle, but instead of seeing an image of a round object in my dreams, it's the gorgeous face of my brilliant tutor. I think I'll be able to do this. Wait. Samuel's rule is Don't Think, Do. That must be his life mantra because it fits his personality.

My mantra is Think, Think, and Overthink. His style works for school but also keeps him in trouble. My overanalyzing keeps me out of trouble but doesn't help in the school department. There has to be a happy medium. That's got to be Sam Squared rule number four.

Chapter Thirteen

Samuel

Mason must have a hollow leg because when my cousin comes over for dinner, my mom has to make twice as much food. He may be a scrawny geek, but he sure does pack it away. At Thanksgiving last year, he ate a whole pecan pie by himself. He kept saying "too much *pi* gives me a large circumference." I just can't deal with his nerdiness sometimes.

After dinner, he stretches out on the sofa in the den, rubbing his belly, then lets out a belch that smells like sour chicken. "Sorry, but man oh man, that feels so much better."

"Loser cousin, you're nasty." I throw him a game controller, which he lets bounce off his stomach and onto the floor.

He searches for it with his foot before his toes latch on to it. Like a monkey, he takes it with his foot and tosses it onto the sofa, never moving out of his supine position. "Not so nasty that I can't whip your butt, moron cousin."

"Bring it."

And he whips my butt. My mind keeps wandering back to my tutoring session. Once Samantha relaxed, she allowed herself to have fun and learn. That part about exercise relaxing the brain was only a half-truth. I was getting too flirty during our session. She's never been interested in me, so I wasn't going to make it awkward between us by seeming like I wanted more.

I love how we were able to run at the same pace and still carry on a conversation. In my mind, I still see the sweat droplets sliding down her neck and between her boobs. As soon as I get rid of Mason, I'm going to retrieve my sketch pad and put her image on paper.

"Must be some fantasy," Mason says, jolting me out of my daydream.

With a shake to my head, I bring myself back to reality. "Huh?"

He giggles like a girl. "I've been pummeling your player with a banana for ninety seconds while you stare off into space."

Fetching two Cokes from the mini fridge, I hand one to Mason while I guzzle from mine.

"I heard Samantha was so pissed at you that she had your nuts in a vise."

Coke spews out of my nose and mouth and onto Mason.

He wipes his face with the back of his hand. "I prefer diet, but thanks for the offer. What's up with Samantha?"

A groan slips out of my mouth as I sink to sit on the floor next to the couch. Mason slides next to me, not missing a beat with the game. He hits his turbo button, and my tank explodes. He lets out a wicked cackle.

I toss my controller on the floor. "That's it. I'm never playing with you ever again."

"Bwa ha ha," Mason says as he clicks the game off.

"Long story short, she asked me to help her improve her grades, and I refused."

"Why?"

"It doesn't matter because I reconsidered. But I promised her I wouldn't say anything, so don't mention it to anyone, especially Craig. We're doing this in private."

Mason takes a swig from his bottle as he processes my confession. "I don't get why it's such a big deal. Lots of people use tutors."

"She's embarrassed. If she doesn't get her grades up, she could lose her scholarship, so there's a lot riding on this."

He stares off, stroking his hairless chin. He grins and says, "I'll tutor her for you."

I reward him with a nipple twist.

"Ow!" He laughs and wags his finger at me. "You're marking your territory. Don't worry, alpha male, I will defer to your greatness."

I go in for a punch, but he curls into a ball to protect his chest. "Stop it, man."

"She asked me, so I'll deal with it. Besides, I made a deal with Henderson I would tutor someone to keep the 'rents in the dark about a certain cheating episode."

"Dude..."

"I know. One day I'll learn."

"So, how did it go?"

"Her hatred for me has come back to its baseline level."

Mason grins as he continues to protect his flat chest. "How did you manage that?"

"We went for a jog, Mr. Smart A-hole."

"Well, that's boring and so not like you."

This ticks me off, so I stare at the ceiling and shake my head. "Why does everyone always think the worst of me?"

Mason takes another big gulp from his drink and burps out "bad boy."

Even my own cousin thinks the worst. And Craig's Goliath-sized warning leaves no room to negotiate a peace treaty. I need to keep my hands to myself, but no one can take away our study sessions. It's mandated alone time, and I'm going to enjoy every minute of it.

Before I forget, I fire off an email to Henderson so he knows I made good on our deal. I need to keep him off my back and avoid having my parents find out about the cheating.

Chapter Fourteen

Samantha

We sit hovered over our usual table in the arts center as I work through another math problem. Mule takes the paper away from me again. I hate it when he makes me do math in my head.

I take a deep breath and close my eyes and do my best to use my athletic mind. "For sine, I think of SOH."

"Go on." Mule's words tickle my ear.

"That means sine equals opposite divided by the hypotenuse." Cringing, I sneak a peek to find Samuel grinning. "Is that right?"

"Of course, it's right. Continue. What about cosine?"

With renewed confidence, I sit up straight in my chair and recite the trick Mule taught me—Indian Chief Sohcahtoa. He really knows how to phrase things so I'll remember them. "CAH is cosine equals adjacent divided by hypotenuse."

He winks, and I embarrass myself by sighing. "If you get the last part right, we'll go shoot some hoops."

Now he's speaking my language. "Tangent function is TOA. Tangent equals opposite divided by adjacent."

When he stands and stretches his arms over his head, he reveals the happy trail of baby-fine hair that leads from his navel toward the waistband of his gym shorts. "Let's do this."

He doesn't have to tell me twice. Mule grabs a basketball out of the supply closet and motions for me to follow him outside.

"Why is there a basketball in an arts closet?"

"I left it here a few months ago. I can only take hearing Tchaikovsky's *Swan Lake* from the next room about twenty times before I go crazy."

"You know classical music?"

He passes the ball to me then collects his hair up in a man bun. "Oh, hush. Let's go."

Right behind the arts center is a decrepit basketball court. From the weeds pushing up through the cracks in the asphalt, it appears as if no one ever uses it.

"Play to twenty-one?" I ask him, bouncing the ball a few times to get the feel of it in my hand. I love the *splat, splat* of the ball hitting the blacktop.

Before I can stop him, he snatches it out of my hand. "If you think you can handle it."

"Absolutely. It should take me about five minutes to whip your butt."

With a jerk of his head, he motions for me to follow him to center court. His teasing expression eggs me on. "Prove it, Sam-Man."

"You're on, Mule."

He passes me the ball, and I bounce it while I try to figure out his strategy. I fake to the right then lunge to the left and scoot past him to do a layup.

"I let you have that one." He gives me a fist bump.

I throw the ball to him. "I think you've been watching too much ballet."

He chuckles as he tries to power past me, but I steal the ball and take a jump shot then toss him the ball, which he easily catches with his large hands. "Reaching if there ever was one."

"Boo hoo."

He dribbles in place and stares at me with a devious expression. "So, this is how it's going to be?"

"Yep. Blame Craig. He taught me how to be aggressive with one-on-one."

Mule dribbles past me to make the shot.

Hands planted on my hips, I huff. "That was a double dribble."

"Boo hoo hoo. Tell me more about this one-on-one." He wiggles his eyebrows. "Sounds fun. Will it involve any *personal* fouls?"

Heat rises from my neck, and sweat trickles down my back. I've seen him flirt countless times with girls, and it always made me want to barf. But I can't get that tingly feeling to go away. Focus on playing ball. That's safe.

"I don't think you're up for it." I sneak past him and hit a three-pointer from the corner. He retrieves the ball and slowly walks toward me, never losing pace dribbling. He has a serious predator expression on his face.

"I am always up for it." His wicked grin slides across his face, and I can't make my feet move.

He slips right past me, but instead of taking the shot, Mule dribbles around me in a circle. I slap his arm, trying to get to the ball, but he keeps his back to me, protecting the basketball from my hands. "Gotta try harder to get to me, Sam-Man."

I snatch the ball from him, but he's hovering over me. Even when I use my elbows, he doesn't back off. His warm breath tickles the hairs on my neck. From behind me, he grabs for the ball with both hands, one on each side of me, and draws me close to him.

"Uh... I think there's a penalty somewhere."

He dribbles the ball with me, his arms around me, his sweaty face touching my neck, and with every smack, my body bounces against his body. I should move away, but his hand grazing over mine, like a finely choreographed dance, is all I focus on. Sometimes, his hand lands next to mine on the ball. Other times, as if on purpose, his hand winds up right on top of mine, making me forget the score. Roundball has never been more exciting.

Mule plants his hands on my hips, and I forget how to dribble. The ball hits my foot and rolls into the grass. He turns me around, hands still on my hips. My chest presses against his. We're both having a hard time catching our breath from... the game, I assume. I could stare at his face for hours and never need to blink. He gazes down at my mouth then to my eyes before licking his bottom lip. I can't stop staring at his mouth.

"Are you going to the dance this weekend?"

"I... uh..." Gah. It's a simple question, but his sweaty body near me makes my brain short-circuit.

With a husky chuckle, Mule jogs away to retrieve the ball. The hottest and smartest guy at school, who also has sweet tendencies, is flirting with me. I shouldn't fall for his moves because I've seen his usual routine—flirt, make out, dump. Rinse and repeat. What would Chief Sohcahtoa do? Throw up, that's what he'd do, all over his hypotenuse.

Chapter Fifteen

Samuel

Samantha drags her heels as we head to Henderson's class for her first of three make-up tests. We've done five practice tests this week, and she has done pretty well, especially after she loosened up around me, but if she doesn't take a breath soon, she's going to pass out. Her usual tanned complexion has an eerie green tint today, so I hope she doesn't spew all over the floor.

"You've got this." I open the door to Mr. Henderson's room and give her a gentle nudge.

A sly grin slides across his face. "I guess we'll see if you were serious about helping."

"What can I say? I'm a people pleaser."

"Are you ready?" Mr. Henderson asks Samantha.

"No." She swings around to flee from the room, but I place my body in the way then slide her into the first desk right in front of Mr. Henderson's.

He stares at me. "You. Leave now."

I clear my throat and throw a playful jab to Samantha's cheek. "Remember what the chief would do?"

She giggles then pops a hand over her mouth.

"Ah, you used the Chief Sohcahtoa trick, huh?" Mr. Henderson asks me.

"It works." I wave at her. "See ya, Sam-Man."

"Bye."

She should do fine if she keeps her breakfast down. I hope she does well because if she doesn't, her confidence is going to tank. She has come so far in the past two weeks, and I hope Mr. Henderson doesn't crush her with a difficult test.

I'm not hungry, but there's nothing else to do, so I saunter into the cafeteria. Jared and Brody harass Paige and Rachel in the far corner. I'm not in the mood for chatter, so I seek out Mason, who sits at the back table with his head in a book. Typical. I sink into the chair next to him, and he jumps, spilling milk on his nerdy T-shirt.

"Make some noise next time." He closes the book and asks, "Is she taking the exam?"

I nod, scanning the cafeteria. I pick up his burger and take a bite out of it. "She's hardly able to sit still, she's so nervous."

"Henderson is tough. I hope he doesn't stick it to her." He snatches the burger out of my hands.

"Hey, I was eating that."

"Get your own." He peers at it, and I guess he doesn't like the idea of eating after me because he hands it back to me and picks at his fries. "You like her, don't you?"

The bite of burger gets wedged in my throat, so I wash it down with his carton of milk. "She's growing on me."

"Yeah, right. You've always liked her. You forgot I've spent a lot of nights at your house. You tend to talk in your sleep."

Busted. "Do not."

He laughs and wags his finger in front of my face. "You protest too much."

We sit in silence for most of the lunch period, and it seems like the longest thirty minutes of my life. Suddenly, Mason's attention fixes on something behind me. "Uh-oh." He motions with his head.

Following his gaze, I turn around to find Samantha standing in the middle of the lunchroom. Her face is beet red, like she hasn't taken a breath in an hour. Her gaze darts from table to table, and as soon as she sees me, she rushes out of the cafeteria, heading to the janitor's closet, no doubt.

"See ya, man," I say to Mason.

"Good luck."

I take the long way to the C hallway so no one suspects I'm following her, and when the hallway is empty, I punch in the security code then slip inside the storage closet. "Sam-Man? Are you in here?"

"Nope. Nothing but us brooms in here."

I flick on my phone flashlight to see her standing in the back. Her breaths are rapid as her chest rises and falls. If she doesn't calm herself, I may have to give her mouth-to-mouth, not that it would be a hardship for me.

"Talk to me." I reach out for her, and she grabs my arm. She crinkles a piece of paper in the other. "Is that your test?"

If Mr. Henderson failed her again, I'm going to punch him into an isosceles triangle. With all the extra effort she's put in, I hope he gives her a few points for trying.

With the force of a skilled athlete, she shoves the paper into my stomach. I move the light so it shines on the paper. In red ink, with a huge circle around it, is an eighty-eight. I swivel the light to her face.

"Sam-Man, you not only passed, but you also almost made an A!" I scoop her up in my arms, and she squeals so loud, I may never hear anything again. She wraps her arms around me so tight I think I'm going to die from lack of oxygen, but I don't care. My girl passed. I swing her around, her foot catching on something on the shelf behind her, so I move her closer to me in case it's about to fall on us.

"I'm so proud of you." I bend my head until we're nose to nose and cup her face. "I knew you could do it." Resting my forehead on hers, inhaling her intoxicating scent, is all I want to do for the rest of the day.

"Thank you so much," she whispers.

"It was all you, Sam-Man. All you."

Mentally, I file her expression away for a future drawing when I have the chance to put it on paper.

She snaps her head up and pushes away from me, causing me to open my eyes wide. I clear my throat to bring myself back to reality. Two more seconds, and I would have pressed her beautiful mouth to mine. "Yes. One test down, two more to go. You've got this."

She nods and glances toward the floor. "I'll never be able to repay you."

I tip her chin up until she gazes into my eyes. "Save me a seat at your first college game?"

The biggest grin grows on her face. She wraps her arms around my neck and hugs me again. "You bet."

I slide my hands around her waist as my thumbs slip under her T-shirt. She shivers and steps away from me, still wearing that gorgeous smile. I love that her spark is back, the one she has on the basketball court when she owns the game. Henderson better watch out. I think I created a tangent monster.

Chapter Sixteen

Samantha

As soon as I mentioned I want to go to the dance but not by my-self, Rachel ditched her date, and I love her for it. She was so excited, she even loaned me one of her fancy dresses. It's a little short for my taste, but she says there is no such a thing as too short. She also talked me into wearing heels, so now I tower over half the guys in our class. Being a five-eleven girl is hard even while wearing sneak-ers.

She slips her arm through mine as we near the gymnasium. I guess she senses my nervous energy because she says as we step inside, "You are gorgeous."

I adjust my dress again, hoping it lengthened two inches since the last time I checked. The disco ball makes the pink fabric remind me of a brilliant multicolored gumball. While my knees knock to-gether, I glance around to see if anyone is pointing at me and laugh-ing. No telling the last time any of my classmates saw me decked out like this.

The DJ plays a rap song, and Rachel is already getting into the beat. Me? I wish I could peel out of these toe-pinching heels and shoot some hoops.

She lifts her hands in the air and shimmies around me. "Come on, girl. Dance. Show off those long legs."

I know my face must be the same color as my dress. I'm so much more comfortable in a basketball uniform than a skimpy pink outfit, but I'm here now. Time to break out of my comfort zone if I don't break an ankle in the process.

Mom said I was beautiful, but she says that even when I'm covered in sweat and dirt. Tonight, I feel beautiful. And it's not the dress or the heels, although that's not hurting my confidence. Something inside me that likes the way I look. For once, my outside matches my inside.

Paige flits in on Brody's arm. When she sees me, her hands cover her mouth. She drops his arm and rushes over to me. "Oh my gosh. Wow."

Pointing to Rachel, I reply, "It's all her doing."

Paige tries to give me a hug, but I have to bend since she's so much shorter than me, and I flash cleavage in the process.

Rachel shakes her head. "I gave her the dress and fixed her hair. The rest is all her."

"I'm so glad you came," Paige says. "I know this isn't your thing, and if it weren't for Brody, you know I wouldn't feel comfortable being here either. Let's dance."

She grabs me and Rachel by the hand, and we do a crazy circle dance, making up moves as we go. Paige waves at Brody, and that's when I notice a slack-jawed Samuel staring a hole through me. He's stopped mid sip of the drink in his hand, and it appears he's not paying attention to the three girls vying for his attention. The more I dance, the sultrier his stare becomes. I wiggle my hips to the beat of the music, and from the way his jaw drops, I'm getting to him. He doesn't move. He doesn't smile. All he does is stare, and even though I try not to peek his way, I do so every chance I get. I have never seen him look at me like that, and it's both invigorating and scary.

Rachel and Paige seem oblivious to the show I'm putting on for Samuel, and I don't care if they catch on. I love the surge of confidence I have, so much so I even have the nerve to wink at him. He motions with his head for me to join him at the punch bowl, where he pours another glass of punch, guzzles it, then tugs at his necktie.

Over the blaring music, I scream to Paige, "I'm pooped. Time-out."

Rachel prances over to Jared, who grins like he is more than happy to dance with her. Paige falls into Brody's arms, and they act like no one else is in the room. I give myself a once-over to make sure my dress isn't hiked up over my butt and I haven't got a boob hanging out. I want to touch my hair to ensure it's still in place, but I'm afraid if I mess with it, the curls will fall out.

I walk across the dance floor as slowly as possible because if I don't, I might fall on my face. Samuel's eyes burn the dress off me.

"Wow."

"You're not so bad either."

He whistles. "Wow. You're hot. I mean you're always hot, but I... I..."

I bite my bottom lip because it's adorable that he, of all people, is tongue-tied over me. "I'd rather be running laps than be here, but what the heck? I'm here now." I pop my hip out for added emphasis.

He jerks his thumb over his shoulder. "We could go for a jog. I'd love to see you do it in that dress, and I would definitely get to my target heart rate in record time."

With a playful punch to his arm, I say, "I didn't spend all that time on this outfit to do interval training. Besides, I bet you say that to all the girls." I smirk, making sure he knows I'm on to him.

All I get for the longest time is one slow, deliberate head shake, and I am positive he doesn't see my dress anymore. He blinks and shakes his head then asks, "Want to dance?"

"Are you as good a dancer as you are..." I wiggle my eyebrows. "You know."

Cringing, he says, "Mom did force me to take dancing lessons, so..."

Mule leads me out onto the dance floor, and thank goodness it's a fast song so not much touchy-feely stuff will happen.

"Follow my lead." He plants my body smack-dab against his, one hand snakes around my waist, and the other holds one of my hands as he leads me through steps I've only seen on *Dancing with the Stars*.

He's so good, all I have to do is lean into him, and he does all the work.

"Same as math. Don't think. Focus on the music."

All I feel is my heart pounding out of my chest. He spins me once, twice, then leads me into him again. To end the dance, he dips me low, my hair brushing the floor. He winks before he gathers me up into a hug.

The sound of clapping surrounds us, and I scan the room to find my friends. Paige's mouth is wide open in shock while Rachel gives me a nod of approval. All the other girls snarl like I've encroached on their territory.

Samuel smiles. "You're a great partner."

I grin so much my cheeks hurt. "I let you do all the work. That was so much fun."

He holds his hands out, inviting me for another dance. As tempting as it is, I shake my head as I back away from him.

Mule pouts, which is kind of cute but doesn't make me change my mind. "Why not?"

"I better not. I think I've made enough enemies for one night."

He scans the gym, his eyes roving over all the gawking girls, then shrugs like he is either totally oblivious to how girls act around him or he just doesn't care.

"You really are like devil's food cake, aren't you?" *I cannot believe I said that out loud.*

A slight blush creeps across his cheeks. First he pouts, and then he blushes. I could get used to that puppy dog face. I offer him a cup of punch and guzzle from my own cup.

Jared enters our bubble and whistles. "Where's mine?"

"Go away," I say, which he ignores. To Mule, I say, "Do you excel at everything?"

He shakes his head and takes a sip from the cup of punch. "You want to find out what else I'm good at?"

My plastic cup drops from my hand, bounces off Samuel's shoe, and sloshes punch all over Jared's pants. His shoe slides on a puddle on the floor.

"I'm so sorry," I say as I grab some napkins and proceed to scrunch down and wipe punch off his pants.

One of the teachers rushes over and takes over cleanup duties, so I rise ever so carefully to avoid slipping in my heels and take a step back toward Samuel.

I poke Samuel in the chest. "Want to find what else I'm good at? That has to be the worst line ever." I groan. "I figured you'd have something slicker than that in your repertoire." When I lean in, I whisper, "Like some sexy, geeky pickup line?"

His response is totally a "don't go there" expression, so I let it go. A slow song begins, and Samuel slides his arm around my waist. He whispers in my ear, "Meet me in your favorite hiding spot in five minutes."

He winks then walks away. My pounding heart is so loud, I can no longer hear the music. Not knowing what I should do, I racewalk through the hallway toward the bathroom and check under all the stall doors to make sure I'm alone, then I turn to face the mirror.

"I danced with Samuel," I say to myself. As I pace the length of the bathroom, I shake out my hands like I'm about to shoot a free throw. I could be totally wrong, but there have been a few times over the past couple of weeks that I felt like he was going to kiss me, but now...oh, yeah, he definitely wants to kiss me. *Do I want to kiss him?*

Turning back to the mirror, I say, "He makes me laugh, and I like being around him." I let out a breathy giggle as I stare at my reflection. "I never thought I would ever say that. But do I want to kiss him? There's only one way to find out."

I smile as I rush out the door. This must be Sam Squared rule number five—"When you see something you want, go for it."

Chapter Seventeen

Samuel

With urgency, I rip out the hairband and release the man bun then scrub a hand through my hair while I walk back and forth through D hallway. What is wrong with me? I'm as nervous as a sinner in church. I've kissed lots of girls, and usually I dive in. I don't do any of this romantic stuff. I need to go in that storage room, kiss the heck out of Samantha, and get her out of my system.

Even I know I'm lying. Nothing about her is usual. She's sweet and kind, and I've wanted to do this since... forever. But Craig...

"You're gonna wear a path in the tile with all that pacing." Mason props himself against a row of lockers. He's dressed like he's ready for a forties swing dance competition with his double-breasted suit and two-toned oxford shoes. At least he isn't wearing one of his geeky math T-shirts.

"What do you want?"

He shrugs and steps toward me, his two-tone shoes making a clipping sound on the floor. "I saw how you undressed Samantha with your eyes, and I'm completely shocked at how clean you kept that dance." He waltzes with a pretend partner, and he doesn't even deserve an eye roll.

Hoping we are not being overheard by anyone, especially Sam, I prop up against the lockers to act nonchalant. "What's it to you?"

"She's sweet, Samuel." He walks up to me, his brow furrowed.

"I know that."

"Not to get all sappy on you, but you can be, too, if you want to be." With that, he takes a step away, I guess in case I take a swing at him.

I bang my head against a locker and groan. "What should I do?"

He clutches his chest and gasps. "You are asking me for romance advice? Dude, you know what you need to do."

Yep, and it's now or never. If I'm lucky, Craig will never have to know.

"What are you waiting for, cuz?"

"I don't know." My feet feel like they are encased in concrete. I want to go, but I'm terrified she'll reject me.

Mason cracks a sly grin. "So, you won't mind if I make a move? I think she's great."

Through clenched teeth, I say, "Stay away from her."

He pushes off the locker and clicks his shoes like he's tap dancing. "If you're not going to do something about it, why can't I?"

With a snort, I say, "You? You couldn't handle her."

He laughs in my face, like only a relative can and live to talk about it. "Like you can."

I hate him because he is dangerously close to the truth.

"I'm right, aren't I?" His grin grows wider.

Sweat trickles down my back as my breath grows rapid. With an angry tone, I reply, "You're wrong."

He shrugs and stuffs his hands into his pants pockets. "I think I'll make out with her."

Now he's gone and done it. If he touches her, I'll make sure he sings soprano for the rest of his life. He must see the steam pouring out of my ears because he raises his hands in surrender.

"Chill, cuz. I'm giving you a hard time. From the way she looks tonight, don't be surprised if at least ten other guys take notice." He bumps me with his shoulder. "All I'm saying is piss or get off the pot."

His words ring in my ears louder than the clicking of his shoes. I stomp into the restroom and splash water on my face. I've got to get control of myself. No girl has ever freaked me out like Samantha.

I stare at myself in the mirror and take a deep breath. I like her. I want her. Now is the time to show her how I feel. I only hope she feels the same way. With renewed confidence, I strut toward Samantha's closet.

Samantha

My confidence boost from the dress diminishes a little more every minute that passes by and he doesn't show. There were at least twenty girls pawing all over him in the gym, so there's no way he's interested in me. And that's why he hasn't shown up. He's found someone better to play with.

I should sneak out of here and slip into the bathroom, then no one will ever have to know about this. I'll be the bad guy, and maybe things won't be so awkward between us on Monday because I'm not quite ready to go it alone in the studying department.

So maybe I'll wait fifteen more seconds because I'd really like to know what those lips feel like. I don't care if it's nothing to him, I have to know. Ten more seconds, and I should leave. Five seconds.

Right when I think he's not coming, a sliver of light makes me spin around. He slips in fast, like he's trying to avoid anyone who might be watching. The bottom of his shoes scuff on the floor as he inches closer.

In complete darkness, I say, "I was about to—"

He grabs me, shocking the breath out of my lungs. He slides one arm around my waist, while the other rests behind my head. His breath tickles my ear as he nibbles on it, leaving a trail of goose bumps down my arms. Every nerve ending tingles with anticipation of what he will do next. He gathers my hair and slides it to the side as he makes his way to my left ear, his lips so warm and soft, teasing me with each touch.

I slide my hands up his chest and clench his shirt. I hope he can't hear my heart, but I know he feels how fast it's beating. His is, too, for that matter. We're forehead against forehead, his rapid breaths warming my face.

With a husky, quiet voice, he says, "I've wanted to do this ever since you held my hand when Nemo's mother died."

"Wanted to do what?" I'm surprised I'm able to speak.

His hands cup my jaw, his thumbs caress my cheeks, then his lips find mine in the darkness. One small, soft, chaste kiss. I slide my arms around his neck and hold him tighter. His tongue dances with mine, and I forget how to stand.

He breaks contact with my mouth and rests his forehead on mine. "Oh, Samantha."

Chest against chest, hips against hips, he walks me backward until I'm up against the wall. A hand slides down my arm, to my waist, and lands on my butt. He gives it a gentle squeeze, making me moan.

My lips find his again, and I slide my tongue over his slightly crooked canine tooth. I can't believe Samuel is kissing me, but I want more than a secret make-out session in a dark closet. I want hand-holding and opening doors. I want snuggle time while we pretend to watch movies and embraces in public that make my foot pop like in the movies. What I certainly don't want is to remember being surrounded by cleaning supplies and a mop bucket during my first romantic time with Samuel, so I can't let anything else happen tonight.

I push him away even though it's the last thing I want to do. He stumbles backward as I move around him. "That was..."

"Amazing." He turns me to face him again then kisses my neck. "You know, whatever I do to one side of the equation, I must do to the other." His mouth finds the other side, and a giggle bursts out of my mouth.

"Only you could incorporate algebra into a make-out session."

"I'm a multitasker."

"I noticed."

His phone buzzes, and he plants a quick peck on my lips before he steps away from me. I already miss the heat radiating from the contact. "Fun time is over, Sam-Man." His fingers trail down my cheek as if he second-guesses his decision to end our moment.

"Yeah, I better go too. Thank you."

Did I just thank him for the kiss? I'm so stupid!

I float out of the closet and straight into the bathroom to catch my breath. That was better than making a three-pointer five times. His lips are magical, and I can hardly breathe thinking about what happened. I still feel every spot he touched. It's crazy to think that Mule likes me. Me! The sweaty tomboy he's known his entire life, the person he's tormented and teased for as long as I can remember. Maybe all that was his silly way of showing he's attracted to me, and I was too blind to see it. Well, my eyes are wide open now.

The water splashing onto my face clears my head. I don't care that all my makeup swirls down the drain along with my pride. I let him kiss the socks off me—if I had on socks—and I liked it. I liked it a lot, and I can't wait for more.

The image of myself in the mirror looks nothing like it did when I showed up at the dance. I have bed hair, and my dress is all wonky to the side, so I shift it back into place and try to smooth my hair into a reasonable shape. I feel like a giddy tweenager getting her first kiss. But wow... That wasn't anything ordinary. It was mind-blowing.

Samuel

After Sam scurries away, I bang my head against the back shelf of the cleaning closet. I reread the text message that interrupted our fun time. Her brother has the worst timing, and he makes me want to punch something.

C: *Heard her tutoring sessions are paying off.*

He really has the worst timing. It's only been minutes since I kissed his sister.

Me: *Yup.*

C: *Can't believe you of all people found her a tutor.*

The corner of my lip turns up. *Oh, I found someone, all right.*

C: *Do you have something you want to tell me???*

He sends me a screenshot of an Instagram post. The pic is of Samantha and me dancing, and my heart stops. Crap. *Stupid, stupid.* I should have known at least one person would post on social media, but it still seems soon. We're still at the dance.

Me: *You spying on me?*

C: *King, there are eyes everywhere. Hands off or I will beat you to a pulp.*

This is not good.

I made out with his sister, and I want to do it a thousand more times. But I can't. Craig will punch out my lights, and on instinct, I will fight back, making things worse. The thought of getting the cops called on me again is enough of a deterrent. I am still popo phobic after the incident at the frat house. Every time a fuzz mobile drives down the road, I come close to having a panic attack, thinking about the frat party near-arrest. Ten minutes in the back seat of that police cruiser—with nothing to think about but my mother's soul-crushing relapse and all the stress my shenanigans cause her—was enough for me to swear off fighting for a lifetime. I can never give my mother a reason to worry about me again. Ever. So hands off Samantha from now on.

Samantha

With his back against a locker, Samuel checks his phone while I drift toward him, still floating on a cloud. I'm ready to ditch the dance and finish what we started.

"Hey," I say, my words a little breathy.

I reach out to take his hand, but he shakes his head as he stiffens.

In my ear, he whispers, "That kiss... It didn't happen. Got it?"

Mule must be joking. It was amazing, and he felt it too. No one can fake a kiss like that. I'm not an expert on the subject, but that kiss ranks up there with those in *Gone With the Wind* and *The Princess Bride,* in my opinion.

He runs a hand through his hair then blows out a nervous breath. "I... I don't think it was a good idea that we did that. Let's pretend it didn't happen. It was all my fault." That jerk chews on his bottom lip and focuses on the floor.

I scrunch my brow as reality sets in. Crashing off the cloud of sheer delight, I land hard back into reality. This was all a cruel joke to him, and I cannot believe I fell for it. This must have been a bet or a test to see if I was gullible enough to fall for it, and I did.

"Wow. Less than two minutes, and you're already regretting it. You're a piece of work, Mule." He better be glad I have some restraint because I fight the urge to punch him in the stomach.

"I didn't say that. What I mean is..."

Mule peers around the hallway. His meaning clicks with crystal clarity. I backpedal, and my high heel slides on the tile floor. He grabs my arm and keeps me from falling, but I jerk free of his grasp. "Nope. We wouldn't want anyone to see us together. I get it."

He scrubs his face, like he's fighting several emotions, but so am I. All he says is "Thanks, Sam. I knew you would understand."

My lips form a tight line. While I would rather claw his eyes out, all I do is nod. "Of course. What are friends for?"

I stomp through the hallway back to the gymnasium, giving myself a mental pat on the back for not breaking down into hysterics. I weave my way through different couples until I find Rachel, her head resting on Mitch Johnson's chest. *Ew.*

"Rachel, I need to go. Now."

She pushes Mitch away. "What happened?"

I shake my head, and we both turn to see Samuel scamper into the gym, scan the crowd, then walk my way.

Paige rushes toward me. "What's going on?"

"I need to go. I think I'm going to be sick." Bile creeps up my throat, and I might spew chunks all over the dance floor if I don't get out of here fast. The sight of that horrible person makes my stomach churn.

Brody, Jared, and Mason head toward us. They all have "what is going on" expressions on their faces. I would like to know the answer to that also.

Brody takes Paige by the hand and asks Samuel, "What's the matter?"

Samuel scrubs his face with his hands. "I swear I don't know. Sam-Man, talk to me."

Of all the nerve!

Brody snorts. "Yeah, suuure you don't. What stupid thing did you do this time?"

Rachel scans my appearance, analyzing every messed-up curl and my smudged makeup. "Don't lie to me. I know a make-out face when I see one."

To save face, I stiffen my spine and let the biggest whopper of a lie fly out of my mouth. "Someone followed me into the supply closet and kissed me senseless. I have no idea who it was, but it was frickin' amazing."

Samuel's jaw drops.

Too bad, Mule. You started this.

"Are you serious?" Rachel takes me by the arm, so I face her. "You don't know who it was?"

I shake my head. "It was dark, but I'll tell you this much. When I find out who it was, we're going to finish what we started." An evil glint in my eye helps solidify the lie.

Brody whistles, getting an elbow in the gut, compliments of Mule.

Rachel takes me by the hand and bounces on her toes. "You leave this to me. I'll figure it out."

Paige grabs my other arm, and together, they escort me toward the exit.

I take one more peek at Samuel and catch him running a hand through his hair. He gives me a slight shake of his head, as if to tell me, *Don't do it.*

Take that, Mister Big Shot. He can take his stupid rules and mess with someone else.

Chapter Eighteen

Samuel

Well, that blew up in my face, royally. If I were to Google *chicken*, my face would be the first result to show up. No need to click on the "I'm feeling lucky" icon. I finally got to taste that sexy mouth, and what did I do? I freaked out, all because of that stupid bro code and the fact I'm so scared of Craig my balls shrink up just thinking about his wrath.

Once my lips made contact with Samantha's, there was no stopping me. I was ready to take it to the next level... in a storage closet. If my phone hadn't buzzed, Craig would have buried me under the doghouse and peed on my grave. Clearly, I did not work through all the steps, but I did show my work, not that Craig would give me extra credit. In fact, he would deduct points by pummeling me.

Brody stares a hole through me like it's my fault his girlfriend ditched him to take care of Samantha. He needs to understand the girl code. They will drop a guy like a hot potato to take care of one of their own.

Brody growls at me, so I ask, "What's your problem?"

He scoffs as his jaw clenches. "I had some serious plans for after the dance, and that's all gone now, thanks to you."

With an innocent expression, I point to myself, like I have no idea what he's talking about. "Me?"

"Yeah, you," Jared says. "Where Paige and Samantha go, there goes Rachel too. She was finally paying me attention tonight." He punches me on the arm. "Two years. I've been trying for two years to get her to notice me."

I grab where he hit me then punch him back. "You and the entire male population at this school."

"Shut up, man. Did you try anything on Samantha? That's what it seemed like in there."

"No, it wasn't me." I pour myself another cup of punch and swallow it in one big gulp. I wish it were spiked, but it's obviously only frickin' punch.

Mason saunters up to us and smirks.

After I scrub my face with my hands and let out an agonizing groan, I say, "Fine, I'll admit I thought about it, but... I didn't."

Mason cocks his head to the side, and I know he doesn't believe me. "Then who did?"

I shake my head. "No clue." *Keep digging that hole, dummy.*

Jared glances between Mason and me, with obvious confusion. "What are you talking about?"

"Nothing," Mason says.

"I need to talk to her." I start toward the gym door. My brain hasn't yet processed what I would say if I caught up to her, but I should at least try.

Brody and Jared block me from leaving. Jared shakes his head. "Whoa. You do not want to get near her tonight. Let Rach and Paige work their magic."

Mason peeks around Brody. "Yeah, she seemed pretty ticked off at you. If you know what's best, you'll give her some space."

I sigh. "I guess you're right. I'm going home."

Jared waves his hand to indicate where five girls stand smiling at me. Their dresses are so short they are more like long shirts. And all that makeup... blech. "They'll help you forget your troubles."

That's what the old Samuel would do. I could snap my fingers, and another girlie would jump at the chance to hook up. Even if I did have to block out the horrific chatter that goes along with that kind of girl, it would help me forget about Samantha. But that is not me anymore. I don't want those girls.

They don't even tempt me a bit. "Not in the mood."

As I walk away, Mason mumbles to Jared and Brody. All three nod. I punch Mason in the arm hard enough for him to get the message but not hard enough to cause damage. He is my cousin, after all, and I wouldn't really hurt him for anything.

I cock my head to the side because I smacked a solid wall of muscle instead of flab. He's still very much on the skinny side, but... "Dude, when did you start working out?"

Mason blushes and walks away, like he doesn't know how to handle a compliment that doesn't pertain to his grades.

On the way to my truck, I send a text message to Samantha. It's a long shot, but I must try.

Me: *Please talk to me.*

Sam-Man: *Nope, you numbskull.*

I slam the truck door and loosen my tie, but the tightness in my chest remains. My phone buzzes, making me jump. Maybe it's her. I glance at my phone. Craig. Another text from the ogre.

C: *Are you being a good boy?*

I want to punch his throat. All I want to do lately is punch something, and I don't like how that feels.

Me: *Yes.*

C: *If you ever touch my sister, I will beat the you know what out of you.*

Me: *Rocky set me up, and you know it. His accusations are disgusting.*

C: *You mean you won't do it again.*

My blood boils. I throw my phone across my truck so hard the case pops off and flies under the seat. I slam my fist into the steering wheel. That was the most knock-your-socks-off make-out session ever, and now, I have to pretend someone else's lips tasted her sweet mouth.

This would be so much easier if Samantha were an only child. I have no idea how I'm going to dig my way out of this mess.

Chapter Nineteen

Samantha

The three of us pile into Rachel's convertible and race away from the madness. I don't know which emotion is the worst—anger or humiliation. Both are pretty top tier to describe my night. My phone buzzes again, but before I answer, Paige snatches it from me. "Nope. Not right now."

I lunge for it, but she hands it to Rachel. "Hey, give it back. It might be important."

"Important, my booty," Rachel says, sitting on my phone while she zooms down Hillsboro Road toward her house. When we stop at a red light, she reads the text. "Pfft." She texts someone back.

"Who was it?"

"Now sit tight. When we get to my house, we're going to kick off these sexy pumps, raid the fridge, then go over every second of what happened back there. I've never seen you this messed up, and you need to spill the tea."

Paige peers over at Rachel and says, "I don't wear sexy pumps."

Rachel sighs. "Whatever. You can take off your kitten heels. You happy?"

Paige gives her a satisfied smile. "Much better."

"But Samantha and I will take off ours."

There is nothing I want to do more than toss these shoes out a window and never wear them again. Without warning, I laugh at the vision of me tossing the shoes out the window right into Mule's stupid face.

"That's what I want to hear," Rachel says, running a yellow traffic light.

I reach over the front seat. "Can I have my phone back?"

She smacks my hand. "Absolutely not."

I play with one of my few curls that isn't a frizzy mess, remembering those big hands tangled up in my hair. His hands were all over my body, and I liked it. A lot.

Rachel turns into her driveway and shoves the gear shift into park.

I clear my throat. "About the guy—"

My feisty friend stops me from finishing. "Hold that thought. I'm hungry."

She leads us straight into the kitchen, where the three of us load up on chips and Diet Cokes then scramble up the stairs to what she calls her "messy room." Half of the upstairs is one big open space with a futon, throw pillows, a pool table, and tons of lounge seating perfect for hanging out. Cool posters cover the walls from when her father worked on the TV show *Southern Tea*. That was before he cheated on Rachel's mother and moved to Los Angeles.

We dump the food on the futon and start stuffing our faces with tortilla chips. We could hole up here for days, and no one would ever find us. Right now, that sounds like the perfect plan.

Paige kicks off her shoes and wiggles her toes freely. "Whew. I hate wearing dressy shoes. So, what's the plan?"

Rachel points to me then to the futon. "Lie down. Close your eyes, and try to relive the moment."

I grab another mouthful of chips and ask, "Is this like a therapy session? Do I learn that all my problems are because of trust issues with my mother?"

"Paige, grab some notebook paper off my desk and write down everything she says."

Before I settle in, I take another swig from my drink. I'm so exhausted, it will be a miracle if I stay awake. It's time to come clean with my friends, at least with part of the story. "Samuel asked me to meet him in the closet."

Rachel chokes on her drink, and Paige smiles. "It was Samuel?"

"No, he didn't show." *Liar, liar, pants on fire.* "Let me finish."

After I spill my guts and remove Mule's name as the culprit, I open one eye to see their reaction to my tale. Rachel's mouth drops. "Hubba hubba."

"I'm not done. It felt like he wanted more, and I didn't want to do anything more with him in a janitor's closet, so I pushed him away then ran into the bathroom."

I balance on my elbows. "When I came out of the bathroom, Mule was in the hallway. He said he was sorry that he led me on and he couldn't go through with meeting me in the closet." *And the bending of the truth continues.*

Rachel drops her drink. Soda splatters all over the walls, but she doesn't even seem fazed by the mess she made. She sits next to Paige on the bed. "Maybe it really was him, and he's too afraid of his feelings."

Man, she's perceptive.

She pushes me back onto the futon. "Details about the aforementioned tongue wrestling. Think about it. What made it significant?"

Other than everything, absolutely nothing.

While I think back over the event, I close my eyes, and the image appears in my mind as clear as the moment it happened. "His hands were strong, and I think his lips were full. His tongue did this circle swirly thing on my lips before he kissed me."

To lead them away from Samuel, I add, "Scruffy chin that didn't so much as hurt but felt... sexy. He seemed tall, taller than me, even with my heels on." I decide not to include his slightly crooked tooth because Rachel will be prying every guy's mouth open to check out their dental situation, and because... they don't need to know that, and I like having at least one piece of the kiss private.

"Jeez, girl." Rachel fans herself. "That certainly was *not* Samuel."

My shoulders slump. "You've made out with him?"

"Yeah, and trust me, it was all hunger and no passion." She juts out her tongue like she's a frog catching flies.

Paige giggles at Rachel's motions. "That sounds terrible. And spot-on. I remember swapping spit with him in ninth grade, and it was... blech."

At least they don't think it was him. But they have it all wrong. He kissed me senseless. I don't know who they are talking about because the version of Samuel who kissed me was very skilled.

Rachel takes my hand in hers. "I don't think it was him either. He's not really that good of a kisser."

I cover my face with a pillow and scream into it. "I told you already, it wasn't him. Please drop it."

"What did his breath smell like?" Rachel starts her pacing again.

To relive the moment, I close my eyes. "Fresh, minty."

Rachel cackles. "Not Samuel. He smelled like smoke."

"Chewing tobacco," Paige chimes in and pretends to gag herself. "I can still taste it."

I stand and sling some balls around on Rachel's pool table. "Enough about Mule. Besides, after his mom got cancer, he quit smoking and dipping. I don't even think he drinks anymore."

She snatches the paper from Paige and reads the list. "We have a kissing bandit at our school, and we need to find out who it is. Operation Mystery Lips starts right now."

Paige bounces on the bed and does a cheerleader clap. "Woohoo! This is so much fun."

Her definition of fun is way different from mine, and I am starting to regret every bit of my lie. It's going to come back to bite me on my behind at some point. I freeze before I send another ball across the pool table. "I don't think I want to—"

Rachel cocks her head to the side. "Are you *afraid* we'll find out who it is?"

I pout. Even though there really isn't a mystery man, I'm too far into this to turn back. I must get over my infatuation with Mule. He'll never be more than my occasional friend and my tutor, if a moment's weakness didn't mess that up. Plus, I have a game tomorrow night. Ugh. If I ever speak to Mule again, I'm going to give him a piece of my mind. Samantha rule number one—"Get over Samuel."

While Paige and I watch *The Avengers*, Rachel taps away on her laptop. She's on a mission, and when she has that intense concentration face and reading glasses perched on her nose, it's best to leave her alone.

Paige leans over to me. "What's she up to?"

"Not a clue, and I'm afraid to ask."

"I heard that." Rachel stands to stretch then snatches the remote out of Paige's grasp.

"Hey, we were watching that."

"Not anymore." She syncs her laptop to the TV, and appearing in front of us is the most spectacular PowerPoint presentation I have ever seen. The words form a heart around two sets of lips.

She waves her hand in front of the TV like she's a game show model. "This"—she clicks her laptop to change the slide—"is the Mystery Lips Project."

Paige giggles at the two sets of lips that pucker and smooch over and over on the TV screen.

"We will determine who those perfect lips belong to, and he'll have to admit his feelings."

I stand and pace around the room. "This isn't necessary. He'll confess at our twenty-year class reunion, probably balding and fat by that time, but he'll finally have the nerve to admit it. I think I prefer it that way."

With a massive shake of her head, Rachel says, "Heck no. In one week, if my calculations are correct... and they always are..." She clicks to the next slide to reveal a pie chart. "I will be able to reduce the list to three guys with a ninety percent accuracy rate." After pointing to the screen, she adds, "I took about a million pictures on my phone at the dance. They were for the yearbook, but we're going to use that as a starting point for our little project."

Rachel flicks to another slide full of photographs from the dance. "These are only a sampling, but I cataloged all the guys who were at the dance."

The next slide shows two columns. The first is a long list of all the guys at our school. The second column is composed of only the names of the guys who were at the dance.

"Based on these photos and my own amazing memory, I decreased the kissing pool from three hundred to eighty-eight guys."

She clicks her laptop and shows the pie chart again, this time with the chunk of non-attendees removed. "Next, I took out the ones who were on the dance floor at the time of the smooch."

Paige nods. "We're at thirty-nine. No, forty."

My mouth goes dry. "That's still a lot of lips."

"Based on your description of this mystery man, you said he was tall and had nice, strong hands." She clicks on the pie chart, and twenty guys disappear. "Those guys are either shorter than you or have bony, frail hands. They have to be eliminated."

Paige wiggles in her seat. "Y'all, this is so much fun."

I roll my eyes. She's got a boyfriend. All I have is the memory of the hottest guy in school being too chicken to admit he made out with me.

"After examining enlarged photos from the dance and last year's yearbook, I was able to remove these because they have thin lips. So that leaves us with eleven. Is it safe to assume Samuel is out of the running?" Rachel glances my way as she waits for my answer, coming close to tempting me to admit it was him. "He is out of the running, correct?"

Not even remotely.

Regretfully, I say, "Yes."

"And" Paige interjects, "remove Brody and Jared. They were with me at the time."

Rachel nods and clicks to the next slide. "That leaves... seven guys." She inserts their photos from our eleventh-grade yearbook onto the screen.

"Ben, Ryan, Keith, Collin, Larry, Jack, and..." Paige gasps. "Mason?"

Our fearless PowerPoint master shrugs. "I cannot rule him out of any of the categories one hundred percent."

Paige giggles. "Wouldn't that be a hoot if it was Mason?"

I shove her, making her fall onto the floor. "Not funny." I turn to Rachel. "So, now what should I do?"

Rachel smiles. "I have a plan."

"Uh-oh. She has a plan," Paige says to me in a funny stage whisper.

Rachel sits on the futon and clicks on her laptop again. "Phase one. We are going to do a palm reading at the annual fundraiser."

"What did you say?"

"Yep." She studies the slide then adds, "I'll take care of it all and get the cheerleaders to help. But when one of the magnificent seven shows up, you will take my place to see if you are able to eliminate any of them."

Paige nods. "That's not a bad idea."

My entire body trembles with laughter. "Are you kidding me? I'm supposed to hold hands with these guys to see if they feel right? Maybe put their hands on my butt to see if it's a perfect match?"

"TMI, Sam," Paige says with a whole-body shiver.

Rachel crosses her arms and huffs. "I have put a lot of work into this. The least you could do is give it a try."

I plop backward onto the futon and stare at the vaulted ceiling. "This is not me."

"I know, but it will work," Rachel says as she squeezes my hand.

Paige pouts. "I think you're reluctant because you really wish it was Samuel."

That is not fair—and totally accurate. She goes right for the jugular, and I do my best to not react. To save face, I draw out a long, agonizing breath and say, "That's ridiculous."

"Surrre," Paige says with a major eye roll. "I think you do wish it was him, and if Samuel gets wind of our plan, he'll get so jealous realizing he missed his chance, he'll regret not making a move with someone who was right in front of his face all along."

More like right on *his face.* I know I have no other choice than to agree with her plan. "What do I have to lose?"

Pumping her fist in the air, Rachel says, "Yes. Operation Mystery Lips Phase I begins Monday."

Paige grabs a stuffed animal and pretends to smooch it, which is both funny and pathetic.

"Ew. Have you no shame?"

She shoves the stuffed animal in Rachel's face, making her squeal.

My friends are impossible, but I adore them. "I can't believe we are doing this."

"It will be fun," Paige says, all perky like. "And Mr. Perfect Pucker might even think it's cute that you're going to all this trouble to figure it out."

"Senior year is supposed to be epic. Mine is going to be one I never want to remember."

"Listen here," Rachel says as she stands over me with hands on her hips. "Miss Poor, Poor, Pitiful Me. This *is* epic. There's a Hottie McHottie Pants out there who is too shy to admit he's into you. Girls dream of this kind of stuff."

"That is uber epic." Paige's expression is hopeful. "Like a real life rom-com."

I side-eye her because only she would think my fake situation is anything like a romance movie. There has to be romance in there somewhere, and I am clearly void of that. But they are right about one thing. If Mule is too stupid to be honest, I'll make him squirm. I know he's into me because that kiss was *hawt*. So, if he's not going to admit it, the least I can do is have some fun with it.

Samantha rule number two—"Make your own epic year."

Chapter Twenty

Samantha

C ome on, Sam. You got this. Get your head in the game.

I swirl the ball around in my hands, once to calm my nerves, another time for good luck. Bounce, bounce. Knees bent, arms over head, release. The ball hits the rim and bounces away. A collective gasp through the gymnasium sends the message loud and clear. Everyone was hoping I could bring us to within four points of the other team, but that isn't going to happen today.

"Sam-Mannn."

Go away.

Paige stands to the right of me on the paint. "Ignore him. Focus on the game."

Yep. Bounce, bounce. Knees bent, arms over head, release. Air ball. My shot isn't even close to the net. The other team takes possession while I process my ten-year-old basketball skills. They score again, and when we take the ball back, Coach calls a time-out.

"Saaam-Maaan." He is so annoying.

With my head hanging low, I jog over to my team as the cheerleaders do some death-defying stunt for the crowd.

Paige pats me on the back. "Are you doing all right?"

I shake my head. Coach chews us all out, but I know the reason we're not kicking the Wildcats' butts is because *I* suck tonight. He draws a play on his whiteboard and points to Parker, a sophomore.

"Parker, you're going in. Sam, sit this one out."

My jaw drops, and so does my heart. He's never pulled me, not even when I was a freshman. "Are you kidding me?"

"You heard me. It's like you're sleepwalking out there. Parker, take point."

Parker's eyes are wide with excitement while mine fill with tears. I've never cried on the court before, and I won't start tonight, so I train my eyes on the court as we break. My team heads out to start the play, and I swallow my pride. The bench is a cold, lonely place, so I bite my lip, adjust my shoelaces, guzzle water... anything to keep from letting my emotions get to me.

Parker makes a layup, and I jump up, clapping for her like she's done so many times for me. I'm happy for her, but I want to be out there. On autopilot, I peek toward the bleachers. Mule's not on his feet like he usually is. He's not even watching the play. He's staring at me.

Yeah, you messed with my head. Thanks a lot. Jerk.

The buzzer sounds, signaling the end of the game, and the Wildcats win. I force myself to walk to center court and congratulate the other team then follow my teammates to the locker room.

Paige pats me on the back. "We've all had bad games."

"Thanks, P." My voice quivers, and tears are on the verge of spilling onto my cheeks.

Coach chews us out, but it's nothing like the lecture I give myself while I change into street clothes. My only consolation is I didn't see the Auburn scouts in the bleachers. With my crappy grades and the way I sucked on the court, there would be no way I could keep my scholarship.

"Are you going to watch the guys play?" Paige asks as she applies another layer of lip gloss then fluffs her hair. She must have a big date tonight with Brody.

"No, that's not such a good idea. I don't want my funk to rub off on them."

"You'll rock it the next game, as usual."

"I think I'm going straight home to have a pity party with my two favorite guys, Ben and Jerry."

She zips her gym bag and slings it to dangle over one arm. "See you soon, and try not to beat yourself up. You know how good you are."

Best friends forever.

Finally, I have the locker room to myself. Thank goodness, because my tears won't stay put any longer. Ugly sobs echo off the metal lockers as I swat one tear after another from my face. My ragged breaths catch in my throat. I should give up playing because there's no way I'll be accepted into Auburn. I'll enroll in the community college and live at home while my friends go off to do great stuff and make incredible memories. I'll end up with a dead-end, sucky job like my mother and always wonder, *What if?*

One more swipe of tears, then I blow out a breath. I push off the bench and fling open the door. Samuel, of all people, stands against the wall. I want to do a one-eighty and spend the night in the locker room. *Ugh.*

"Mule, not today. I know I played like crap."

"Yeah."

"You don't have to rub it in. Besides, it's your fault."

"I know, but if you had been more—"

I poke him in the chest with my finger. "Don't give me the play-by-play. In case you don't remember, I was there. I felt every missed basket, heard every gasp, so shut up." Poke. Poke.

He touches my cheek, but I swat his hand away. "Go find another girl to mess with."

Mule blinks. "It's not like that."

Stomping away from him, I yell, "I don't care. I've let you get under my skin long enough. Is that Samuel rule number three? To see how much you can torture me?"

"Number three is to trust—"

"Stop!" I swing around to give him my full fury.

He hovers over me, and his expression is unreadable. "I'm sorry I got in your head and messed up your game. It won't happen again."

"You got that right."

"See you Monday after school?"

I focus on my bag and shake my head. "It's no use." I bite my lip to keep it from trembling. "I appreciate the help so far, but I don't want to waste any more of your time."

"Sam-Man, please."

"Bye, Mule."

Chapter Twenty-One

Samuel

Sam-Man didn't answer one frickin' text all weekend. I sent about twenty, and she's probably thinking I'm a stalker by now. If she ignores me this morning during class, I think I'm going to pull my hair out. I go in search of her and find her with her head in her locker. She doesn't notice me walk up to her. Even though she's wearing jeans and a baggy T-shirt, the memory of her hot body in that tight dress is seared into my memory.

When she sees me, she lets out a huff. "Go away."

I rub the back of my neck, trying to choose my words carefully. "Come on. Can't we talk about this?" I'm a horrible friend, and I should let her calm down, but I'm an idiot. It was a childish move chickening out like that, but there is more at stake here than an amazing kiss. She needs me to help her jack up her score... and I need her not to be mad at me anymore. I can't stand the way she's shutting me out.

Sam-Man shakes her head so hard *I'm* dizzy. "I made a complete fool of myself. First, the you-know-what in the closet then my lousy game, so please, don't make this worse than it already is."

Even though she stomps away from me, I can't leave well enough alone, so I add insult to injury. "Fine, if that's how you want it, but what about Auburn?"

She screeches to a halt and slowly turns around then stalks back up to me. "I hate you."

"At least you're talking. That's a good start."

I grab her arm when she tries to move around me. "Where are you going? Your class is the other way."

She jerks her arm out of my grasp. "To talk to Mr. Henderson. Maybe he'll find me another tutor."

Even though she racewalks away, I stay on her heels. "You don't need to do that."

"I wouldn't want to crimp your style."

"I think the word is cramp."

Sam snarls as she flings open the door to Mr. Henderson's room, letting the door shut in my face, but I pull it open again. "I need to speak with you," she tells him. "It's an emergency."

He stuffs the rest of a bagel into his mouth and mumbles, "What's the problem?" He motions for us to sit.

Pointing a finger in my direction, she says, "I cannot work with him anymore."

"Your grades show that whatever he's doing is working."

Not my finest moment, but I let out a chuckle. Samantha throws darts with her eyes.

"Shut up." She smiles at Mr. Henderson. "Sorry. Not you. Him."

I sit on the desk next to her and let my book bag slide to the floor.

With a deadpan expression on her face, she pins me with steely eyes. "We are incompatible."

With a gulp of his soda, he says, "So don't marry him."

"Ugh. Bite your tongue." The flush across her neck says she doesn't really think the idea is that gross.

"He must be doing something right, so you need to keep it up." He glances in my direction. "I thought it'd be a cold day in Hades before I defended you, but here we are."

It's not like me to beg, but I think it's time to grovel. "Sam-Man, come on. We can work this out."

"Nope."

Mr. Henderson takes a gulp of his coffee then lets out a deep sigh. "Miss Baughman, I think you need to check your pride at the door."

Sam-Man closes her eyes and clenches her fists. I'm assuming she's trying to settle her anger. "It's more than pride. It's... self-respect."

"Well, tell your self-respect to get over herself and remind it what you have at stake."

Maybe letting out a low whistle is not the best idea because she smacks me on the arm. "Ow."

"You two please kiss and make up, or create dark memes, or whatever teens do these days, but get the heck out of my room. This is my only quiet time the entire day."

Samantha and I stare at each other. She stands, stiffens her spine, and walks toward the door, making sure she steps on my foot on the way out.

Our teacher shakes his head. "What'd you do?"

"Being an idiot, that's all." I throw my arms up in an "it is what it is" move.

"Oh, so nothing new?"

"Ha ha. Funny guy."

He tosses his paper cup into the trash. "She picked you to help her. Get her to pass. You are really good at this. And believe me, it is incredibly hard for me to admit that. Plus, we have a deal, remember?"

I'm glad he doesn't hear me mumble my not-so-friendly comment when I turn my back to leave.

Samantha stomps into the arts center and throws her book bag onto the floor with a huff. I'm ecstatic she showed up, but I'm not going to rock the boat by saying something sarcastic. My attempts to lighten the mood haven't worked so far, and I don't think today is going to be any different.

"No jogging today?" She snaps her fingers. "Oh, that's right. Someone might see us together. We can't have that. I guess rule number six is 'Be a jerk and a coward.' That's a lot for one rule."

"Stop it." I stand up and take her by the hand to walk her outside. She snatches her hand away, so I grab her around the waist.

She breaks free and walks away from me toward one of the exhibit halls. "You go for a run while I check out these paintings. I noticed them last time and didn't get a chance to really take them in."

"No!" I yell louder than I mean to.

She slips right through my grasp and enters the exhibit hall to our right. "Why not?"

"Because."

"I know I'm a jock, but even I appreciate art." She walks into the room, and I know as soon as she sees it because she freezes. In slow motion, she turns to me, her mouth gaping open. "What is that?"

"Let me explain."

Slowly, like she's afraid to make any sudden moves, she walks toward the painting. My painting. My painting of her, to be precise. She reaches out to touch it, but her hand stops in midair. Then she inches closer to read the signature. A faint gasp comes from her mouth, I guess when she realizes it's my name.

"Don't be mad."

"Mad?" Her mouth hangs open, and shock is in her eyes. "Confused maybe, but not mad."

I tug her onto the bench in front of the paintings, and we both stare at mine. "This was the day you got the email about your SAT scores. The day your life was turned topsy-turvy. It's seared into my mind."

"But how could you... It was only a split second."

"Photographic memory." I focus on my shoes. "Every moment I've spent with you is stored inside my mind."

It seems like her brain cells are churning, trying to process what I told her, and I'm certain she doesn't believe me. "That's not a line, I promise. It's the truth."

"I had no idea." Her words are so frail, so soft I barely hear them.

"Yeah, I'm full of surprises." My nervous laugh confirms I'm in uncharted territory.

"Pfft. So, that whole thing about waiting on your cousin during her dance class was a lie."

I shake my head. "That part is factual. Truth be told, it's how I found out about this place. I always doodled, but when I saw the art that regular people created, I thought I'd give it a shot. Caroline, the director, encouraged me to try it, so I did. She says my pottery is better than hers."

"You do pottery?" Her voice screeched two octaves higher than normal.

I grinned. "Yep."

She walks up to her portrait and fingers the edge of the frame. The smell of oil paints wafts around the room, making me itch to draw the image of her gazing at her picture. "You should study art in college."

I snort. "My dad would freak if he heard you say that."

"Why?"

"He thinks I should use my 'talent' for math and science to be a doctor like him."

She gets a goofy grin on her face. "Well, you've broken enough hearts. Maybe you could make a career out of fixing some."

Clutching my chest, I feign shock. "Hurtful, Sam-Man."

She sits beside me again on the bench, and our knees touch, sending a warm sensation through my leg.

"I'm sorry I messed up your game. I never meant to. I... I'm not good for you, Sam-Man. You have to understand that."

She nods.

"It *was* pretty painful to watch."

She balls up her fist, like she is going to hit me. "It was a train wreck, I get it. You don't have to remind me. It's like there's a game tape playing over and over in my mind. I can't unsee my awful game."

I wave my arm in the air to the art surrounding us. "I don't want anyone to know this part of my life. I like having something that's all mine. I trust you to keep this between us. And can we move past the..."

A large groan escapes her lips. "As long as you admit it was the best kiss of your life." She peers over to me, her eyes sparkling.

I hold up six fingers. "Rule number six—'Never admit anything that might be held against you later.'"

She nudges me with her shoulder. "I will accept your answer as an admission of the facts."

I stand and help her up. "Let's jog and talk about tans and secs."

Red splotches spread across her neck. "Sex?"

"S-E-C. Math, silly. Jeez, Sam-Man. Get your mind out of the gutter."

After two miles, she's finally relaxed enough to focus on math. And she aces another practice test. Sam holds her hand up for me to high-five, which I gladly oblige. I'm thrilled I didn't destroy her confidence because that's the last thing I want to do. She's smarter than she realizes. I take a swig from my water bottle as she packs up her bags.

"I need to go soon. Rachel is planning this palm-reading session at the school fundraiser to help me find the mystery kisser."

Water goes down the wrong pipe, and I let out muffled coughs. "Excuse me?"

She pats my back to help me breathe again. "When you were too chicken to admit you smooched me, Rachel said I needed to meet the mysterious person who did."

A lazy smile falls across her face, and my heart does a happy dance since I know I'm responsible for it. "Why?"

Her neck flushes pink. "Because."

I snatch the pencil from her and start drawing her lips across her practice test. I can't help it. "Because why, Sam-Man? Tell me. I need to know."

She groans. "Because..." She flops back in the seat like she's exhausted.

My bottom lip is going to be bitten in two from my teeth clamping down on it. I can't smile, but wow, what a compliment. "That good, huh?"

Staring at the ceiling, she exhales a happy sigh. "Yes. Are you happy?"

I've made out with a lot of girls, and I've never had one blow my mind like she did. "Are you telling me I gave you the best kiss of the century?"

"Yep." I love the way she pops the *P* in her one-word answer.

Jutting my chin high in a snooty position, I say, "You should thank me."

She rolls her eyes at me. "Oh please. It's always all about you. Anyway, Rachel used an algorithm to eliminate every guy in our school except for seven, and step one of her crazy scheme is for me to check out their hands."

My body rumbles with laughter as I lay my head on the table. "Hands? Sam-Man, this is hilarious. Does Rachel really think you'll find out who it is by looking at their hands?"

"It's not what they *look* like, Mule. It's how they felt... on my butt, to be exact. You should know. You were there."

I snap to attention when her words sink in. "You'll let random guys touch your butt?"

She cringes. "Well, I didn't think about it like that. But no. I'll at least eliminate some that are too bony."

I hold out my hands, knowing good and well they are the guilty digits. "Would mine pass?"

She pushes them away. "You're not in the running for two reasons. You eliminated yourself from the beginning, hence the reason for this stupid escapade anyway."

"And what's the other reason?"

Biting her lip to hold back a laugh, she adds, "Rachel and Paige both say you are a terrible kisser and your breath smells."

Boom. Ego is straight in the toilet now.

"Seriously?"

She giggles. "It's true. They say you're all jabby tongue and you smell like smoke. Actually, Paige said it was chewing tobacco. So, not minty." She sticks out her tongue at me. "Ha. You're not one of the seven."

"Who is?"

"Not telling."

"I'll find out."

"Leave my lips and my mystery smoocher alone. When this is all over, I'll have found my perfect person."

"No matter what you do, they'll never figure it out because..." I point to my mouth then wink.

"I might find someone even better. Someone who is not a chicken. Bwaak bwaaak."

Her words make me flinch, but I try to cover it up with a smile. "Let's hope it's not Chris Framingham. I heard he has oral herpes."

Her face blanches. "I need to check the list."

"If you're finished obsessing about your future make-out session, can we get back to more important things? Like sec?"

"Ha ha." Her smile drops. "You mean SEC, right?"

I grin. "Maybe."

Why can't I be honest with her about how I feel? She's accepted that I'm smart and artistic, so why is it so hard to admit my feelings to her?

Because Craig would kick my teeth in.

Because of me, she's going to hold a bunch of hands and tongue wrestle with other guys when she should only be with me. I'm so close to her, I could move a centimeter and brush my lips against hers to remind her this charade is fruitless. I want to, and by the way her pupils dilate, she does too.

But I can't. It would ruin everything. She said I was a good kisser, but that doesn't mean she likes me as more than a friend. And I only have myself to thank for her slamming me all the way back into the friend zone. She deserves to be happy, and I can't make her happy. Rule number seven—"Happiness isn't for wimps."

Chapter Twenty-Two

Samantha

Craig is home again and, as usual, hogs all the food. We grab for the last yeast roll at the same time, and when he pouts, it reminds me of when we were little. He used to make that face every time he didn't get his way, and I would give in because I'm the good little sister.

"Aw, Sammy. All I get to eat is dorm food all the time. You don't want me to get all skinny, do you?"

I growl but concede the roll to him. While he's moaning through a bite, I kick his shin. "Ow."

"Doesn't seem like you're missing any meals. That freshman fifteen's a real thing, isn't it? Looks like you gained a solid twenty pounds, if you ask me."

"Bug, you wait until you get to Auburn," Dad says. "No matter how good the food tastes, it will never be as good as your mom's cooking."

He kisses Mom on the cheek, making her smile. Craig and I cringe at the parental show of affection.

"Being married to the best cook in the world does have its advantages."

My brother does a full-body shiver. "Dad, we don't need to see this."

He knows better than to say anything about Dad's displays of affection to Mom because that only adds fuel to the fire. When my father takes her hand and smooches it, working his way up her arm, Craig covers his eyes. "Guys, get a room."

Mom's eyes twinkle. "Actually, we have one reserved."

I drop my fork while Craig stuffs his flushed face with carrots.

"It was a joke." Mom pries her hand away from Dad's grasp. "What I mean is, I'm going with your dad to Los Angeles for the CMA awards this year."

I snap my head in her direction. "Really? You hate that stuff."

She shrugs. "It's been a while, and he promised not to leave my side this time."

Confusion washes over me. He hasn't worked in the music business for six months. "But Dad, they laid you off and you're still going?"

"I fought to sign Rose Phillips, and now she's up for an award. She insisted I be there."

Craig chuckles. "Mom, the last time you went, you fussed for two weeks afterward."

I nod. "And remember Mom's words about the dresses?"

"Yep."

Together, Craig and I say, "Wretched capitalist excess."

Dad belts out a laugh. "This time her secret crush, Benjamin James, is up for an award, too, so there is a bonus incentive to go."

"Ah... now I get it." I side-eye my brother, and he cracks a grin.

"Oh, hush." Mom's face flames with a massive blush.

My brother raises his fork to his mouth like he's holding a microphone and sings in a falsetto voice, "Every day with you is a dream come true."

I add, "Come true. Ooo, come true."

Craig and I slap palms while Dad pinches Mom's cheek.

She sits taller in her seat. "I'm going, but he left out one major detail. Your father is also up for an award this year."

I snap my head around to look at Dad as my mouth hangs open. His face is red. "Seriously?"

He nods. "Don't you ever read the news?"

My brother and I reply with a resounding "No."

"Well, you should," she says, giving my dad another peck on the cheek. Ugh, more PDA.

"To Dad," Craig says, raising his glass in a toast.

We lift our glasses and clink each of them. "To Dad."

"So, who will referee in your place?" I certainly hope it's not Tony Anderson. He's such a stickler, especially when it concerns me. I can't do anything right in his eyes.

"Sorry, kiddo. It's Tony."

Figures. That's just my luck.

Craig sucks in a breath. "He didn't get the nickname the Enforcer for no reason. Better bring your A game, sis."

"Actually, Craig," Mom says, "I was hoping you could come home that weekend and hang out with Samantha."

"Mom, I'm not five. I don't need him to babysit me." My pout doesn't help my case, and neither does my torn, dirty T-shirt and mismatched socks.

"Yeah, she's like at least... seven." Craig thinks he's so funny.

I ball up my napkin and throw it at him.

Dad clears his throat. Oh boy. When he does that, it always means a change in tone and that he has some important announcement.

"The Martins got broken into a few days ago."

"That's awful." A shiver goes up my spine. The Martins live only two doors down, which means the break-ins keep getting closer.

"And last week, the Franklins were robbed. Sheila was home, and they scared her really bad. Took off with her grandmother's jewelry."

Nibbling on a fingernail, I mentally count the neighborhood break-ins in recent weeks. Stealing is one thing, but doing it while someone is home means the person is getting bolder.

Craig glances over at me.

I shrug.

"Sure," he says. "I'll make it a point to come home."

"Thanks, honey."

As much as I don't want to be treated as a child, I'm relieved Craig will be here when our parents are gone. He could scare Ted Bundy away.

"Is school going all right?" Mom asks me, making me drop my fork like a fool.

I swallow the lump of food and take a swig of tea. Why is she asking? Does she know something? Craig stuffs his mouth full of pot roast.

"Sure," I squeak out. Suddenly, I wish we could talk more about the thief. Anything would be better than discussing school.

After we clear the table and I retreat into my room in hopes of having a moment of silence, Craig pops in. "Everything all right?"

I drop my phone. "Yeah, so far, so good. Tutoring is working. I wish I had done that a long time ago."

He peers behind himself into the hallway before he asks, "So you'll be ready to take the SAT again soon?"

"I think so. My tutor knows how to explain things so I understand. Turns out, I'm not as dumb as I thought."

"That's good. Anyone I know?"

Why does he have to be so nosy? "You wouldn't recognize him."

He waves as he leaves my room. If I told him Samuel was my tutor, I'd never hear the end of it, especially if he knew Mule and I did more than work a few math problems.

My phone rings. I blink at the name of the caller to see if I'm hallucinating. Samuel never calls me. If he wants to aggravate me, he sends a text. Maybe I should let the call go to voicemail, but like a hangnail, I can't let it go. "Hello?"

"Hey, Sam-Man."

Before Craig comes back, I close my door then pace my room. "What's up?"

"I, uh... wanted to make sure we're good."

"Of course. Why wouldn't we be?" He's being weird.

His husky laughter ripples through my ear and down my spine. "The K-I-S-S."

"Oh, that. I forgot about it. I'm good. I'm better than good. Yep, I'm super good." *Liar, liar, pants on fire. Again.*

"Super good?" I hear the laughter in his voice, and it gets my anger up.

I stomp my foot on the floor because I hate it when I sound so girly. "Very good. You really think I'd stay mad?"

"Uh, yeah."

As if he could actually see me, I stick out my tongue. "You have a very high opinion of yourself, don't you?"

"Yes, but I also know you."

"No. You. Don't. Will I see you at the palm reading?" I snap my fingers. "Oh, wait. No need because you're not in the running."

Silence. It's the best sound all day.

"See ya around," I say.

"Uh, yeah. Sure."

"Bye, Mule."

Punching the air with my fist to celebrate my minor victory, I give myself a virtual pat on the back. It's not very often I get the upper hand on Mule, but tonight I did, and it feels awesome.

Samantha rule number three—"When Samuel gives you lemons, squeeze the heck out of them and make sure you aim the juice in his direction."

Chapter Twenty-Three

Samuel

Brody is the last person I trust to drive me anywhere, but at least with the top down on his Jeep, it feels like we are driving faster than the actual speed. That helps to lighten my mood... a bit.

"Where are we going?" I ask as he drives. "Burger Heaven?" I could use a hamburger about right now. Please say it's so.

He shakes his head. "Nope, we're going to the fundraiser."

My head falls back on the headrest. "Why didn't you tell me? I would have stayed home."

"That's why I didn't tell you."

I stare out the window and ponder what to say. "The palm-reading thing is a stupid idea."

"Probably. Wait. How did you know about that?"

"Your girlfriend can't keep a secret."

He nods and drives in silence for a bit, then he asks, "Don't you want to see who your competition is?"

Rubbing my temples just like my dad does when he's frustrated, I say, "You're a jerk."

He gasps. "Pretty much every day. You could stop all this foolishness by confessing."

I'm going to grind down my molars to nubs before this conversation is over. "I don't know what—"

Brody holds his hand out to stop my words. "Shut up, man. I'm not stupid."

Even though the top of his Jeep is off, I suddenly feel extremely closed in. If Brody, the clueless one in our friend group, is figuring out I kissed Samantha, I'm doomed.

"Why did you do it?" he asks as he turns a corner.

"I'm not following you."

He chuckles. "Since you're in denial, let's skip to question number two. What are you afraid of?"

It's no use trying to hide anything from the master of romance, especially since he's one of my best friends. After I let out a huge groan, I say, "Me and Samantha... not a good match."

"Let me get this straight." He drives into the school parking lot and cuts the engine. "You kissed her, and by the way you've been acting lately, I would bet money that you liked it... a lot."

I give him the evil eye, but he continues anyway. "You lied about it because you're too cool for her."

"Yes. No. Not at all. Wait. I never said—"

"Stop. Enough with the lies because you suck at it. You get this twitchy muscle in your cheek. It's a dead giveaway. You should thank me that I've never told any teachers about it."

After we have a stare-off that feels like it lasts for an eternity, he smiles.

I glance away before I crack a smile too. "It's complicated."

"No, it's not."

I groan. "You want the truth?"

He nods. "What's standing in your way?"

With one last huff, I admit the truth. "Craig."

His mouth forms a huge O as he processes my reply. "You... are afraid of Baughman?"

"Partially. His sorry excuse of a college buddy told him I did something, and Craig believes him. He won't let it go, and he threatened to pulverize me if I touched his sister. So I promised him I would keep my hands off. If he ever found out about that kiss"—I point to my mouth—"these teeth will be mangled. I don't think my parents will pay for braces a second dorme."

He pouts and wipes fake tears off his cheeks. "Poor baby."

"It's not funny. He's an oak. Besides, I gave him my word."

Brody giggles like a girl. "Since when does that mean anything?"

"Shut up, man. It's a code."

Grumbling, he fidgets with his keys. "Just be honest with Samantha. I bet she's not afraid of her brother."

He has a point, but I promised her I wouldn't tell anyone about the tutoring, and I don't want to get her in trouble with her coach. These are things Brody cannot know.

"She has no idea what Rocky is telling people. She'd be mortified. Besides, I can fight my own battles, and I figured if I keep my mouth shut long enough, the problems with Craig will blow over. He'll get over it, then maybe I'll be in the clear."

Brody slides out of the seat, and I follow him across the parking lot to the school, where we can hear music playing at the fundraiser. I lean against the brick building, postponing my next interaction with Samantha as long as possible.

"So you're going to wait it out? You'll never go out with anyone else?"

My shoes are suddenly very interesting. "Maybe."

Brody snorts like that's the silliest idea he's ever heard. "Yeah, sure you are. I believe you." He glares at me. Moonlight reflects off his face, and it's obvious he's dead serious. "Don't count on her to wait for you."

The pit of my stomach feels like I ate a boulder as I let his words sink in. If I play it safe and keep Craig on my good side, I might lose my chance with Samantha. But if I make things right with her, I risk losing my friend and getting beat up along the way, not to mention disappointing my mother. And this is all assuming Sam wants me at all. I could make a grand gesture and get turned down *and* beat up all on the same day. Nothing seems like a good path forward.

Brody motions with his head for me to follow him into the school, breaking me out of my internal monologue. Maybe I should walk home and forget going inside because this is going to suck.

Chapter Twenty-Four

Samantha

If anyone on the planet can rock a gypsy costume, it's Rachel. Her colorful bohemian skirt swooshes every time she moves, and her white ruffled blouse slips off one shoulder far enough to entice half the guys in our class to line up to get their fortune read by Madame ZZ. Chunky bracelets accentuate her henna-stained hands. Her blond hair is away from her face and covered by a vivid pink scarf, showing off huge hoop earrings that might rip holes in her earlobes at any minute. She's gone all out, and the guys are eating it up. They'll eagerly give a dollar for Rachel to hold their hands and tell their futures, ones they all hope will include her.

George, who has already been eliminated, sits in front of her. Paige peeks over at me as I fidget in my own gypsy costume. I don't rock it like Rachel does, and poor Paige is dressed like she raided a kid's dress-up closet, but it's the thought that counts. Rachel smacks her gum as she strokes George's palm.

"I see you have been using diz hand for bad things. Madame ZZ sees bad things for you. But!" she yells, making Paige and me jump. "There is time to make all things good. Stop playing with yourself, and you'll find the luuuve of your life."

She winks and motions toward the donation box. "Dollar in the donation box, bud."

"Uh, sure." He throws a dollar bill into the box and stands. He shifts his jeans and glances around. I'm sure everyone in the hallway knows what he's trying to hide. "Thanks, Rach."

When he's out of earshot, she mumbles, "And remember what I said. Stop playing with yourself."

Paige bends over the table, giggling so much she loses the scarf covering her head. "That was awful."

"I know, right? Who's next?"

"Ben Sanders," Paige says.

"Ooo. He's on the list." Rachel pushes me into the chair. "It's time for Madame Sam to do her magic."

"This is silly." If my brother could see me, he'd laugh his butt off.

"Maybe so, but you'll be able to eliminate him, so do it."

Ben walks up to our table, all smiles. He's one of those dudes who doesn't really fit into any of the typical high school categories. Ben's not a jock, but not a geek, and certainly not a skater boy. He just exists. When he sees me sitting at the table in front of the snow globe disguised as a crystal ball, his grin fades. "When is Rachel back on the clock?"

"Ben, sit," Paige says, pointing to the chair. "You don't get to pick your fortune teller."

He harrumphs and plops down in front of me then holds out a pale, sweaty hand. Ick. His fingers are so long and skinny, I could break them like toothpicks. Those hands would never be able to hold me. I reach out to touch his hand and... yep. Cold, clammy digits.

Not able to think of anything unique, I say, "You're going to live a long and fruitful life if you stop playing with yourself."

He slumps back in the chair. "Dang it. How'd you know?"

With a straight face, Paige says, "It's not safe to ask too many questions. Dollar in the box, please." She shoves the box under his nose. He groans and does as he's told. As he walks away, he stares at his hands.

"Well?" Rachel asks.

I shake my head. "Definitely not him."

"Whew. Thank goodness. One more eliminated. Six to go. Let's do this."

Brody and Samuel are next in line. Brody plants one on Paige's cheek. "Can I get my fortune told by you?" he asks as he nuzzles her nose.

"Absolutely."

Samuel stares at me then rolls his eyes. I chew on the inside of my mouth to keep from laughing.

"Hey," Rachel says. "Happy couples are bad for business."

Samuel throws a five-dollar bill into the box. "I want her to tell my fortune." He stares at me like he's undressing me with his eyes.

I shake my head. "I'm off the clock."

"Come on, Sam-Man. I've already donated money. No take-backs."

Ugh. He is so obnoxious. "Fine. Sit."

He holds out his hand, and I glance at it, not daring to touch it because I know what those hands are capable of. I peer over the table as I plan my next move. Not waiting for me, he rests his hand in mine.

I turn his over so his palm is facing up. "Madame Sam sees a long life."

"Madame Sam?" He quirks an eyebrow, his mouth twitching in a faint smile.

"Shh," Rachel and Paige say at the same time.

"Yes, I see a long life. Many years of school." I run my finger down the middle of his palm. "Doctor, lawyer... artist. Madame Sam cannot tell for sure." I sneak a peek up, and he gives me a warning look. "Ooo, and kids. Many, many kids. Five... No, wait! Six."

He jerks his hand from me and stands. "All right. I'm done here."

Paige does a cheerleader clap. "Good one, Sam."

Mason is next in line, his hands stuffed into his pockets. We haven't ruled out Mule's cousin, but it is highly unlikely Paige and Rachel will leave Mason in the running after today. He's wearing a Math Is a Piece of Pi T-shirt, so his hands can't be too yummy.

When he retrieves a dollar from his pocket and hands it to Rachel, she flinches. She unfolds the damp dollar and throws it in the box then points to me. "She's on the clock. Sorry."

"Go ahead, Rach. It's cool with me." I will gladly give up my position.

She shakes her head. "Madame ZZ sees bad things. I do not wish to share."

"Fine, I'll do it. Sit," I grumble to Mason.

He obeys and holds out his hand. It's nice and strong, certainly not what I was expecting from the president of the physics club. "Strong hand, strong heart." Like I received an electric shock, I jerk back, losing contact with him. "That's all I've got."

With a pout, he mumbles, "Hardly worth a dollar."

We all watch as he leaves the table. He bumps into the wall while he tries to walk and check his phone at the same time.

"Please tell me I can cross his name off the list," Rachel says.

If I didn't know better, I'd be convinced he was the one. So, to throw her off, I say, "I don't know."

Paige gasps. "Seriously?" She points in his direction where he just tripped over his own shoelace. "That guy?"

I throw my hands in the air and admit defeat. "He has strong hands." I then whisper, "And minty breath."

Rachel and Paige both suck in their breaths. We sit in silence for the longest time, all afraid of what this might mean. It wasn't Mason who kissed me, but if I didn't know better, I would think it was him—and that is beyond bizarre.

Finally, Rachel breaks the silence. "We'll note him as a maybe."

Chapter Twenty-Five

Samuel

Brody can't keep his hands off Paige over lunch in the cafeteria with the usual crowd. I know she's cute in a short, tomboy kind of way, but I don't want to see all the affection while I'm trying to eat. Rachel rolls her eyes, and I can only assume she's as annoyed at the lovey-dovey couple as I am. She smacks her gum while working on her physics homework.

She glances toward the lovebirds. "Paige, no offense, but could you two please stop lip locking over there?"

Paige lets out a sappy sigh. "Sorry, I get carried away."

Her doe-eyed boyfriend wipes his mouth and chuckles. "She's jealous she isn't getting any."

Rachel wheels around and gives him the stink-eye. "Dude, I'm able to get any guy I want. All I have to do is snap my fingers." She snaps her fingers, and as if on cue, Mason walks up.

"Hey, guys."

I hold on to the table to keep me from falling out of my seat laughing. Brody rests his head on the table and belts out a belly laugh. We both receive kicks in the shins, compliments of Rachel's stabby high heels.

"What's so funny?" Mason asks.

"Nothing." I motion for him to sit with us, so when I slide over to make room, I stretch out my legs under the table, nudging Samantha's foot with mine. She's situated directly across from me but totally ignoring me. She snatches her foot away.

Mason glances over the table and taps Rachel's physics homework with his finger. "I could help you if you want. I finished it already."

She shakes her head. "I got it."

With a defeated expression, he stuffs his mouth full of pizza.

At the other end of the table, Brody nibbles on Paige's ear, and she giggles.

It sends a flashback of my make-out session with Samantha. I still taste her ear, her neck, and that delicious mouth. She stares at me, biting her lip. Is she thinking about the kiss too? We gawk at each other for a moment, and I wonder if she believes I'm not attracted to her. That is not even close to being true.

With concern etched across his face, Mason says, "Samantha, I heard about your neighbor getting attacked. That's awful."

I snap my gaze back to those eyes of hers. "What happened?"

"Michelle from across the street went for a jog around the block, and somebody grabbed her."

Paige covers Samantha's hand with hers. "Did she get hurt?"

"She fought him, and when a car passed, he took off. She's banged up but not as bad as it could have been."

Paige squeezes Samantha's hand. "You jog through your neighborhood all the time."

"Yep. Usually at about the same time too. My mom practically has me on lockdown now."

I clench my fists. The thought of someone scaring her, maybe even hurting her, makes my blood boil. "Did they catch the creep?"

"No, but they have a good idea who it might be."

"If you want to stay with me for a few days, let me know," Paige says.

"Me too," Rachel adds. She smacks Mason's hand away as he's trying to point out another mistake in her homework.

Samantha stuffs her face full of chips. "It's all good if someone else is there. No biggie. But Dad won't let me jog alone anymore, not that I'm complaining." She shivers. "It's creepy. At first it was only a few things stolen, but now..." She plasters on a smile, but I've spent enough time with her recently to know it's fake. "It's only a matter of time before they catch the loser. I'm not too worried."

Sam stares at me again, and I see fear in her eyes. I have this strange desire to protect her—if she would let me. If Craig was home from school, I'd feel better about everything, but with him gone, she doesn't have anyone to be there for her.

I text Craig.

Me: *Did U know about the attack in your neighborhood?*

C: *Yup. It's creepy.*

My fingers twitch as I decide what I should say next.

Me: *Want me 2 keep an eye on Sam?*

Please say yes, I pray. Please say yes.

C: *Yeah.*

Yes! I have an excuse to spend even more time with her.

If only Craig would believe me over his sorry excuse for a roommate, maybe he would be more understanding. He'll never accept that Rocky was the one talking smack about his sister, not me. In fact, when Rocky told me what he wanted to do with Samantha and didn't even care if it was consensual, I was so frickin' disgusted, I flipped out. At least I got in one good punch to his face before the cops showed up. To this day, I still have a knee-jerk reaction every time a car drives by that resembles a police car.

My phone chimes again.

C: *But keep your hands off!*

I growl and shove my phone back into my pocket. He is such a buzzkill.

Chapter Twenty-Six

Samantha

Mule will not shut up about math in our study session today. While I appreciate his help, especially because it's working, I'd still rather be doing what I'm good at—sports. When he gets into geek mode, he's a force to be reckoned with. As soon as I free myself from all the talk of tangents and triangles, I zoom across town to the Nashville Youth Center. Mom doesn't like that I drive there to help coach basketball, but if I text her when I get there and when I leave, she doesn't fret too much.

This old, run-down gym makes me forget about my petty problems. These kids have it hard. They'd laugh in my face if they heard how I made such a fuss about my scholarship. The worst thing that could happen is I'd have to go to junior college, where I wouldn't get to play basketball. These kids will be lucky to go to any college, so I guess I like coming here to help them get closer to getting what I already have. Because I really do have it good, even if I don't get everything I want.

The door creaks open, announcing my arrival. Six giggly teenage girls race over to me and hug me, all at the same time.

Coach Owen waves. "Let's start with some drills. Samantha, you take Sue, Trish, and Vanessa, and I'll take LaTonya, Kristen, and Jane."

Jane groans. "Again? I always get you."

I laugh. Jane doesn't need much coaching. She has an older brother who plays for Duke, so she pretty much has her very own private coach. But she still comes here every week to play ball.

My trio follows me to the far side of the court as I bounce the ball to get my head in the game. The thump of the basketball on the gym floor is one of my favorite sounds. It calms me better than any meditation out there.

"First, let's work on the two-on-zero drill. Sue, you're on point. You yell 'ball' when you're ready to make a layup. Remember, no dribbling on this drill unless it's for the layup. And the last pass is a bounce. Let's run, not jog. Go."

My group sets up the play on the court, and by the third time, they've pretty much mastered it.

"Good job, y'all. Let's see if you can do it with some defense. Coach Owen, is your team ready?"

"Let's do this."

The girls all yell, "Yay!" and we set them up. My team lines up and maneuvers around the other three girls, working the ball until it's past them. Trish bounce passes to Sue, who makes a perfect layup. My girls squeal and jump around like they won the NBA championship.

"Good job, team. Let's take a break."

The girls sit on the bleachers, laughing and guzzling water. They are having so much fun, they don't even need to stop to check their cell phones. Their social outlet is right in front of them.

The coach blows his whistle. "It's scrimmage time. My team against Samantha's."

The coach and I run the court, acting as referees for the next thirty minutes. I'm winded, but I don't care because I love this. I forget about failing Trig, and I do my best to forget about Samuel and how only a week ago, I thought he was into me. *Silly girl.*

The door slams shut, causing me to jerk my attention in that direction. Samuel stands against the wall in the corner of the gym, arms crossed over his chest and a big scowl plastered on his face.

I'm not paying attention to the game, and the ball whacks me in the stomach.

Coach calls a time-out. "I think we've had enough for one day. Get ready for study time." As if on cue, the group protests.

"Ah, Coach, do we have to?"

"We don't have homework."

"I'll do it later."

Coach shakes his head. He's heard every excuse in the book. "Let's do it. Grab a snack, and meet me in the conference room in five."

After our scrimmage, my hamstrings are in urgent need of a good stretch, so I prop my foot on a bench and bend over. Sue and Trish approach me.

"Is that your boyfriend?" Sue asks.

I snap my head around. "Absolutely not."

"Why not?" Trish stage whispers.

"I know, right?" Sue says. "He can be my boyfriend any day of the week."

I don't think so.

I point to the conference room. "Go."

"See you next week," Trish says as she waves to Samuel. He stalks toward me with a disapproving scowl.

I pretend not to care and start placing basketballs on the rack but ask, "Hey, what are you doing here?"

He picks up one of the balls, bounces it, and sinks a shot from the free-throw line. It swooshes in, not even hitting the rim. I really hate that he's so freaking good at everything.

"Uh... In the neighborhood?"

As I roll the basketball rack to the side of the court, I shake my head. "I highly doubt that."

He comes over to me and touches my arm. "This is not a safe part of the city to be in after dark."

Yanking my arm away, I glare at him, hard enough for him to take a step back. "Maybe you should leave then. I wouldn't want anyone to hurt that pretty-boy face." I pat his cheek for emphasis. The third pat makes a nice smacking sound.

As if his scowl isn't bad enough, it gets more menacing. "I'm serious. Do you come here a lot?"

As I face him, I cross my arms over my chest. "If it's any of your business, yes, I come here once a week. It's fun and... I help kids with something I'm good at."

"You shouldn't be coming here alone. It's not safe." The furrows in his brow are going to stick if he doesn't lighten up soon.

"No worse than my own neighborhood lately. What's it to you?"

I stomp over to the bench and snatch my purse. Ignoring his brooding, I walk past him with keys in hand, march to the exit door, and shove it open. I stride to my car, which is parked under the streetlight that's been burned out for over a year.

He jogs to my side, his hand sliding around my arm again. He's got to stop touching me like he cares. I wave him off and ask, "You followed me here, didn't you?"

"Maybe."

Ugh. I swing around and bump into that muscled chest. "Why?"

He blinks. "Because you left our tutoring session in such a hurry. I was... worried."

"Worried about me? I doubt that." I let out a scoff to emphasize my words.

He takes another step closer, so close we are only inches from nose to nose. My heart skitters. We've been down this road before, and I'm begging my hormones to not show their ugly heads.

"I am worried. After what happened to your neighbor, I don't want you to be scared. I care about you."

My brain doesn't register anything after he says, "I care about you." He could be yammering on about Trig or his latest painting, but my ears can't process anything else, so I stare at the pavement. I hate that he reads my mind. Maybe I am a little scared, but that doesn't give him the right to follow me. "You are not allowed to care about me."

He scrunches his nose. "Excuse me?"

I shake my head. My ponytail whips around my face. "Caring is limited to my family and close friends. And you, buster, are not either of those. You're my... tutor. Caring people aren't afraid to admit when they kiss me."

His spine stiffens, and a thrill runs through me because I think I hit a nerve.

"That's complicated."

"You had your chance." With my finger, I draw an imaginary circle around my mouth. "You can kiss your chances goodbye of ever touching these lips again."

That sounded better in my head than how it came out. *Gah.* "Figuratively speaking, of course."

He blows out an exasperated breath. "Let me explain about that ni—"

"Don't. Care." I hold up a hand and walk backward toward my car. Before I unlock the door, I say, "Go home, Samuel. If I needed your help, I would have asked for it. Come to think of it, I will probably never ask you for help again."

He follows me to my car and puts one arm on each side of me, caging me in against the door. He stares into my eyes, but it doesn't have the same effect on me as before. I no longer melt into a puddle.

"Why not?"

As if he has the right to ask.

I hope he doesn't notice me sniffing him because I really like the way he smells. *No, I don't. Focus, Sam.*

"Because I had to practically beg you to help me. I shouldn't have to plead." I focus on the ground. "Go home, Samuel. I wouldn't want you to be seen with me."

"Ouch."

I push away from him, giving me a chance to slip into my car and slam the door. I don't need him, and I certainly don't need his protection. I've got a very big brother for that.

Samantha rule number four—"Never let them know you're scared."

Chapter Twenty-Seven

Samuel

When I turn into my driveway, still fuming about how Sam blew me off, Mason's car is in my parking space. I don't need this, but his family has a standing dinner date with mine every Tuesday. Maybe I'll fake a stomach virus, and no one will want me near them.

"'Sup, cuz?" he asks, walking from his car with a casserole dish in his hands. His little sister, Michelle, bounds past us to the house, twirling like a ballerina, making Mason teeter on the steps. He takes one gander at my scowl and asks, "Dude, who peed in your cornflakes?"

"I am not in the mood. What's for dinner?"

He lifts the lid, and the savory aroma of roasted herbs wafts over me. "Um. Chicken Divan."

I peel back the foil, and my eyes roll back in my head. "Did your mom make those homemade dinner rolls too? I love those things."

"Yeah, but there aren't many remaining. I got hungry on the way over here."

"You know how much I like those." My pout doesn't make him seem the least bit sorry about his binge.

The back car door opens, and my aunt walks out. She takes the casserole dish from Mason, and I give her a quick peck on the cheek.

Aunt Jamie gives me a cheesy smile. "You know I made an extra batch of rolls for my favorite nephew." In a stage whisper, she adds, "I had to hide them from the family hog."

"Ha, take that, Mace."

My mom and Aunt Jamie are like two peas in a pod. They are identical in appearance, act like each other, and both married surgeons. Mason and I were also born only two weeks apart, so I guess twins do think and act alike.

She adjusts the clip in her dark hair and pats me on the cheek. "You seem stressed. Want to tell your favorite aunt all about it?"

Hoping to get some help from my cousin, I glance over to Mason. We may have different attitudes about our intellectual abilities, but we are aligned like brothers when it comes to our moms. They are both over the top in everything they do.

He holds his hands up. "Samuel, run. She loves to psychoanalyze every minute of my day. It's a shock I haven't been committed yet."

I pop him on the arm and hold the door open for Aunt Jamie. Mom stands in the doorway, more peaked than yesterday. The dark circles under her eyes are a little more prominent, too, which makes me want to ask how she's feeling, but I know she'll blow me off and insist it's just a lack of sleep. "Hi, Mom."

"How was your day?"

"Uh, same as always. I need to take care of some school stuff before dinner." I head down the hallway in hopes of figuring out what happened with Sam. She's never been so... defiant before.

"Dinner will be ready in twenty minutes," she replies as I walk away.

I climb the stairs two at a time because I need to get away from civilization and figure out why I'm still ticked. My bed bounces when I fall onto it, then I give my pillow a quick punch.

"At least that's not my face you're hitting." Mason props himself against my doorframe, his legs crossed at the ankles.

"It will be if you don't leave."

He proceeds to enter my room uninvited and sits on my desk chair. He steeples his fingers as he swivels back and forth. "You know, you don't scare me."

"You should be scared. I'm not in a good mood today."

He gasps as he feigns shock. "No, I didn't notice. What is wrong with you?"

If I don't tell him, he'll pick and pick until he figures it out. "Argh. It's Samantha."

"Who didn't see that one coming? There is so much tension around you two that it could cause a fire."

"She takes risks. Dangerous risks. I don't like it."

"So?"

"She goes to Claiborne Street to help with inner city kids."

"And?"

I sit up on my bed. "That's the most dangerous street in town. Someone got decapitated in a street fight a few months ago. That's how bad it is."

Mason lets out a slow whistle. "Man, I need to watch the news more."

To keep my hands busy, I pick up a baseball lying at my feet and toss it from one hand to the other. "It's not safe."

"Wait a second." He grins, and it's as if I can see the lightbulb turn on in his brain. "You hooked up with her, didn't you?"

I shake my head. "No, of course not." I throw the ball to him. He fumbles it but eventually catches it before he tosses it back to me.

"Well, something's going on because she and her buds are acting so strange lately, more than usual."

"Pfft. She wants to know who kissed her until her toes curled." I spin the ball on my finger then send it back to Mason.

"Ah. So that's what the fortune-telling stuff was about." He stares at his hand and chuckles.

"They are trying to narrow the suspects."

He throws the ball back to me, and I lunge to the left to catch it before it crashes into my bedside lamp. "I need to brush up on my roundball skills. Anyway, Samantha must remember something about the hands. I wonder if I'm on the list." He winks.

I stand over him, still tossing the ball from one hand to the other. "You need to stay away from her."

"Why? Jealous much?"

"Mason, don't go there."

He stands, and we're eye to eye. He's grown three inches since summer and has just about caught up to my height. "You don't want her, but you don't want anyone else to have her either. Thinking about someone else kissing her is driving you crazy. Isn't it?"

"Shut up." The truth hurts, big time.

He chuckles and plunks back in my desk chair. "I'm right, and you know it."

"If you weren't family, I'd deck you right now."

The chair squeaks as he spins around in it. "No, you won't. You've never laid a hand on me before, and you aren't about to start now. Besides, I don't know what your problem is. Heck, I'd ask her out if I didn't think you were so into her."

"Wise."

"You either think she's not good enough for you, or you're pissed someone else got to her first."

I stand and stretch my arms over my head. "You are worse than your mother." I give him a playful shove, knocking him out of the chair. "I'm hungry."

"Answer me one thing." He pulls himself to a standing position.

"What is it?"

A sly grin slides over his face. "Am I a contender for the mystery smoocher?" He puckers his lips and pretends to kiss me.

As I lead him out of my bedroom, I mumble, "You wish."

I've never been jealous a day in my life, and I'm surely not going to start now. Samantha has me so messed up. I should never have made out with her. Forget that thought. I should kiss her again.

Samuel rule number eight—"If you see something you want, go for it."

Chapter Twenty-Eight

Samantha

Mule says I need to think like a ballplayer today. I wish I were on the court right now, but as I sit in the parking lot of the testing center, I want to hurl. Sweat trickles down my back, and my hands shake so much I've dropped my keys on the floor of my car twice. I do not want to take the SAT today, but it's my last chance to improve my score.

Something out of my peripheral vision catches my eye, and when I notice a human standing next to my car, I let out a squeak. Realizing it's Mule, I groan. "I told you not to come."

He backs away with his hands out in surrender. "Would you believe it if I said I was in the neighborhood... again?"

"Nope."

"Busted." He leans against my car and stares down at me while a lock of hair falls over his eyes, distracting me from my pre-SAT jitters. "You've got this. What are Auburn's requirements for admission?"

I blow out a raspberry as I open my car door. "The coach says I need to make six twenty on the math part and a total score of at least eleven eighty." I shrug. "That math..."

He lifts my chin with a finger. "Hey, you've got this. You've always had it. I only showed you how to use it."

My cheeks warm. "Thanks." I close my car door and blow out another breath. "It's showtime." I walk away, but when I get halfway to the testing center entrance, I turn around and find Mule resting against my car, a faint smile on his face.

"You're not going to wait around here all day, are you?"

He crosses his arms and gives me a huge smile. "Are you telling me to leave?"

"Pretty much." I wave to him as I check my purse for the fifth time to make sure I have my driver's license.

After I use the restroom and splash water on my face, I follow the crowd to the check-in desk. I hand the person manning the table my admission ticket, and he verifies my information as I clench my number two pencils with a death grip.

"Good luck," he says, handing me back my license.

I'm going to need it. This day cannot be over fast enough.

I wish the test started with math so I could say goodbye to Chief Sohcahtoa, but I have no choice but to endure the English section first. I hope I don't worry so much about math that I mess up English. When the math part begins, I close my eyes and try to remember all the tricks Mule taught me, but all I see is his face, smiling. He believes in me. It's time to believe in myself, that I can do this.

Come on, Sam. Remember the Samuel rules. Think like a ballplayer. Always show your steps. Samantha is smart. Trust Samuel. Don't think, do.

I should take another try at question forty-seven. That one really tripped me up. As I scan my answer sheet, I feel Mule telling me to stop. *Dang it, Mule. Get out of my head.*

With more force than I intend, I slam my pencil on the desk, signaling I am done with the exam. My heart races like I've finished a basketball game that went into overtime. When the agonizing three hours are up, the administrator gets to my station. I hand him my test papers but keep hold. He has no idea my entire future lies within those answers.

"Miss, you've done the work. It's time to let it go."

I release my grip and slump back into my chair, waiting to be dismissed. For the first time since I sat my butt in this seat, I brave a look around the room. It's filled with people who wear expressions reflecting exactly how I feel—hopeful, fearful, exhausted.

The administrator organizes the test booklets, answer sheets, and our scratch paper before he dismisses us. Everyone in the room bolts for the door, leaving me all alone. I wish I felt like I did better this time, but I don't know. Dread comes over me because it was my last shot. I have no more chances, and the next few weeks will be agonizing until I get the notice my scores are posted.

With my head hanging low, I slog out of the building and toward my car. Mule rests his tall frame against my VW Bug. His thumbs fly across the screen of his phone. He's obviously unaware I am nearby. I clear my throat to signal my presence.

A wicked grin spreads over his face. "How'd you do?"

"What are you still doing here?"

With a shrug, he replies, "Like I said. I was in the neighborhood."

"Mule..."

He motions with his head for me to follow him to his truck. "I figured you were too nervous to eat breakfast, so"—Mule opens his truck door and holds out a Music City Sandwich Company bag—"I got your favorite sandwich."

The smell of sourdough travels to me, and I'm pretty sure I purr. "Black forest ham?"

"It has light mayo, lettuce, pickle, onion, and a dash of oregano." He pulls out the sandwich and hands it to me. "I also got you salt-and-vinegar chips and a Diet Coke."

It's so sweet that he knows exactly what I order from the best sandwich shop in town. He helps me into his truck, and we munch on food. The only sounds are the crunching of chips and gulps while we drink. We've spent so much time together lately that we don't have to use words to communicate.

He catches me watching him eat, and he winks. "I bet you made a twelve hundred this time."

"You think you're that good, huh?"

With a tap to my nose, he says, "Not me. You. And you are on track to get at least a 3.0 GPA if you get B's on the rest of the Trig tests, which will be a piece of cake."

I snort. "Let's not get ahead of ourselves." Finishing off my sandwich and taking the last gulp of my drink, I toss all my trash back into the paper bag.

Samuel burps. "Sorry."

"Classy, Mule."

We sit in silence for a moment, then he says, "I can't help it if I'm myself around you."

Aw. When he's mean I have no trouble snapping back at him. But when he's nice... I clear my throat to tamp down the bubbles erupting in my chest. "Thanks for the lunch. It hit the spot. And thanks for..."

"Any time."

An odd sensation comes over me while we stare at each other. I swallow hard and glance away. "I better be going. Paige is making cookies for me."

He waves a hand toward the door. "By all means. I can't compete with cookies. See ya, Sam-Man."

"Bye, Mule."

I climb out of his truck and run to my car to keep myself from wrapping my arms around him and thanking him with a massive kiss. With a full stomach and the memory of Mule's smile, I feel better about how I did on the test. I hope I did well enough because if I didn't, I don't know what I'll do.

Chapter Twenty-Nine

Samantha

Rachel plays with a strand of hair as she goes over her updated mystery smoocher presentation. She jabs Paige in the side. Startled, Paige topples off the futon. I disguise my yawn behind my hand because all this fuss is for nothing. Rachel is awesome, but she is like a dog with a bone when she puts her mind to something.

"Here's the next item on our list." Rachel changes the slide to one with the faces of the seven remaining guys. She hits the keyboard, and a big red tomato splats Ben in the face. "Ben's out due to sissy hands."

Paige sits up and takes the laptop from Rachel. "Samantha and I talked about it, and we both decided Keith and Collin are out. There is no way either one would ever have minty breath."

"Are you sure?"

Paige grimaces. "Trust me. I am sandwiched between them in European History. I've actually gagged a few times. I even gave them gum one time, and they'll even make Coolmint Ice Breakers non-minty, so I'm positive. They are off the list."

Of course they are off the list. There is no list, not really.

Paige hits the space bar, and tomatoes smear both of their faces.

"If you say so," Rachel says. "Four more to go."

"So, what's the plan now?" I must admit her system would come in handy by eliminating some real duds—if our quest was necessary. But the closer my friends get to finding out who the mystery smoocher is not, the more nervous I become. I'm not sure how Rachel will react when she finds out this is all for nothing.

Mule frustrated me when he followed me to the community center the other day, but the more I think about it, the more it makes me all gushy inside. If he didn't care, he wouldn't have tried to keep me safe and he wouldn't have camped outside the testing center, waiting on me to finish the SATs. He does care in a strange and twisted way. Something is holding him back, and as long as he keeps this up, I'm going along with this ridiculous game.

None of the remaining four guys really *do it* for me. Ryan's kind of shy, and I don't know much about him except he talks about playing Dungeons and Dragons a lot, which falls into the *ew* category. Larry and Jack are on the lacrosse team, and that's kind of cool, but most of the lacrosse players aren't serious athletes. At my school, lacrosse is an entry-level sport. I really shouldn't judge because I bet they don't have any trouble getting into their first-pick colleges.

I'm not sure either one would know I sometimes go into the janitor's closet, and I surely don't think they would have the guts to deliver a mystery kiss. They may have strong hands—I'm not sure about their breath—but there's no way they could give me a kiss as good as Mule's, even if I didn't know who I made out with.

After a long, exasperated sigh, I say, "So, master planner, what's next?"

"I had this great idea for phase two, but the principal put the kibosh on it. So we'll have to put phase three into action."

My phone buzzes in my lap.

"Ooo, maybe it's Mystery Lips himself," Paige says, wiggling her eyebrows.

My phone displays it's from *brother*, my fake name for Samuel in case anyone ever sees our messages. "Hardly." I'm getting all too comfortable lying to my friends, and it needs to stop soon.

Mule: *How'd U do on the latest Trig test?*

I grin as I think about the results. I've been dying to tell him about the exam I took earlier today but didn't want to seem like a puppy, waiting for a pat on the head. I need to give him space because he does have a life outside of tutoring, which probably includes every cheerleader in the school.

Me: *I did all right.*

Mule: *I need a number, Sam-Man.*

Since I got a good grade on the first make-up exam, he probably assumes I'm capable of that every time.

Me: *82*

I nod at whatever Rachel is rambling on about, hoping she thinks I'm paying attention.

My phone buzzes again. Samuel sends a smiley face, a heart-shaped smiley face, a high-five, and two more smiley face emoticons.

Mule: *Why didn't U tell me?*

Me: *Because I didn't think you'd B happy.*

Samuel sends me an eye roll emoticon, and I snort with laughter.

Mule: *Nonsense. That's great. Happy 4U. Boy... I'm gooood! JK ;)*

Me: *Now I'm doing an eye roll. Thx.*

Mule: *Pretty soon, you won't need me anymore :(*

Me: *LOL. You wish. Your secret(s) are still safe with me.*

Mule: *Thx. I am pretty handy, huh?*

Oh no, he didn't go there. That little rat.

Rachel clears her throat to get my attention.

"Sorry." I put my phone on the floor and smile.

My phone buzzes again.

She slaps her hand over it. "Don't. You. Dare. Now we have got to ramp up phase three of our investigation." With a clickity click of the keyboard, she pulls up a drawing of a wooden structure with hearts and lips painted all over it.

Paige scrunches her nose. "Are we going to build a lemonade stand?"

"No, silly. It's a kissing booth to raise money for Second Harvest Food Bank," Rachel says as she crumples a piece of notebook paper and slings it at Paige.

My phone buzzes again, and Rachel raises her eyebrows, daring me to answer it. I bite my lip to keep from smiling.

"Excuse me?" I do not like where this is going. Not at all.

"We need to eliminate more guys, and the best way to do that is for you to kiss them." She points her finger at me and smiles. I am so glad she's my friend because she could easily use her planning powers for evil, and I wouldn't want to be on the receiving end of that.

"I don't know about this. How many creeps will I have to smooch before I get to the ones left on the list?" The thought of tongue wrestling with some of the guys in our class makes my stomach churn.

My phone buzzes again.

She blows off my concern. "I have kissed most of them before, and the others would pay a dollar for the privilege." She gasps. "That sounded way more conceited than I meant. I'll take a few for the team. But you'll owe me after this is all over. And just like during the palm reading, when someone on the list shows up, you'll step in to complete your assessment." She turns to Paige. "Do you think Brody would help with the construction of the booth?"

Paige shrugs. "I'm sure he would. It is for a good cause. Maybe Jared and Samuel could pitch in too."

Rachel bobs her head as she types on her laptop like someone has a gun to her head. "It would only take one afternoon. I've already got the plans downloaded, and it's a pretty simple design."

Once again, my phone buzzes, causing Rachel to throw her hands in the air. She gets up and stands over me. "Oh, for the love of all that's good in the world, answer it."

I grab it and read all the messages from Samuel.

Mule: *I'll always need U.*

Mule: *RU ignoring me?*

Mule: *Answer, or I'll start painting another portrait.*

A giggle slips from my lips. Paige glares at me like I've grown horns. "Sorry. Craig said something silly."

Mule: *There are ten types of people in this world. Those that understand binary and those that don't.*

I snort and am shocked that I got the math pun.

Mule: *Parallel lines have so much in common. It's a shame they'll never meet.*

Oh, that was so bad. He has gone down the geeky path and can't stop now.

Mule: *Why did the chicken cross the mobius strip?*

Mule: *To get to the same side.*

Oh my stars. The nerd has been let loose, and it's adorable.

Mule: *What's your sine? It must be 2/1 because you R the 1 :)*

My ears burn. I text him back.

Me: *LOL. Enjoyed your geekiness. Sorry. I was busy.*

Mule: *2 busy 4 me? I'm not being obtuse. You're an acute girl. Hee hee. Get it?*

Me: *Shakes head.*

Mule: *CU at the arts center at 3 2morrow?*

Me: *Sure.*

Mule: *Bye sec c.*

That last text makes my hands shake. My phone falls to the floor with a thud. Rachel and Paige stare at me. "Sorry. I haven't talked to my brother in a long time."

"Whatever," Rachel says. "We start on the project Thursday."

"Sounds good to me," Paige says. "Let's call the boys over to bribe them into helping us. Not Samuel because he's too broody."

I nod, but I'm not really listening to her anymore. For all I know, she could have told me my next assignment was to bungee jump off the Natchez Trace Parkway bridge. My mind is still back on those silly texts from Samuel.

Rachel's thumbs fly over her phone screen at breakneck speed. "Making a note to text Mason for help with physics and Jared to tell him I need a shoulder to cry on. Once I hit Send, they'll be over here in record time."

"You're awful." I suck in a breath when an evil idea clicks in my brain. Calling Mason over here isn't a bad idea at all. I might have an idea of my own.

She points to Paige. "And you are going to get Brody in on it too?"

"He'll do anything I ask," she says with a cheesy grin that makes me want to gag.

If Mason agrees, I know exactly how to get under Mule's skin.

Samantha rule number five—"All is fair in love and war."

But he called me sec-c...

Chapter Thirty

Samuel

Tired and sweaty from a game of two on two, Mason, Brody, and Jared follow me into the kitchen in search of grub. As expected, Mom fetches all the food from the refrigerator, and we stuff ourselves while we sit around the bar. She loves having a house full of kids. Mom is in her element when she's making others happy, and in this house, that usually involves food. That's her love language. Until recently, any smell would make her nauseous, so this is a great sign she's feeling better.

"Thanks for the food, Mrs. King."

"You're welcome, Jared Wayne."

A red flush spreads across his neck. Mason giggles like a girl until Mom shushes him with a glance. "If y'all will be here for a while, I'll whip up a batch of my no-bake cookies."

"Yes!" we say in unison. The four of us have never been so like-minded about anything in our lives. Mom's concoction of chocolate, peanut butter, and oats is straight from the gods. I can't remember the last time she made a batch. Within a minute, she's located the ingredients and tied aprons around our necks. "This time, you all are going to learn how to make them."

"Where's the fun in that, Mom?"

She smirks at my disgusted reaction. "It won't be long until I'm not... I mean, until you're off at college. This is the perfect late-night treat. You can even cheat and make them in the microwave."

She tries to hide her slipup with a smile, but my heart stutters inside my chest. I cannot think about life without her. I need her. She settles Dad in a way no one else can, and we both love her.

Brody and Jared nod politely, but I share a glance with Mason, and his face reflects my fear. He's been around through all the treatments, all the lousy CT results, and every one of my angry outbursts when things didn't go Mom's way.

"C'mon," she says, bringing me out of my dark place as she hands me a wooden spoon. "I'll show you how."

Before long, she has us all doing a step of the recipe. Jared melts the butter. Mason is on chocolate duty, but he eats as many chocolate chips as he melts. Brody is at the ready with the peanut butter and sugar, and I man the oats station.

"You see, boys, the secret is how long you cook the ingredients on the stovetop. If you are too quick, they're too gooey. If you take too long, they become like concrete."

I shake my head. "They taste great no matter how they turn out."

I think back to the times I tried to make the cookies for her when she was recovering from chemo. Sometimes the cookies were the only things she had an appetite for. My batches usually ended up in the soupy category, but she always said it was the thought that counted.

Mom hip bumps me. "Do you remember we would eat them straight out of the pan?"

I grin, thinking back to my childhood. "Yeah, Dad would make the batch too hard, and I would make it too thin."

She ruffles my hair, and my friends smile. "It never mattered. My two favorite men made them for me, and I loved that."

She takes the saucepan from me after I add the oats and dollops the mixture onto waxed paper, fanning it with a dish towel. She swats Mason's hand away as he goes in for a cookie.

"Let them cool. You know, now that I think about it, these cookies are a lot like girls."

Jared drops the spoon he's licking. "Ouch, that was hot."

"I'm serious. Girls are very sweet, but if you mess with them while they're steaming, you're going to get burned."

"Tell me about it." Brody reaches for a cookie but gets the stare down. Did he not hear anything she said?

"You have to let girls chill, and then, well... then they are just right."

Make her stop.

She waves the dish towel over the cookies again to speed up the cooling process and leans in to inhale the chocolate goodness we created.

Mason holds up a finger. "But if you wait too long, they're cold. And that's no good either."

We stare at him, and I ponder his analogy. He's on to something, which is a shocker. It's always been obvious he's a genius with math and science, but it never occurred to me that he had a knack for philosophy too.

He glares at me, and I know what he's thinking. I stuff a cookie into my mouth, not caring if it burns. "What are you looking at?"

"Nothing," Mom says with an unconvincing tone.

Jared and Brody fist-bump, and it's like everyone in the room except me is in on a joke, one I don't want to be included in anyway.

Mason's phone chirps. His face brightens as a smile slides across his face.

Then Jared's phone goes off, followed by Brody's. They each get an "oh, crap" expression on their faces. Brody jumps off the stool and steals a cookie before he runs upstairs. Jared stuffs his phone back in his pocket and kisses my mother on the cheek.

"Where are you going?" she asks him.

He swallows. "Rachel says she *needs* me. I'm not passing that up."

Mason rushes around the kitchen and snatches his keys. "I have to go too." My cousin bolts in front of Jared, trying to leave the kitchen.

Jared pushes Mason out of the way. "Nuh-uh. She says she needs *me*. Last one there eats my dust."

Jared and Mason hightail it out of the house, leaving Mom and me to stare at each other. I shrug because I really don't have a clue what is going on. Brody stumbles back into the kitchen, one shoe on and the other tucked under his arm.

He grabs a cookie. "Paige got in a big fight with Rachel. I gotta go before they yank each other's hair out."

When the kitchen quiets, Mom and I stand on opposite sides of the bar with the cookies between us. We both lunge for them at the same time. She giggles as she stuffs her mouth full of sweets then moans. "Best batch ever."

"They snooze and lose, right?"

She nods and feeds me a cookie. I don't care what my friends needed to race off to do. I'm in my kitchen, enjoying perfectly made cookies with my mother. We sit in silence as we eat the warm treats and slug down cold milk. And right now, nothing else matters.

Chapter Thirty-One

Samantha

Fooling the guys into helping us is new to Paige and me, but apparently, Rachel does this quite often because guys seem to drop everything to help her. She says it's harmless to play with their feelings, but I still don't like it. She peeks out the window to stare over to Mason's house across the street.

"His car isn't there. Jason, Brody, and Mason might all be at the same place. Ooo. I think I see headlights." Screeching tires on the pavement announce someone's arrival. "Get ready."

The doorbell rings, and Rachel goes downstairs. I can hear a deep, muffled conversation then the sounds of heavy footfalls on the steps. I sneak a peek at Paige. She nibbles on her bottom lip, and she seems as nervous as I feel. I'm working my way through all the nails on my right hand. If they don't get up here soon, I'll have to start on my left.

Rachel opens the door to her room at the same time Mason stumbles past Jared. He lands on his stomach like he's sliding into second base. Brody rushes past him with Jared hot on his heels.

Coming to a screeching halt, Jared slings his long hair out of his eyes and stands tall. He winks at Rachel. "You... need me?"

"Ugh," she says but recovers quickly, plastering on a fake smile.

Brody takes Paige by the hand to lead her out of the room. "C'mon, I'll take you home, and we can sort all of this out. I'm sure it's just a big misunderstanding."

She digs her feet into the carpet as she peers over at Rachel. "We're okay now, aren't we?"

"We're good. Have a seat." Rachel motions to the futon.

Jared and Mason obey like well-trained puppies. Brody stands with his arms crossed, clearly not under her spell.

"Or... stand if that's your preference. Guys, Samantha needs your help."

All eyes focus on me, and I wave like I've never met them before. This idea is insane. Getting them involved is even crazier.

"She has a problem and needs help from all of you. This falls under the *cone of silence*."

"Uh... sure." It's no shocker that Mason is the first to volunteer.

Rachel flashes a brilliant smile at him. "As you know, we are on a mission to find out who made out with her at the dance."

Like puppies being scolded, Brody and Mason keep their gazes trained on the floor. In fact, the dust bunny behind the television gets more of their attention than I do.

With a snap of her fingers, Rachel brings their attention back to her. "I had this elaborate, scientifically designed procedure to determine who the mystery kisser is."

"What's your P value?" We all glance over at Mason, who has a serious expression on his face.

I sneak a glance at Paige as she scrunches her brow. She seems to not understand what he's talking about either.

With no expression in her voice, Rachel says, "If you must know, it's 0.001."

We stare at our smart friends like they are speaking Yiddish. Mason nods and turns to me. "That's very good."

I shrug. "Oh, good to know. I guess."

Rachel has a "told ya so" smirk on her face. There is so much brain power in this room, I feel very silly that such intelligent people are wasting their smarts on such a stupid project.

He clears his throat. "Wait a sec. You don't need my help with physics?"

"No, I do not."

Paige swallows a snicker as Brody plunks down in a beanbag chair. He mumbles to her, "He will never learn."

Jared whips his hair out of his face again. "What do you need us to do?"

I take a deep breath and stare at Rachel and Paige. They nod in support. "It's stupid, but we need your help constructing a kissing booth."

Rachel settles in on the futon between Jared and Mason to seal the deal. Jared sits taller and puts an arm behind her while Mason's chest rises and falls. If he doesn't watch out, he's going to hyperventilate.

She focuses on Mason first since he's clearly the easiest to convince. "What do you think?"

His face loses all expression as he turns to Brody. "I, uh, me? I'm not much help with power tools, but I'll do what I can. Anything for you, Rach."

I inwardly groan, but Brody lets out his exasperation loud and clear, making Jared chuckle.

Large and in charge, Rachel stands to resume her pacing. "There are four guys left, and only one is *the* one who kissed Samantha in the closet."

In his typical by-the-book fashion, Mason raises his hand and asks, "Am I on the short list?"

She tugs on her necklace then stops in front of him. "You haven't been eliminated yet."

He leans back and laces his hands behind his head. "Ha. And you think it's me, right?"

"Doubt it," Rachel says. "I think you would have confessed by now, and... I certainly don't think you fit the description Samantha has given us."

He grins at Rachel as he wags his finger at her. "You're *hoping* it wasn't me."

"I didn't say that." She gets all twitchy, and I love that he is getting to her. If she would get over herself, she and Mason would make a cute couple. An odd one, too, but they have more in common than they care to admit.

He snorts, and I love that he has found his confidence around her. "Ah, but you're thinking it."

"I'm not getting involved," Jared tells Rachel.

She stands in front of Jared and runs her hands through his long hair. He gulps. I see his Adam's apple bobbing from across the room.

"If you help us construct the booth, you get one date. Me and you. One real date."

People as far away as Kentucky can probably see his wide grin. "Abso-freakin-lutely. Count me in."

She moves to Mason and taps her finger to her lips. He watches her every move like a kid waiting in line to see Santa. "I know you need me to show up at the booth more than you need me to help build it. What's in it for me?"

Like she is spitting venom, she groans then says, "You get a date too."

"One date? Come on, Rach. You can do better than that. I could very well be the mystery man. You know you want to find out if these are the lips that caused all this commotion."

I cover my mouth to hold in the laugh because he's so full of himself, plus I know he wasn't the one, but I don't blame him for using Rachel's uncertainty to his advantage. It's obvious he carries the same swagger gene as Samuel, and that could really come in handy with the seed of an idea I have.

She blows out a breath and says, "Fine. You get three dates." She bites her lip and glares at me with a "you owe me big time" expression.

We all wait for his response. Mason opens and closes his mouth like a fish gasping for water. "Nope."

She steps back. "Really?"

A wide grin forms across his face. "Since I am one of the final four, I want three dates *and* an additional date... to the prom."

Like a bug flipped on its back, Brody rolls over and out of the beanbag chair to hide his face. Jared plops back on the futon, punching a pillow.

Paige mouths, "Oh my."

With fists clenched by her sides, Rachel turns her back on Mason and stares at me. I plead with my eyes. She closes her eyes, and through gritted teeth, she replies to Mason, "Fine."

He collapses onto the futon then slides to the floor as Paige giggles. He gets a playful punch in the gut from Brody.

Paige stops Brody from smacking him again. "Is that a yes?"

All Mason does is nod. A lot. He kicks his feet in the air as he lets out a "woo-hoo."

"Dude. Not fair," Jared says, like someone beat him at Fortnite.

Mule is going to flip when he finds out I am using his cousin to get back at him, but that's what he deserves.

Chapter Thirty-Two

Samuel

Humming one of Samantha's favorite songs doesn't snap her out of her fog. Talking with a British accent doesn't do it either. Even tapping on her paper doesn't get her attention. This is going to be a tough study session.

"Come on, girl. Focus."

She stares at the paper then draws some squiggly lines on it. She erases and draws again. When she erases it this time, she rips a hole in the paper.

"Chill, Sam-Man. What is up with you?"

She bangs her head on the table. "Sorry. I have a lot on my mind."

I slide the notebook from under her head and place it in my backpack. "I don't think you're going to get any serious studying done today."

"Sorry, but I can't stay focused."

"What's going on that's making you so jumpy?"

She stares off, her hands shaking. I've never seen her this off before. "As much as I hate to admit it, I don't think I should go to the Nashville Youth Center today. There was a robbery across the street from there yesterday. It's making me a little paranoid, especially with all the crap that's been going on in my own neighborhood."

I growl. "I don't like it when you go there."

She smiles. "That's very sweet of you—"

"I'm not sweet. It's a fact." *Liar.* "Rumor has it, there's a pickup softball game this afternoon at the park." I mimic swinging a baseball bat. "I know you want to go."

She taps her pencil on the table, considering my offer, so I throw in some tempting tidbits.

"The crack of the bat. The smack of the ball in your glove. Come on. Brody's bringing Chase, Louie, and Carter. They aren't exactly the best players in the world, but at least it would be even... if you come too."

I stand and stretch my arms over my head, making my T-shirt rise. She bites her bottom lip as she stares at my stomach. *Love it.* Her eyes scan my body then lock on mine. When her face brightens into the most perfect shade of pink, I melt. She quickly glances away. Man, she is so adorable.

"You drive a hard bargain." She retrieves her phone from her pocket and types a message. "There. I wrote to the director of the center that I can't make it today. It wouldn't hurt me to hit some balls around."

I punch my fist in the air and say, "Yes. What are we waiting for? I'll drive, and we'll study along the way."

She jumps from her chair so fast it falls backward. "Well, come on."

Samantha picks up a bat and taps the instep of her sneakers before she struts to the makeshift home plate, which is made from a scrap of cardboard. I'm behind it, playing catcher. With her bat, she points at me then to the infield. "Hey, genius. Shortstop is out there."

I pop my glove with my fist. "Yeah, but the view is much better from here."

She grins as she swings her bat a few times, each swing getting closer to my head. "Smarty pants." she says. She winds up and kicks dirt behind her into my face, making me cough.

Paige is the pitcher and lets the first pitch fly into my awaiting glove. Samantha doesn't try to hit it.

"Strike."

She turns to scowl at me. "Maybe if I was bowling."

On the next pitch, the bat cracks as she makes contact with the ball. It sails over Mason's head into the outfield, which is no shocker. She does a girly bounce before she darts toward first base, but I grab the back of her T-shirt.

Her feet move, but she's not going anywhere as she swats at my arms. "Let me go."

Paige doubles over in a fit of laughter. When Mason catches up to the ball, I let Samantha free, and she's like a wind-up toy. She rounds first base and heads for second. Mason slings the ball toward Jared, who is covering second base. She does a half slide then pops up to stand on the base.

Rachel, playing first base, yells to Samantha, "Nice job."

Paige throws her hands in the air. "She's on the other team, Rach."

There is a reason why my team has one extra player. Neither Rachel nor Mason are jocks, so to make it even, Samantha's team only includes Brody, Louie, and Carter. It's the best we can do on such short notice.

"Oops," Rachel says. "My bad. But it was still a good hit."

Brody saunters to the batter's box, bat slung across his shoulder.

"This isn't *Project Runway*. Do you remember how this game works?" I love throwing Brody's modeling gig in his face every chance I get.

He swings a few times. "Shut it." Brody points his bat at Paige on the pitcher's mound. "Hey, cutie, you won't throw anything too hard at me, will ya?"

She lets one zing past him, and it lands in my glove. I return the ball, shaking out my hand wearing the glove. "Ouch, that hurt."

"I guess she has no problem with playing hardball after all."

Brody winds up again. He hits the next pitch, and Samantha runs toward third. For some strange reason, Rachel takes off running toward second base even though she's playing infield.

"Rach, you're not a runner." Paige flags Rachel, pointing toward first base.

"Sorry. My bad."

Brody jogs past Rachel and blows Paige a kiss.

With Brody on second and Samantha on third, Louie takes a practice swing. Not that I'm paying much attention to him. I focus on every deep breath Samantha takes as she waits to run toward home plate, toward me.

Louie hits a line drive, and she races off with the intensity of the serious athlete she is. When she is five feet from home plate, Jared throws me the ball. She rears back and slides toward me, feet first, aiming to take me out and to score the run. I'm ready for impact, I think.

Her feet hit my ankles with more force than I anticipate, so it tosses me forward. The ball pops out of my glove, and I land with a thud on top of Samantha, my gloved hand under her head to cushion the fall for her. "Oof."

"Safe," Carter yells.

I rise up to my elbows, gazing at this beautiful, sweaty mess of a girl underneath me. Her hands rest on my waist, not allowing me to move—not that I mind.

Brody jumps over us to touch home plate. "Woo-hoo!"

Samantha stands then holds out a hand to me, which I take because only a fool would reject that. She could be completely covered in dirt and sweat yet still be the sexiest girl on the planet. She cracks a smile while she fixes her ponytail, and I know I'm a goner.

We play for another hour, but afterward, I don't remember anything else about the game. I'm not even sure who won. I drag my feet until all our friends leave the field. Samantha and I walk back to my truck together in silence. She sips from her water bottle before she hands it over to me.

"Thanks. I, uh..." I can't remember the last time I had trouble talking to a girl.

She pats my sweaty back. "This was fun."

"Yeah."

She scrunches her nose and stares at me like I've grown horns. "You're acting weird."

"I'm not."

"It's like you're having a silent conversation with yourself."

Isn't that the truth? I rest my back against the bed of my truck and gaze toward the setting sun for guidance. "Sam-Man?"

She grins, and my heart melts a little more. "Yeah?"

"Would you be mad if I told you..."

Her eyebrows rise. It's time to tell the truth and face the consequences.

I blow out a breath. "I, uh. The night of the dance." *I can't form the words to complete the rest of my sentence.*

Her mouth turns down. It's not a frown but more of a disappointed reaction. She shrugs. "It's fine."

I shake my head. "No, it's not. Would you..."

Her eyes show her surprised reaction even though she tries to tamp it down. She takes another step closer to me. "Would I what, Mule?"

The way her eyes are so big and brown, I'm reminded of how much her appearance is like a female, way-prettier version of her big brother, the dude who will lose his mind if I touch his sister.

Stifling what I want to say, I focus on the ground and take a deep breath. "Nothing. We should go."

"I really should get going. I promised my parents I would be home before dark while they are out of town."

"Yeah." A light bulb goes off in my head. "They haven't caught the guy who attacked your neighbor, have they?"

In the smallest of voices, she replies, "No."

"I'll take you to get your car then follow you home to make sure you're safe. I mean, if you want me to."

Her face breaks out in a big smile. "You'd do that for me?"

"What can I say? I'm a pushover for those big brown eyes."

She lunges at me and grabs me around the neck. I encircle her waist with my arms, and any visions of Craig are completely gone.

"Thank you so much."

"No problem, Sam-Man."

"I can always stay with Paige because I don't want to put you out."

Put me out? She's being ridiculous. I'll always be there for her, and Craig might even thank me. "Nonsense. Let's get you home."

Chapter Thirty-Three

Samuel

Samantha wrings her hands and follows so closely behind me as I go room to room that she's bumped into me at least five times. I understand her concern, but the chances of someone being inside her house and hiding in a random closet is close to nil. Convincing her of that, however, is not going to be an easy task.

"There's nothing under your bed. We've checked the basement and every single room. All the windows and doors are locked. I am confident that you're completely safe."

By the way she nibbles on her bottom lip and focuses on the floor, I'm sure she isn't as certain as I am. "You think I'm a big chicken, don't you?"

I rub circles on her lower back, kicking myself for enjoying the touch when she's obviously so tense. "It's perfectly normal to feel this way."

She rolls her eyes and grins. "What do you know about being normal?"

"Ha ha."

"Anyway, thanks."

"Always. Set the house alarm when I leave, and you'll be fine."

Her next smile melts me. I better get out of here while I'm able to control myself, but she latches on to my arm when I turn to leave. "How about a movie?"

As much as I'd love to spend time with her, I reply, "I'm really beat. Maybe some other time."

Sam's face becomes stoic, and I give myself a mental kick in the butt for not staying a bit longer.

"What time will your parents be home?"

"They're in Los Angeles until Sunday."

Her eyes don't land on one place for more than a second before they dart to another.

"Craig's coming home, right?"

She shakes her head. "He was supposed to come home to hang with me, but I guess he forgot because he went camping with Rocky, his jerk-face college roommate."

Way to go, Craig. I groan. I can't leave her like this. I'm a jerk, but I'm not *that* big of a jerk. "Do you think he'll care if I crash in his room?"

Relief washes over her face as she shakes her head with vigor. "No, he won't care. He won't even have to know. I promise I won't bother you. And I trust you... to not try anything."

I cock my head to the side. "It's not a bother, and on my honor as a gentleman, I will be a good boy." For emphasis, I take a deep bow.

She lets out a snort, then after I lock the front door, she sets the alarm, nibbling on her lip. If she wants me to keep my oath, she really must stop doing that, or I'm going to break the golden Craig rule—"Thou shalt not touch my sister."

"Come on." We start up the stairs, and she turns around abruptly, knocking me off-balance. Before I tumble down the steps, she grabs me by the waist.

"Sorry. Are you sure all the doors are locked?" She swallows hard.

I point up the stairs to keep her moving. "Positive."

She starts up the stairs again, and I don't mean to, but I get a handful of booty. With a warning glare, she passes her room and heads to Craig's. When she opens his door, she covers her nose and grimaces. "Gah, this place is disgusting. Good luck finding the bed."

Craig's room is as messy as I remember. The dirty laundry strewn all over the floor and an empty pizza box on the dresser make me feel right at home. "If I didn't know better, I would think it was my room."

"Guys are so gross. The bathroom is across the hall, but you already know that. I'm... I need to take a shower." She crosses her arms over her chest. "Mule..."

"Good night, Sam-Man. I'm right here. No one will hurt you. I promise."

She walks up to me, and I'm reminded of how our bodies match so perfectly. She puts her hands on my arms as my hands find her waist. If she gives me one centimeter, I'm going to take it. *Craig who?*

When she closes the gap between us, I stop breathing. She plants a quick peck on my cheek, but before I turn and get those lips on mine, she scoots into the bathroom, slams the door, and locks it. Sam may be afraid of intruders, but I think she's even more terrified of me.

Across the hall, the sound of water rushes through the pipes, and I imagine Samantha standing under the pulsating water... naked. This is going to be harder than I thought it would. But everything in this room reminds me of Craig, and that takes the wind out of my sails, so to speak.

I clear a path of grungy clothes to the bed then empty a space so I can watch some television. The clock on the wall shows nine o'clock, but I'm already beat. I pick up a baseball bat sitting by the bed and tap it against my palm while I wander around the room. A Nerf basketball is settled in the corner, begging me to toss it into the tiny rim anchored on the back of the bedroom door, but then I catch a whiff of my armpits. No wonder she doesn't want to be in this room. It stinks, and I stink worse. I even disgust myself.

Craig's taller than me, but we're about the same size otherwise. I'm not above wearing someone else's boxers, so I strip to my boxer briefs and cast around in Craig's dresser in search of something clean. I locate a pair that seems sanitary. Only he would have green underwear with a four-leaf clover on the front and Kiss My Barney Stone written on it.

Tucked in the back of the drawer is a bag from The Chill Pill, a hemp store in town. Peering inside, I find a stash of special gummies. Typical Craig. I bet he forgot he left them. Otherwise, he would have consumed them a long time ago.

The water from the shower stops running, and a moment later, I hear Samantha's quick footsteps pass Craig's room and get fainter before her bedroom door closes with a soft click. I was hoping for one more "good night," but it's probably best this way.

I stare at the bag of gummies, thinking of my options. The old me would swallow all of them at once and chill out. They would help me relax and clear my mind from thinking about Samantha, kisses, and thoughts of making out with her, but I don't partake of THC anymore. The new, improved me puts the bag back in the drawer and goes in search of a long—and maybe very cold—shower.

Chapter Thirty-Four

Samantha

With deep breaths in and out, I practice mindful imagery like Coach taught us. After ten minutes, I'm actually getting a little drowsy until a knock on my bedroom door makes me let out a bloodcurdling scream. I jerk up the sheet to cover my boy shorts and tank top, as if that's going to protect me from getting killed.

The door creaks open, and Samuel says, "It's only me."

I blink to get my bearings and see that the big bad wolf is indeed Samuel and not someone even more scary. I let out a breath and turn on the bedside light. He sits beside me on my bed, shirtless. Shirtless, shoeless, sockless... void of everything except for some boxer briefs. Holy cow. I knew he had a good body, but... *nice*. He should walk around like that all the time. If he dressed like that in our tutoring sessions, I wouldn't learn any trig, but I sure would get a lesson or two in biology and chemistry, and I would ace human anatomy. I don't mean to, but I lick my lips, making him chuckle. *Cocky jerk.*

"You scared me." I sit up and attempt to conceal my chest that's only covered by a tank top. I cross my arms, but he's already gotten an eyeful. The skin from my toes to my ears tingles from his scorching hot gaze. "What are you doing in here, other than taking a few years off my life?"

He sniffs his armpit. "If it isn't completely obvious, I need a shower, but I didn't see any towels lying out."

"Oh." I flop the sheet off and walk out of my bedroom to the bathroom. I bend in front of the sink and dig around under the cabinet. He lets out a groan, and I realize my butt is sticking up in the air. *Real attractive, Samantha.*

I pull out a washcloth and towel and hand them to him. "Here."

"Thanks." He holds the towel in front of him as he shoos me away with his hand. "I need my privacy… unless you want to join me."

I jerk up to a standing position, banging my knee against the cabinet door. I hobble around, stepping on his foot before I scoot out into the hallway. "Good night."

"Night, Sam-Man." Before the door is completely closed, I catch him shaking his head. I'm sure he thinks I am ridiculous, which is not far from the truth.

My stomach lets out the loudest growl, and I realize I haven't eaten anything since lunch, so I descend the stairs in search of a snack. The neighbor's dog barks, and I jump a foot off the floor. Roscoe never barks. A shadow falls across the kitchen window, and I let out a squeak. Grabbing the bag of Oreos, I run back up the steps to my bedroom and retrieve my baseball bat and phone then skitter down the hall toward the sound of the shower running. I shouldn't have let Samuel leave his car in the garage. If he had left it out in the driveway, maybe we'd be alive tomorrow morning.

With shaking fingers, I call the non-emergency police phone number to report the weirdness as I pace enough to wear a hole in the carpet. The operator who answers the phone says the police will check it out, but it might take a while. Since there is no immediate threat—their words, not mine—they will canvas the neighborhood when they're free, which probably means next Tuesday.

Thanks for nothing.

After a long, deep breath, I open the bathroom door to be completely consumed with steam. I move the towel resting on the toilet seat cover and sit, cradling my bat with the towel in my lap, and place the container of cookies on the vanity. If we are going to get attacked, at least we'll be together. I stare at the doorknob, praying it doesn't rotate. When a hand touches my shoulder, I flail like a fish out of water while I let out a scream.

Samuel jumps and slides the shower curtain open, exposing his completely naked body.

I yelp. His feet slip on the wet bathtub floor as his eyes widen. With a quick jerk, he whips the shower curtain around him in a feeble attempt to cover his manliness. "What the heck, Sam. What are you doing in here?"

"I, uh... I heard something outside."

He grabs the towel from my lap and wraps it around his waist.

"Give me that." He snatches the bat from me with a huff. "Did the alarm go off?"

"No, but—"

"Then we are safe."

I grab the box of cookies, if for no other reason than to keep my hands from shaking. "Are you sure? I think we should call the cops again."

"Again?" Samuel's jaw drops as his eyes grow wide. "You called them, and they're on the way?"

I cringe. "Well... like I said, I heard a noise. Then something walked past the kitchen window and..." I bite my trembling bottom lip. "I don't think the police are coming. They said they would when they got a chance, so maybe you could..."

"What do you have in mind? Take on a robber wearing nothing but a towel?" He laughs. "I guess I could always moon him. That might scare him off."

"C'mon, Mule." I'm not humored by his lighthearted tone. Even the thought of his hot naked booty can't distract my thoughts from our imminent danger.

After a moment, he lets out a deep sigh and walks out of the bedroom, still only wearing a towel. He descends the stairs with me only an inch behind him. A thump, thump sound from outside the kitchen makes my heart skitter. Mule freezes.

In a whisper, I say, "See. Someone. Is. Out. There."

We hear the noise again, then Mule snorts. He peeks out the back door to catch an opossum trying to get into the garbage can. "That 'someone' is an animal in search of food." He chuckles. "Girl, you need to relax. My mom would say you are wound up tighter than a three-day clock."

Without waiting for me to follow, he heads back upstairs and into the bathroom, but I fall into step right behind him. "I guess I should call the police to tell them not to come out."

Mule makes a swirling motion with his finger. "Turn around unless you want to see that full moon I was talking about. I can't believe you called the cops because of an animal in your garbage."

While I slap a hand over my eyes, I do my best to breathe normally again. "Well, it seemed like it was a real threat at the time, and it very well could have been. Gah. I can't stop over-thinking everything."

"Got any Benadryl?"

"Yes, but it makes me real sleepy."

Mule makes a '"duh" expression. "Exactly."

"I mean I get totally zonked if I take that stuff. And I don't want to be completely out in case... you know. You never know when we'll have to take off on foot."

He stares at me like I have lost my mind. It's as if he can't decide if he wants to laugh or hug me. If he does both, it won't offend me.

"How about some alcohol, only control the amount?"

I shake my head. "Nope. My parents are teetotalers. And before you ask, I'm sure if Craig had anything stashed in his room, he would have taken it with him the last time he was home."

Samuel leads me to my room, and with firm hands on my biceps, he sits me on my bed. Even though I shouldn't be turned on right now, the sight of Samuel's near perfect body in nothing more than boxer briefs is a sight—even if he is wearing the Kiss My Blarney Stone underwear someone gave my brother as a dirty Santa gift last year. I'm still grossed out Craig showed them to me. Not wearing them, of course. *Ew*.

"Do you want me to buy you a six-pack?"

"No!" *I didn't mean to say that so loud.* "Don't leave me. Besides, you're too young to buy beer."

A mischievous smile slides across his face. "You have to know the right places."

I don't want to know the "right places." "Thanks, but no. I don't want to compromise the integrity of the perimeter."

"You watch too many cop shows."

Pressing the heels of my hands into my eye sockets, I flop back onto my bed. "I cannot get my mind to shut off."

Samuel yawns. "I've got another idea, but you're probably not going to like it."

"Whatever. Tell me."

"You could eat some... special gummies." His voice trails off like he's afraid I might hit him.

Like a bolt of lightning, I sit up so fast, we bump heads. Holding my forehead, I ask, "You have drugs on you? Do you always carry illegal substances?"

"I used to, but I haven't done anything like that in a very long time. I'm only saying, I bet we could find some in this house if we look hard enough." He coughs the word "Craig" before he adds, "And... they aren't illegal if you're twenty-one."

I gasp as his words sink in. "Are you accusing my brother? Because he's not twenty-one."

He laughs. "Yeah, but he looks it, and he uses that to his advantage. I found some tucked neatly inside his..." He points to Craig's underwear he's wearing, and now I'm gazing at Mule's package. *Stop staring, Sam.*

My hands continue to shake, so I do need something to calm my nerves and to help keep my mind off every creaky floorboard.

Since he's not offering up his body as a living sacrifice, I guess eating a few edibles is my only option. "I've never done that before. Will it make me pass out?"

He shakes his head. "It will help you relax. It's not my thing anymore, but I think you could use some right about now."

I move close to his ear, and I swear he sucks in a breath. He smells like soap and goodness, and I want to stay right here and breathe in his fresh, clean aroma. In a hushed tone, I ask, "You promise not to tell anyone?"

He holds out his little finger, and we pinky promise like we are back in second grade. "It will be one more of our little secrets."

This is the dumbest idea ever. I should tell him to take a hike and that I don't need pharmaceuticals to relax. The only drug I want is him, but that's worse than illegal. It's toxic. Besides, he's not offering any magical Samuel medicine, so I need to put that thought to bed.

I glance up at him, and he has an expression that makes me think he's reading my mind. "Why not? I bet it won't make a difference anyway."

Chapter Thirty-Five

Samuel

In my crouched position resting against the side of Samantha's bed, I try my best to conceal my laughter. She's the funniest greened-out girl I have ever seen. I didn't get one nibble of an edible before she downed them all. They must be super potent because she is hilarious. I was afraid she'd puke them up, but she seems to have a tolerance for the amount she ate. It's fine that I'm totally sober because I want her to relax, and if I get stoned with her, I might not have a filter on my words or actions. One thing is for sure, she is going to kick my butt in the morning.

She slings her head over the side of her bed, slapping me with her long hair. "This stuff isn't working. I feel so stupid. I'm such a chicken. Chicken. Chicken. That's a funny word, don't you think?"

All I do is nod.

"When's this stuff gonna kick in? Kick in. Chick-en." She snatches the bag of Oreos from me and shoves the remaining broken cookies into her mouth. When there are no more cookies, she pitches the bag over her shoulder and pops open a container of Pringles.

I double over with laughter while she chugs the chips like she can't get enough. She has no idea how funny she is. I roll over onto my back as my entire body trembles as I snicker.

She slams the round chip container on the bedside table and huffs. "I'm serious. I'm a chicken. But not a food chicken. I'm a scaredy-cat chicken." She slides off the bed and slithers over to me, sticking her face right next to mine. With the seriousness of a heart attack, she asks, "Can a chicken be a scaredy-cat?"

That's when I lose it. I hide my face between my knees to compose myself as my body rumbles with laughter. She taps me on the knee. When I look up, she has the cheesiest grin. "Is it working yet?"

"I, uh, I think so." I crawl onto her bed, throwing a pillow over my face. She snatches it and fluffs it under her head to settle on. She's solemn, and I'm one nanosecond from losing it again.

"I'm a pothead now."

"No, you aren't."

She nods like one of those bobblehead dolls. "Am too. I'm a druggie, and it's all your fault." She punctuates every word with a poke to my gut.

"Me? Blame it on your brother."

She nudges me in the ribs. "Yeah, but you knew he had some. And now... I'm a druggie."

"Sam-Man, a couple of edibles doesn't make you a druggie."

I wasn't prepared for her to roll over and place her head on my chest. It takes every ounce of control not to wrap her in my arms. "Ever heard of a gateway drug? Next time, you'll probably slip me some heroin."

Her head bounces from my chuckles. "I promise I won't do that." I slide my arm around her, and my hand rests right above her hip. She doesn't shove it off, so I know for sure the drugs have kicked in.

She closes her eyes and yawns. "Am I flat chested?"

I fling my eyes open. "Sorry? What did you say?"

"Rocky, Craig's college buddy, said I was." She holds up a finger to make a point. "But he liked them because he told me more than a mouthful was a waste. He was good at snogging, but nothing like you."

Bile rises in my throat at the mention of Rocky. When I visited Craig one time at college, he asked me about Samantha, and in a drunken state, I confessed how much I liked her. He started talking about what he wanted to do with that "tall drink of water," and I blew a gasket.

"I hate that guy."

She taps me on the cheek to get my attention then flops onto her back and drags my hand with her.

"What do you think? What size bra do you think I wear?"

When I'm too shocked to answer, she clears her throat. "Well? I'm waiting." In all of my years of knowing her, I have never heard her use a singsongy voice.

"Answer the question, Mule."

"Uh... they are fine." *Someone, help me.* All this talk about her breasts is driving me out of my mind. I want to do the right thing here, but she's making it extremely hard, and I'm not just talking about what's in Craig's underwear.

When I decide to do the right thing and move away from her, she swats my hands away, like this entire conversation was my idea. "Who cares anyway? I've got chicken boobs. Chicken, chicken, chicken." She lets her arms rest above her head and closes her eyes. "Go to sleep, Mule. You're bothering me."

"Oookay."

A satisfied smile slides across her face. "You're so pretty."

Hmm. I've been called good-looking, handsome, and—if I hear the word one more time, I think I'll puke—hot. But pretty? I kind of like that, especially coming from her.

"So are you," I whisper in her ear, covering her up with the sheet.

"I like your nipples."

"Uh..."

She lets out a yawn. "Chicken nipples."

Adorable.

She curls into a ball and throws an arm over my bare chest. I guess I'm not sleeping in Craig's room tonight. "Samuel?"

"Yeah?"

Her breathing slows until it's at a nice, rhythmic pace. It's so slow and even, I think she's drifting off to sleep. I've never spent the night with a girl. Knowing Samantha trusts me enough to sleep curled up next to me makes my heart swell.

"I know all of your secrets." Sam holds up a finger as her eyes flutter closed.

"Yes, you do."

"You're a great kisser."

My face hurts from the huge grin I can't hold back. "So are you."

She's going to be so embarrassed in the morning when she realizes what she did and, especially, said tonight. She may not remember a thing. Even if she does, it will be another one of our little secrets. They keep piling up, and soon, we'll have so much stuff on each other we'll have to be a couple to keep everyone else from finding out.

As soon as I think she's fallen asleep, she slides off the bed then stumbles around the room until she comes across her backpack. She turns it upside down and tosses all her stuff on the floor. A hairbrush, hair ties, her Trig textbook, and a wad of paper scatter across her floor.

"Ah, there you are." She waves her phone in the air as she bounces back down on the bed. "Speaking of secrets and Rocky and... where was I going with this?" She blinks then adds, "Oh yeah." Her fingers slide across her phone, and when she finds what she's looking for, she shoves it in my face. "Rocky drunk FaceTimed me last semester, and I recorded it."

Seeing his face on her phone and hearing the disgusting words come out of his mouth about wanting to hook up with her makes me want to punch him again. I ball my fists for a second and close my eyes to picture pummeling Rocky's cocky grin off his face. It's a good thing I'm not in the same room with that dolt because I would go to jail with the beating I would give him.

When the realization of what she's showing me clicks, I snap my eyes open. Finally. I finally have proof that my attitude toward Rocky is valid. It sucks to see and hear the things Rocky says to Sam-Man, but if Craig sees this... I grit my teeth. No. He and I have been friends for a long time. He should believe me over Rocky even without proof.

"Did you show this to Craig?"

"Nope." She pops the P in the word. "I forgot I had it until now. Here, I'll send it to you, and you can have the pleasure."

My phone pings as Samantha tosses her phone on the floor and snuggles in beside me. While I lie there steaming about Craig, I wish I could forget about the Rocky situation and focus on what's lying next to me. Right now, I only want to enjoy how her soft body feels tucked next to mine. She burrows deeper, and the waft of her shampoo filters through my nose. She smells so fresh, like peaches and soap. It's more intoxicating than any drug out there, and I'm totally addicted.

As soon as her breaths become slow and rhythmic, I slip out of her warm grip and stand. For a moment, I watch her sleep. The old me would slide back in to snuggle next to her, but I'm not that guy anymore. I don't even know that person. After one final glimpse at my girl snoring like a freight train, I snag a blanket off the bed to make a pallet on the floor.

Chapter Thirty-Six

Samantha

"What are you doing in my sister's room?"

Morning sunlight filters through the blinds, and I squint to focus on the large human hovering over me. I raise my head enough to figure out that the booming voice above me belongs to Craig. My room is littered with cookies and chip containers, and crumpled chips are all over the floor. My brother's words don't make sense until I notice a muscular human is sacked out on the floor, sprawled out on his stomach. Samuel, who only wears underwear, yawns and sits up from the hard floor, grimacing.

Holy crap. This is bad. Really bad.

My feet won't move fast enough to get me out of bed. When my legs catch on the sheet and I kick Samuel in the process of untangling myself, he snaps awake, falling back with a thud.

In a nanosecond, Craig is on Samuel. He snatches him up and dumps him on my bed like he's a five-pound bag of flour.

"What are you doing?" I yell. Craig's face is red, and a vein in his neck pulsates.

"Teaching this loser a lesson." Craig rears back, but I pounce on him and pinch the daylights out of the skin on the back of his arm. As I squeeze and twist his skin, like I've done many times over the years, his knees buckle.

He lets out a girlish yelp. "Sam. Stop."

"Not until *you* stop."

"But—"

I twist some more, making his eyes water.

"Fine. I promise."

I let go while standing on the mattress, hovering over him. His eyes grow big, then he squeezes them shut. "Samantha, put some clothes on."

I peek down and realize I'm only wearing my boy shorts and my skimpy tank top that's skewed to the side, showing way too much of my chest. "Oh my." I grab a pillow to cover my exposed boobs. To Samuel, who looks like he's ready to flee at any moment, I ask, "Why are you in my bedroom?"

Craig growls through a clenched jaw. "You better choose your words carefully, King."

Samuel holds out his hands in defense. "Man, let me explain."

"Start talking." He crosses his arms, his biceps bulge, and I am reminded of how menacing he can appear.

"It's not what you think," Samuel and I say at the same time.

Mule stands in slow motion, probably afraid to antagonize my brute of a brother any more than he already has. "Where are my pants?"

Craig jerks a thumb to the door. "You left them in my room." He squints. "Are those my..." He shakes his head and, with an evil chuckle, adds, "I don't want to know the answer. Somebody, start talking."

I hold up a finger so he'll wait a second while I go in search of clothing. I retrieve a sweatshirt from my dresser and jerk it on, wrong side out. Next, I grab a pair of sweatpants, and after three attempts, I finally slide them on. If I could find a winter parka, I'd put that on, too, but I would still feel totally exposed.

"I'm waiting," he says, arms still folded across his chest.

"It's not what you think." I know my words aren't going to calm my brother down, but I don't know what else to say.

"You said that already."

I pace around my room, trying to figure out what happened and how to explain it to my very large, overprotective brother.

I poke Craig in the chest. "This is all your fault." This is the best deflection ever in the history of passing the buck. Here's hoping he buys it.

"How so?"

"If you weren't off camping with that disgusting friend Rocky, I wouldn't have gotten scared, and then Samuel wouldn't have hung out with me, and he wouldn't have tried to get me to relax, and then I wouldn't have eaten your edibles."

"Come again?"

I stare at the floor. "Uh, I didn't think this through, but they did the trick."

"Apparently." Craig towers over me and yells, "Did King force himself on you?"

My brother's head snaps backward when I slap him across the face. My blood boils from his words. "What a horrible thing to say."

The silence is deafening compared to the loud argument we just had. I sit on my bed as he rubs his cheek. Samuel stands frozen where he's flattened against the wall, and I don't blame him for staying still. After I've had enough time to talk myself out of stringing my brother up by his nut sack, I say, "All he was going to do was check the house to make sure it was safe and then leave. But I was terrified."

Craig scrubs his face as realization sets in. "The attack. I forgot. Sis, my phone croaked, then Rocky's car battery died, and he didn't have any jumper cables. We couldn't get a tow until this morning."

"Craig, you know how much I can't stand the sound of your roommate's name. Anyway, Mule planned to stay in your room, so I don't know what the big deal is."

"It seems like he ended up here... in my underwear. I never want them back, just so you know."

I step up to Craig and touch my handprint on his cheek. He flinches at my contact. "I couldn't sleep because I was way too keyed up. Samuel suggested lots of things to get me to relax, but the only thing that we found was your little bag of gummies... in *your* room. So, again, this is all your fault."

Craig cocks his head to the side. "He found my stash?"

"Yep."

"Why didn't he use his own?"

"Maybe he doesn't do that stuff anymore. It stunts your growth and makes you impotent. I'm just saying."

My brother growls at me. "I don't care about his fertility issues."

This conversation has gone on long enough, and I'm tired of explaining

Samuel's innocence to my overbearing brother. I point to the door. "Get out of my room."

Craig stomps toward the door. "King has some explaining to do anyway." He stares at Samuel until Samuel follows Craig out of my room.

With a sneer, I wiggle my fingers under my nose. "Don't make me use these pincers again."

They leave, and I'm left thinking about everything that happened. I cannot believe I spent the entire night with Samuel. The memories I do have seem innocent, aside from the gummies, but Craig catching us really ups the awkwardness.

Mule didn't try anything. Maybe he's not the bad boy everyone claims he is, or maybe he's trying to be a gentleman, which is super sweet. Or maybe he's not into me at all. Regardless of the reason, I liked how his hand felt on my skin. It was warm and protective. I have the vaguest memory of using his chest as a pillow, so no matter what, I had the best sleep of my life.

Craig shouldn't be so mad at Samuel. We didn't do anything he wouldn't do. Craig really does need to get laid, or maybe stoned, or both.

Chapter Thirty-Seven

Samuel

Craig tosses me across his room like a football and slams the door behind him then locks it. This is as bad as it gets. I've seen his anger flare before, and it's not a pretty sight. Looking like he's about to rip my arms off, Craig asks, "What do you think you're doing?"

In slow motion, I snatch my shirt off his floor and throw it on over my head. "Man, I told you the truth. Nothing happened."

He paces like a caged animal. "You were practically naked in her room."

"I promise, I slept on the floor the entire night." I back up to avoid his approaching stalk.

"And that's supposed to make me feel better? How many times do I have to tell you not to touch my sister?"

I stuff my clothes into my backpack and find my phone on the floor, all the while keeping one eye on Sam's deranged big brother. "Why is it so important to you that I not get involved with your sister?"

"You know why. You don't deserve her."

"I'll never deserve her."

"Good. We're on the same page, so leave her alone."

I shake my head and fling the hair out of my eyes. I've got nothing to lose at this point. He caught me asleep in his sister's room, practically naked, so it can't get much worse. "I don't know if I want to do that anymore."

He picks up his baseball bat next to his bed and taps it against the palm of his free hand, like he's trying to decide if he's going to take a few practice swings with my head as a ball. "You better watch what you say."

"She doesn't always need you towering over her. She's sweet but doesn't take crap off people, including me."

Banging on the bedroom door startles us both. "Craig, open this door. Now!" Samantha yells.

With an evil grin, he replies, "I'm having a little chat with your sleepover buddy."

When Craig cocks his head to the side and puts on a "you better go along with me" expression, I add, "It's all good, Sam-Man."

"Are you sure, Mule?"

No. "Yeah."

"If he hurts you…"

"I'm fine."

"Craig, if you lay one finger on him, I will tell Mom and Dad everything."

From his frozen stance, I'm certain he knows Sam has him right in the palm of her hand and will make good on her threat, if necessary.

Not taking his steely eyes off me, he replies, "I promise, sis. No harm will come to him."

As soon as we hear Samantha's bedroom door clicking shut, he runs a hand through his hair. "I know how you toss girls out when you're done with them, and you're not going to hurt Samantha that way. I won't let that happen. You promised to leave her alone, and you better not break that promise. I'm going to give your little sleepover a pass because of the break-ins, but if I hear of you messing with her again, I will beat you to a pulp."

I march up to him and point my finger in his face. "She's not ten anymore and in need of your protection. She's smart and can hold her own."

Craig blinks at me, like he's processing everything I said. I've never stood up to him, and I bet no one has, so this must be a new feeling for him.

I sink back onto his bed and put on my socks and shoes. "Craig, we've been friends for a long time, and I would never do anything ever to hurt your sister. She's funny, beautiful, and a whole lot smarter than she even realizes, and..." I stop short of telling him I feel things for her I have never felt before.

He kicks my backpack and curses under his breath. "She's a good kid. I want her to have her chance at college. Maybe find a nice guy there."

I roll my eyes. "A nice guy like Rocky? Yeah, that's exactly what I'd want for her too."

"Don't start with him again. I *know* what happened." He crosses his massive arms over his chest. "Get out of my house."

I pick up my backpack to leave. Now isn't the time to continue this fight. I have to show him I'm serious, that I'm not using her as a placeholder until someone better comes around.

My patronizing bow doesn't do anything to improve my situation. "Riiight," I say, sarcasm dripping from that one word. "You think you know everything, don't you? There is at least one thing you *don't* know. Keep believing Rocky's lies. Ask your sister if you don't believe me. In fact..." I retrieve my phone from the floor and forward him the video Samantha sent me before I can talk myself out of it. I didn't want to be the one to prove it to him, but he leaves me no choice. "Check your messages."

While I still have the courage, I add, "Look, maybe you are right. Samantha deserves more than I can offer."

"You finally came to your senses. I guess you aren't as stupid as you seem."

I flip him off because it's what I do.

"Screw you, Samuel."

I pucker my lips at him. "You're not my type." I rush out of the room before he has a chance to take back his promise not to hurt me.

Chapter Thirty-Eight

Samantha

The house suddenly becomes quiet right before the tires on Samuel's truck squeal as he pulls out of the driveway. I didn't think he and Craig would ever stop arguing. While I'm glad my brother is protective, he tends to go overboard. At this rate, I'll never have a boyfriend.

Craig's lying on his back, staring at the ceiling, when I knock on his open door. "Come in, my little juvenile delinquent."

"Ugh. Stop it." I sit next to him on his bed. "I cannot believe you were going to beat the stew out of him. What got into you?"

"And I cannot believe you ate my gummies."

"Will you please move past that? He was trying to help because I was on the verge of a panic attack. Craig, I promise, he was a perfect gentleman. And that's no excuse for violence. What's your problem?"

He snorts. "I'm sorry, but Mule being a perfect gentleman is a little hard to believe."

I pick up the Nerf ball and toss it into the hoop over his door. "He's never been anything but nice to me. Ever since he started tutoring me—"

"What did you say?" His face loses all expression.

"You heard me correctly."

Craig grits his teeth. "Son of a..."

"He's my best shot, so get over it. That's right. I bet you didn't know he was smart. Like annoyingly, genius kind of smart. Anyway, I've seen a side of him that he keeps hidden from most people, and I like it."

Craig rises from the bed and picks up the Nerf ball, sending it sailing into the net. "Sam, you don't know what you're dealing with."

His lack of confidence in me hurts more than any punch to the gut. "I'm not stupid, you know."

He freezes and stares at me. "I never said that."

My reflexes are quicker than his, so I steal the ball from him. "You didn't have to. You make me feel like I'm too dumb to make smart decisions."

Regret crosses his face. "I never meant it that way. I don't want you to get hurt." He shakes his head.

While I shrug, I say, "It may be Samuel or some other guy who hurts me, but there's a good chance I'll get hurt at some point. Caring for someone is worth it."

He brushes the hair from my face. "Oh, Sammie. I know, but you're supposed to still be seven, and I'm the big brother who doesn't let anything bad happen to you."

"So that's why Freddie Templeton went radio silent on me in middle school."

He cringes. "Guilty."

"Ugh. You are horrible." With outstretched arms, I say, "And you saw me wearing very little this morning, so it's safe to say, I'm not seven anymore."

He covers his eyes. "Don't remind me." He peeks through his fingers. "You promise nothing happened?"

I shake my head. "Like I said. A perfect gentleman."

"Hmm."

While he's not paying attention, I bonk him in the face with the Nerf ball. "You need to stay out of my business. I'm serious. I'm able to think for myself about guys, no matter who they are. Got it? Back off."

I wiggle my fingers under his nose to remind him of what they can do.

"Stay away from King. He's trouble."

Before I lose my nerve, I need to spit this out. "I like Samuel. Deal with it."

Whew. I don't breathe while waiting on his response. Craig's deer-in-the-headlights expression says it all. His brain hasn't caught up to my revelation. "What did you say?"

"You heard me. I like him. A lot." I tap my toe as I wait on his reply. "And if you don't back off, I'll tell Mom I found—"

"Truce, for now. You've made your point."

Samantha rule number six—"If it's important, stand up for yourself."

Chapter Thirty-Nine

Samuel

Sitting in my driveway, I take a deep breath, realizing how close I came to getting the crap beat out of me. So far, Craig has only issued threats, but that angry fire in his eyes was on a totally different level. I'm pretty sure if Sam hadn't intervened, I would be in the emergency room right now.

I spent the entire night with her and didn't even try anything. Thinking back to her stoned antics brings the biggest grin out of me.

My phone buzzes with an incoming text.

Sam-Man: *Are you okay?*

Me: *Yes, thanks to you.*

Sam-Man: *Sorry about the Spanish Inquisition.*

Me: *He doesn't scare me. Fine, maybe he does a little.*

Sam-Man: *I've never seen him get so angry.*

I have. Many times. He must hide it from his family well.

Me: *He's only protecting you.*

Sam-Man: *Eye roll.* You *were protecting me last night. Thx.*

Me: *Anytime.* You *protected me this morning, so I guess we are even. BTW, I enjoyed... *weed emoji**

Sam-Man: *I'm never going to live that down, am I?*

Me: *Our little secret.*

Sam-Man: *They keep piling up. Got any more you want to share... sec-c?*

I've turned her into a geek.

Sam-Man: *Not at the moment. Gotta go. CU later.*

Me: *Don't forget to wear a shirt... or not.*

She sends me a text message with a smiley face shooting me the bird.

I bounce out of my truck and go inside. As soon as I round the corner into the living room, I stop in my tracks because I realize I'm the worst son on the planet. I didn't call, or text, or even send a smoke signal to let my parents know I wouldn't be home last night. Even a lie making them think I was at Brody's would have been better than keeping them in the dark. Mom and Dad sit on the love seat. The real Spanish Inquisition is about to start, and I deserve it this time.

Dad throws his hands in the air. "Where have you been? You had us scared sick."

Mom gets up and hovers over me. "We were so worried when you didn't come home and you didn't answer your messages. And…"

"I'm all right, Mom. I'm sorry. I meant to call, but I crashed at Brody's house. I guess I was more tired than I thought."

She collapses on the couch next to me as tears fall down her cheeks. Here's yet another example where I have caused my mother to worry. If I could, I'd beat *myself* up.

Dad hangs his head low and sighs. "I called Brody's house, and you weren't there, so I'm going to ask one more time. Where were you?"

I cut my gaze toward my mom, and she silently pleads with me to tell the truth. If I want my parents to start believing me, I need to start being honest with them. "I was at Samantha's house last night."

Mom blinks a few times then says, "You were with Samantha? Like *with* her?"

"No, not like that. We didn't *do* anything."

I continue to tell them everything, except the edibles part. I leave that out because I'm in enough trouble as it is, and the edibles have nothing to do with why I was there.

Dad scrubs his face with his hands. "Craig threatened to beat you up?"

"Yeah, but he thought he was protecting his sister. We're all good now. At least I think we are."

Mom coughs once, twice, then gets up and grabs a tissue. "Sorry."

My dad's gaze ping-pongs between Mom and me. "Honey, why don't you get some rest? Samuel's home and all in one piece."

She wipes her eyes and nods. "I love you, Sammy."

I soak it in every time she says those words, not knowing when it will be my last chance to hear them. "I love you, too, Mom."

When she leaves, I turn to Dad. "What's going on?"

"She's worn out from worry. Now back to you. How are you?"

With a cocky grin, I say, "I'm fine. He didn't lay a finger on me, thank goodness."

"I mean emotionally. Craig's browbeating couldn't have been easy, especially in front of the girl you like."

I pick at a hangnail. "I didn't say I like her."

"You don't have to." He pats my back. "You look like you didn't get much sleep last night. Take a nap. We'll talk later. I'm glad you're safe."

"Thanks. Me too."

I hate making my parents worry, but it feels amazing to finally be honest with them. As I collapse on my bed, I realize how pooped I am. Thinking about how close I came to losing all my teeth, I do a full-body shiver. Craig's a jerk, but I would stay with Samantha all over again if it meant keeping her safe.

Chapter Forty

Samuel

My growling stomach wakes me from my snooze. When I pass my parents' room, I hear them speaking in hushed tones. Their door is cracked open, enough for me to see my mother lying in bed with a thermometer in her mouth. Dad listens to her lungs with his stethoscope.

Without knocking, I burst into their room. "Mom?"

Dad raises a finger for me to hold that thought until he's finished. Thirty seconds seems like an eternity. He takes a deep breath. The thermometer beeps, and he retrieves it from her mouth. His brow furrows when he checks the reading, and it's as if he's aged ten years overnight.

"He's only being cautious," she tells me with a weak smile, but I know by her sweaty, pale complexion, there's more to the story.

"Ninety-nine point five."

"See? Nothing to worry about." She shivers.

I perch on the side of her bed and slide the comforter around her.

"Thanks, sweetie."

"Dad?"

He sighs. "It's a low-grade fever, but her right lower lobe sounds aren't clear. I'm going to call in an antibiotic to be on the safe side."

She shakes her head. "I'm fine. I just overdid it yesterday."

His lips form a thin line. "Humor me this time."

She rolls her eyes. "Yes, Doctor."

While Dad calls in the prescription, I take in my mother's brave face. She's the strongest person I know. Others would have given up the fight long ago, yet she somehow finds the strength to weather every battle thrown at her. I don't know what I'd do without her, and I hope I don't have to find out anytime soon.

The front door slams, and footsteps barrel up the stairs. Aunt Jamie rushes in like a tornado.

Mom sneers at her twin sister. "What are you doing here?"

Aunt Jamie plants her hands on her hips. "Making sure you don't cash in your chips before you get a chance to return my favorite sweater."

Mom laughs, but Dad walks away and faces the dresser. He fidgets with his wallet then pinches the bridge of his nose.

Aunt Jamie says to Dad, "Danny's wrapping up his last surgery case but said not to hesitate to text him if you need a second opinion."

My Uncle Danny has been as helpful to Dad as he's been to Mom. It's nice to have a doctor in the family who can evaluate Mom's condition as a more impartial third party when Dad can sometimes overreact to every little blip, not that I blame him. I can't stand the thought of my mother being sick, and I certainly don't want to imagine life without her.

"That won't be necessary. Right, Adam?" Mom asks, breaking the fog that he's in.

He clears his throat then hands me his credit card. "Samuel, will you pick up your mom's prescription?"

"Of course."

His glassy eyes indicate he's only seconds away from losing it. If he breaks, I know I will. He nods as he walks out of the room. "I need some air."

I did this to Mom. The stress of not knowing where I was all night has sent her health spiraling out of control. The tension in the room is so thick, I can't move.

My phone buzzes in my pocket, and a text from Mason shows up on the display.

Mason: *I'm in your truck.*

Mom and Aunt Jamie are in their own little twin world, finishing each other's sentences and joking about how awful Mom looks, so they don't even notice when I leave the house. On the porch, I pass Dad, who's holding his face in his hands as his entire body shakes. Not knowing how to console him, I pat him on the back before I descend the steps to the driveway.

Mason's face scrunches like he ate prunes. "You're a mess."

"Long story."

He and I ride in silence to the pharmacy. Mason has been around for every cycle of chemotherapy, every emergency room visit, and every infection scare. At times like this, we don't have to talk to communicate. He doesn't feed me the "everything is going to be fine" lies like everyone else does, and I appreciate it. It's times like this he's the brother I never had. And I really need a brother right now. Losing my mother would ruin me.

"Do you want me to go in and get her meds?"

"Yeah, thanks." I hand him Dad's credit card and watch as he enters the store. The silence in my truck kills my ears, so I text Samantha.

Me: *Mom's sick... again.*

Sam-Man: *Oh no. :(What can I do?*

Me: *You are already doing what I need. This is all my fault.*

Sam-Man: *No, it isn't. I'm here if you need me. I can ask Craig to get us more gummies.*

Me: *That would not be a good idea right now, but I appreciate the thought.*

I close my eyes and fight a sudden craving to have her with me. Samantha would wrap her arms around my neck, and even though she wouldn't say a word, she would make me feel better. She's always had a piece of my heart, but she's taken it hostage now, and I am completely fine with that. I get another text.

Sam-Man: *If you want another distraction, I'm here for you.*

My grin is so big it hurts my mouth. Before I reply, she adds: *We'll talk about triangles and sec. :)*

I can't help but grin. She is adorable.

Mason pops in the truck, holding the pharmacy bag. "Are you okay?"

I nod. "I am now."

He smiles as he retrieves two supersize candy bars. "I figured as long as I had Uncle Adam's credit card, I'd treat us to a snack."

"You read my mind."

It's times like this that family and special friends are all a guy needs in this world. A giant-sized candy bar doesn't hurt anything either.

Chapter Forty-One

Samantha

I think I would be more comfortable at a cotillion than at my tutoring session today. It's the first one since our little sleepover, and it's awkward at best. My face has to be covered in red splotches. My gaze stays fixed on the paper in front of me. The memory of Samuel's strong hands on my boobs, my butt, and my skin takes me back to the dance and our slumber party.

"What's up?" he asks.

"I'm fine." I squeak out, my voice way higher than usual. "I can't focus today. A lot on my mind."

His face falls. "You and me both."

"How's your mom?"

He scrubs his face with his hands and lets out a deep sigh. "I think Dad caught the infection in time. We'll know in a few days when the antibiotics kick in."

"That's good. I'm glad."

He stares at the desk and clears his throat. "I appreciated your text distractions earlier."

I yawn, and I'm sure I'm a total dork. "Anything for a... friend."

With a quick swivel, he turns my chair toward him and positions his legs between mine. His hands rest on my thighs. "We need to talk about what happened."

This is not a conversation I want to have. I shake my head. Was I wrong about what I told Craig? "Did we, uh... you know?"

The cutest grin pops out, and I'm kind of hoping he's going to say we did. "No, I would never take advantage of you. But you were so funny."

I scoot my chair away from him and sneer. "Craig was in a mood all weekend because of what happened."

Samuel points to my homework sheet, and I have no choice but to start working on the third problem. "He'll get over it. We didn't do anything."

"Except for the whole edibles thing. And the boob exposure and you grabbing my butt. Nope. We didn't do anything. At. All."

His chuckle makes my heart go all thumpity thump.

"Good thing, huh?" I scribble some numbers on my paper. "You don't need me to mess up your life, do you?"

Samuel scrunches his brow. "What do you mean?"

To keep my hands from shaking, I doodle on the piece of notebook paper in front of me. And I hope to goodness the green-eyed monster doesn't peek through my words. I want to tell him how I feel, but I can't form the words.

"If word gets out you slept with me—even though it was only *sleeping* and on the floor, at that—everyone will think you're off the market. The girls will stage a protest. The cheerleaders will slash my tires. Either that, or one of them will burn me at the stake."

Mule sits back in his chair. "They can think whatever they want."

I tug on the collar of his Green Day T-shirt to peek at his neck.

As he wriggles away from me, he asks, "What are you doing?"

"I think an alien has hijacked your body, making you say things you wouldn't normally say."

"Will you stop?"

"Whatever. You shouldn't let me stand in the way of your reputation." I smirk, signaling I'm only partially kidding.

He lets out a sexy chuckle and pinches my cheek. I try to back away, but he grabs me around the waist and gathers me close. Since I'm not sure where to put my hands, my arms hang by my sides.

He leans in close to my ear, and my heart pounds—again. He better speak loudly, or I'll never hear him over the sound of my heartbeat thudding in my ears. "Maybe I have a thing for chicken nipples."

I gasp and push him away. "I can't believe you brought that up. And I asked you what you thought my bra size was." I cover my face, humiliated. "I am never eating those things again."

"Good policy, but I like the laid-back Samantha. You should lighten up more. You are so adorable when you're silly."

Mule called me adorable. I don't know how to reply to that.

He clears his throat. "I mean... Never mind."

To keep myself from wrapping my arms around his neck, I force my gaze from his and focus on the paper, but I couldn't concentrate on trig if my life depended on it—and it does.

To tease the daylights out of him, I say, "The quest to find the mystery man is progressing nicely."

I think I struck a nerve because even though he recovers quickly, I caught him flinching. My words must hurt more than Craig's fist ever could. "Is that so?"

"We've narrowed it down to four guys, and Rachel is in the middle of planning this really adorable kissing booth for phase three of the mission."

As though a lightbulb is going off in his mind, he snaps his fingers. "That's what those texts were about. I saw a bunch from her, but she's always trying to rope me into doing stuff, so I usually delete them without reading."

"Do you think it will work?"

Mule rolls his eyes. "You know it's ridiculous."

"Harrumph. Jealous much?" He's been so noncommittal that I need to force my hand to get him to admit anything.

"Yeah, right." He points to the paper again.

I point to my lips. "Right now, you are thinking about all those guys who will be experiencing these, and you won't be one of them."

His eyes bore into mine.

I hit a nerve.

"Maybe I *will* help Rachel with the booth after all, and I also might be the first in line. What do you think of that?" His eyebrows dance.

"Ha. We both know you'd never kiss me in front of other people because you are way too embarrassed. But I will let Rachel know you're willing to help out with the cause."

I'm not sure if I've ever seen his face get that bloodred before. His jaw muscles flex.

To add insult to injury, I add, "Don't forget to tell Mason about it. He's one of four left on the list."

He sputters. "Excuse me?"

"Oh yeah. He's got great hands, so he passed that test. He's been known to have minty breath on occasion, so he's in the maybe category. The big test is the kiss." I pucker up. "I never thought he had it in him, but you know those intellectual types. They surprise you sometimes." I wink, and if I don't lay off, he's going to blow a gasket. I pat him on the chest. "Relax. I'm only giving you a hard time, but Mason *is* on the list."

He shakes his head. "He is not your guy."

"He could be."

Samuel chuckles then freezes. "There's no way."

"How are you so sure?" I never thought I could pull off a singsongy voice, but it seems appropriate right now.

He snaps his head around to stare at me. "Are you telling me you're into him?"

I shrug and stuff my Trig notebook back into my bag. It's clear we won't be getting any more work done today now that Mr. Mark His Territory has gotten his dander up. "I never thought about it before now, but it could work."

"No."

With that, I cock my head to the side. "Excuse me?"

"No, it wouldn't work."

"Why? Because the more we talk about it, the more I like the idea."

His chair screeches when he stands, then it crashes to the floor behind him. "Let's call it a day."

I wave my hand in the air like I'm flicking a fly away from my face. "Sure thing, tutor. See you next time."

He growls as he marches toward the exit of the arts center. *Ha!* Now I see why he likes to make people squirm. It's so much fun. To see him get so jealous of Mason is hilarious. He opens the door for me to leave, and all the way to my car, Samuel's big bad wolf breath tickles my neck.

"Should I call Mason, or will you do it for me?" When I turn around, I bump into him. "Never mind. I'll tell him myself. You don't need to get involved."

With a clenched jaw, he takes a step backward and grinds out, "You do that."

He returns my girly wave and slams his truck door closed. When I put my car in reverse, I swear I see him pummeling his steering wheel. I love being in the driver's seat of this... friendship.

Mission accomplished. If he doesn't figure out his feelings for me soon, he's going to lose his chance.

Chapter Forty-Two

Samuel

The last person I want to see when I pull into my driveway is Mason. He is sitting on the hood of his Jetta, messing with his phone. He's probably playing some geeky math game or Tetris. His T-shirt reads "It's all fun and games until somebody divides by zero."

He smiles. "Hey, loser cousin."

"Hey, moron cousin."

Mason slides off his car's hood and raises a fist for me to bump. I walk past without returning the gesture then slam through the front door, passing by Aunt Jamie and Mom, who wears a surgical mask.

I hear my mother ask Mason, "What's got him in a tizzy?"

He mumbles some kind of answer, then I hear his footsteps behind me. I do not want to see him today. When I try to close my bedroom door, he stops it with his size-eleven shoe. "What do you want?"

"To hang, that's all."

He follows me into my room, and we proceed to play video games in silence. He beats the crap out of me in the first round of *The Legend of Zelda*. His choice, not mine.

Breaking the silence, he asks, "What's up with you?"

"Samantha."

"Ah. We're back to that. Will you kiss her again and get her out of your system?"

"It's not that easy." I toss the game controller onto the bed and groan. "Rachel's planning a kissing booth to figure out who the mystery guy is."

"Oh yeah. I heard something about that. And since you're in denial, who are they focusing on?"

When I don't answer, he lets out a slow whistle. "Me. Because I'm a suspect."

I can't believe I'm saying this, but he'll know if I'm lying anyway. "It appears that way."

"Woo-hoo." He prances around the room like a peacock. "It's music to my ears to hear you admit that."

"You didn't do anything with her. We both know that."

He whistles, and I know he caught my slip. He puts his hands up in surrender and gives off a low chuckle. "But *they* don't know that." He gets a big grin on his face.

"Shut up and play."

He rolls over on his back and kicks his legs in the air like an overturned bug. "Woo-hoo. I get to snog Samantha."

"Or Rachel."

"Even better."

I shoot him a warning stare.

"It's a win-win. I'll get a smooch either way, something you won't be getting. Ooo, this is going to be fun." He rolls over to sit up and rubs his palms together like he's already plotting his next move.

I throw a pillow at my nerdy cousin. "Shut up. We both know it wasn't you, so you'll embarrass yourself when they throw up after you get them in a lip-lock."

The hamster wheel in my cousin's brain is turning, and I don't want to know what he's thinking.

With an evil grin, Mace says, "Hmm, let's see. If you're so sure Samantha won't say it was me, do you dare make a wager?"

He lobs the pillow back at me, missing me by a mile. "Here's how I see it. If Samantha kisses me and says it was me, you'll kick my butt, but it will be worth every black-and-blue mark."

"That's—"

His outstretched arm stops my reply. "Let me finish. Or she'll kiss me and confess it wasn't me in the closet, and I'll take my lumps. If she's truthful, you get to make me do something embarrassing. But if she says it was me... you will have to wear one of my geeky T-shirts to school and post your grades all over the Internet."

"No problem. And you get to streak across the gym during a basketball game if she doesn't think it's you."

He swallows. "Streak, as in..."

"Yep, nothing but your birthday suit, your butt cheeks flapping in the wind." I wink. "How confident are you, cuz?"

"How confident are *you*?"

"Oh, I'm positive it wasn't you in the closet."

"What are you going to do about it?"

I pick at a fingernail as I try to formulate my response. "I don't have to do anything."

Mason snorts. "Yeah, keep telling yourself that. So, what's it like to kiss Samantha? No, wait. I'll find out for myself soon." He has the nerve to add an evil cackle.

"You're such a loser."

"You're going to be the one who loses if you don't watch it."

I drop my game controller as I process his words. "I'm not following you."

With an exasperated groan, Mason says, "Sometimes you are so smart but stupid at the same time. It doesn't take a genius to see how you feel about her. What's so hard about this?"

It drives me crazy when he's right, but of course, I'd never tell him that. She's too good for me. As much as I would love to be more than her friend, it's best that I don't make a move. I would only ruin her life. "You know what? I'm going to take your bet, and let's see who comes out smelling like a rose."

He licks his lips over and over then puckers up.

"Dude, what are you doing?"

"Getting ready for the big day. This will be the most action I've ever gotten."

"Shocker."

He laughs. "Which shirt do you want to wear? The one that says 'Never trust atoms, they make up everything,' or 'You underestimate the power of the dork side'?"

"None of those."

I'm walking a fine line between getting my butt kicked by Craig and losing the girl. I need to grow some balls soon, or it's going to be too late.

Mason cups his hand to his ear. "I think I heard your dad come home."

"Great. Thanks for the warning."

He peeks out my bedroom door and mumbles, "He's coming this way. It was nice knowing you." He takes off. "Hey, Uncle Adam."

"Hey, Mace."

Three seconds later, Dad stands in my doorway, his scrub shirt halfway tucked, still wearing a surgical cap on his head and booties on his feet.

"Tough day?" I point to his head.

He reaches up to snatch the cap off. He groans and collapses into my desk chair. "The worst." His eyes close, and for a second, I think he's fallen asleep. "Can I give you some career advice?"

Not today. "Go ahead. You're going to do it anyway."

He snorts before a yawn escapes his mouth. "Don't be a surgeon."

I burst out a laugh, making him grin.

"I'm serious. I work at least twelve hours every single day. I order people around like an ogre. I've got insurance companies and people in suits yelling at me constantly about how I am supposed to document my cases, or they tell me I used the wrong ICD-10 code. It's not what I thought it would be." A sad smile crosses his face, like he has lots of regrets. "Plus, I'm missing out on all this family stuff."

I cock an eyebrow. "Seriously?"

Dad stretches out his long legs, kicking off the booties onto the floor. "Yeah. How's your mother today? She tells me she's fine, but I'm pretty sure she's telling me what I want to hear."

"It's hard to tell, but she's cooking, and the smells don't seem to bother her. She's wearing the mask, so I think she's taking it seriously this time."

We are quiet for a while, and it seems like he's got a million memories running through his brain. "She's so tough."

"Too tough sometimes."

"Yeah." He stares off then continues, "I know I ride you hard about school. Just find something that uses your talents but also something you'll enjoy doing for the next forty-plus years."

I relax back in my chair and fake a shocked expression. "What have you done with my father?"

He chuckles, and his eyes get a little misty. "I do miss you and your mother so much. More than you'll ever know. When she's sick and I can't be by her side every minute of the day..."

This is more than he's said to me in years that wasn't about grades or my out-of-control behavior.

"Well, if you repeat this, I'll deny it, but... we miss you too."

He snorts a laugh. "What have you done with my son?"

Tossing him a game controller, I ask, "Got time for me to whip your butt?"

"Bring it, smarty-pants."

Dad chooses the game, and I even let him beat me the first few rounds before I ramp it up and wallop the daylights out of him. After he's had time to relax from his exhausting day, I get the courage to bring up school.

"Dad, I have an idea about a major for college."

"Yeah? What is it?" His eyes never leave the television.

"You won't like it."

"I'm trying to be open-minded. Hit me."

Here goes nothing. If he shoots holes in this idea, we're back to square one. "I know I'm good at math."

"Brilliant is a better word."

Typical. "But I love art."

He rests the controller in his lap. "Go on."

"I've been doing some research, and I, uh... What if I found a way to combine the two?"

"I'm listening."

After I blow out a breath, I run a hand through my hair and figure it's now or never. "Architecture."

He smiles, and his eyes twinkle, so I know it's a genuine response. "Sounds right up your alley."

Shock runs through me so much I drop my controller. I think he gave me the green light to pursue this. "Well. I, uh... I'll check into it and see what schools offer that program."

He yawns and stretches as he stands. "Keep me posted. Right now, I've got to get some food then hit the sack with my girl."

"Dad, that's so—"

He waves me off. "Now is not the time to keep feelings hidden from the people you care about."

What just happened? He is either mellowing out in his old age, or he's terrified about losing the one person who means the most to us both. Whatever it is, I'm going to take full advantage and move forward.

Chapter Forty-Three

Samantha

It's hysterical seeing Rachel with her reading glasses perched on her nose. She only uses them when she's in a serious mood. She chews on a pen cap as she paces around her room.

Samuel hasn't sent me a nerdy text in two days. I guess I really ticked him off talking about Mason. Serves him right. It's time to put Rachel's plan into action. When this is over, I need to focus on passing Trig, securing my scholarship, and running as fast as I can to Auburn and away from all this drama.

But that kiss...

"The guys have agreed to build the booth using repurposed lumber from last year's spring theatre production. A little paint, a few nails, and we have our booth." Rachel points to Paige. "Did you get approval from Principal Hughes?"

A huge grin consumes Paige's face. "He said if the money goes either to a local charity or to the student benevolent fund, he's fine by it. He rolled his eyes, and when I tried to explain, he shut me down. I guess it's one of those 'don't ask, don't tell' situations."

"Good." Rachel high-fives Paige.

"I'm starting to think this is a bad idea," I say as I rub my temples.

Rachel points her perfectly polished index finger at me. "Don't think that way. I've put a lot of time into this project."

I bury my head in a pillow. "This is so embarrassing. I can't kiss random guys in front of everyone. I'll never be able to pull this off."

Paige nods. "I have to agree with her there."

Rachel, in complete control again, throws back her shoulders and starts her pacing once more. "I told you I'll kiss them for you. No need for you to get grossed out."

"I really am so thankful it's been you helping me with this boy stuff. With anyone else, it would be so awkward, even more than it already is. But this is not me. I only want to be the center of attention on the basketball court. This is not in my comfort zone."

"At least it's not Samuel, so you won't be too grossed out."

I squeeze my eyelids shut. I can't believe I'm going to ask my friend this question, but I need to know. "Did you and he…"

"Yuck, no. Ew. No, no, no. We only went on a few dates before we figured out it wasn't working." She swats my arm. "What kind of person do you think I am?"

Guilt rushes over me at how I accused one of my best friends of something that is completely none of my business. "I'm sorry. That was mean and totally inappropriate, but I get the impression he's slept with half the class."

Paige snorts. "Oh please. I'm convinced all those girls started that smack about sleeping with him because they think it raises their social status."

"That's disgusting." Although the thought makes my stomach turn, it does make sense.

"I know, but I wouldn't be surprised if he hardly gets any. All talk. And it's not him doing the talking."

Maybe he isn't the stud I built him up to be in my mind. It makes sense because the Samuel on our jogs, or when we're studying, is not the hot mess of a guy he lets people think he is. No matter what his real deal is, I'm going to be kissing a few frogs soon, and none will turn into the prince I want. Maybe I need to have a hand in writing my own fairy-tale ending. As much as I appreciate Rachel and Paige, I need different reinforcements this time.

Time to beg Mason to help me out.

After several failed attempts, I finally muster up the courage to knock on Mason's front door as I contemplate my plan. Bad idea. Bad idea.

He answers the door, hair dripping wet, only wearing a towel around his neck and a pair of gym shorts. My jaw drops as I take in his muscles. Not bad. He's not as buff and ripped as Samuel, but his physique is way better than I assumed.

"Oh, I didn't expect you." He backs up, glancing around.

"Is this a bad time?"

He shakes his head but holds out a hand. "Let me get a shirt." He motions with his head for me to follow him.

As he takes the stairs two at a time, I follow him to his room, which is as messy as Craig's but without the stench. And instead of alternative rock band posters on the wall, Mason has Albert Einstein and *Star Wars* posters lining his walls. He rifles through a drawer then slips a T-shirt over his head. Now he's more like the Mason I know. The "Talk nerdy to me" shirt clenches the deal.

"So, what's up?"

I close the door behind us. "I need to talk to you about helping with the booth."

He shakes his head. "I don't know if I am able to. You've got Brody and Jared to do all the—"

"I'm not talking about building the booth. I'm talking about helping *me*."

"Help you do what, exactly?"

I shuffle from one leg to the other and do my best not to sound so girly. I'm not a girly girl, but that's exactly how this feels right now. "I need you to help me make Samuel jealous."

After a beat of silence, he blinks then says, "I'm sorry. I'm not following you."

"He kissed me in the closet then freaked out."

Mason's mouth turns into a big O as he collapses onto his bed. "Yeah, I kinda figured as much."

"He ran like a scared child afterward, and I need to make him confess."

We sit in silence for a moment as he focuses on the ceiling. Finally, he blows out a breath. "He's an idiot, that's for sure, but more than that, he's my cousin. Plus, he's my best friend."

I sink down on his bed beside him, and guilt washes over me for even asking him to do this. "I know it, and I feel terrible asking you to do this for me, but I have to make him admit whether he likes me or it was only a weak moment."

He covers his face with his forearm. "Samantha."

"Do it for me, please. You know he's changed. This may be the nudge he needs to prove it to everyone."

He moans.

"You already agreed to come to the kissing booth anyway. Don't forget three dates *and* the prom with Rachel." I waltz around the room with an imaginary partner.

He slams his fist onto the mattress. "You don't fight fair."

"I hate that you're in the middle of this, but there is one more thing. We must make it appear authentic."

"I'm not going to like this, am I?"

On the inside, I cringe. I shake my head. "We need to go overboard, and if he doesn't confess it was him who kissed me, we might need to keep up the fiction for a few days."

His mouth drops open, but he says nothing.

"Remember, three dates *and* the prom."

He clenches his teeth and kneads his gym shorts with his white-knuckled hands. "Anything else?"

"Yeah."

He whimpers and whispers, "Three dates, three dates, three dates."

"I think we need to practice."

His laughter rumbles out of him, earning him a smack to the arm.

"Not funny."

Abruptly, he sits up, slinging his long legs over the side of the bed. "All my life, I've watched Samuel go from bad to worse on the outside. In private, he's not that way."

"Exactly. It's time." I nudge his knee with mine. "I like him." I bet I have the goofiest grin on my face, but I don't care.

"No duh. And for the record"—he whispers in my ear—"I'm pretty sure he likes you too."

Bubbles form in my stomach because I'm hearing this from the person who knows Samuel better than anyone. I'm hardly able to sit still. "Are you sure, because I'm not smart and—"

"Stop." He lets out a groan. "Both of you have put yourselves inside these boxes, thinking you're only allowed to be one thing. You think you are only good at sports and you can't possibly be anything but a jock. That is not true at all. You're athletic and funny and beautiful... and smart."

I never realized I was pigeonholing myself, but I guess I am. And so is Samuel. We are more alike than I thought. "So, you'll help me?"

"Sure. I guess it'll be fun to get one over on him. That hasn't happened since... ever."

I sit up straight. "Are you ready?"

He shrugs, cracks his neck, then lets out a sigh. "Let's do this." He closes the gap to kiss me, but I block his advance.

"Whoa. Wait a second. I need to describe what happened so you'll be able to duplicate it."

"Yikes."

"To make this seem like you were the one from the closet, you have to do it exactly like he did that night."

He covers his face with his hands. "Three dates, three dates."

"And prom."

I explain in full detail what happened that night and how he needs to proceed. By the time I'm done, Mason is laughing his butt off.

He taps his chin. "Let's work this problem one step at a time. First, the kiss, then we'll master where all the appendages should go." He lunges forward and plants a peck on my lips then jerks away. "Well, what did you think?"

I shrug. "Nice lips. No zing, but I didn't expect one."

"Ouch."

"This time, slower, longer. Let it linger."

After he lets out a breath, he slides a hand around my neck to bring me closer. His soft lips meet mine, and when his tongue enters my mouth, there's a slight zing. He cups my face in his hands to deepen the kiss.

Right when I start to respond, he snaps back and holds up a finger. "Wait right there."

He scrounges around until he finds a scrap of paper and a pen in his desk. He scribbles something onto the page.

"What are you doing?"

"Shh."

I bite my tongue to keep from laughing, waiting on him to finish whatever he's doing. He slams the pen and rotates back toward me, taking my face in his hands again, going in for another kiss. No zing at all this time.

"Hmm. Which one was better?" He grabs the paper and scribbles something else on it. "I want to get this right. I mean, I'm helping you, but you're helping me too."

Before I protest, he goes in for another lip-lock, but this time it's all tongue and sloppy. I can't get away fast enough. "I think you should exclude three and four completely. They are too all over the place." I shake my head. "Can we focus on one problem at a time?"

He crumples the paper. "I was hoping I could get some pointers while we made Samuel squirm."

"For the record, the second one was awesome. Whatever you were feeling, use it. It was really... nice."

He sits up taller. "You didn't think it lacked the proper amount of tongue?"

"No, no. Not at all. Too much tongue is all lizardly."

"So I've got the kiss mastered. What else?"

Everything he does is with a scientific mentality. "Uh... It wasn't an ordinary kiss. It was..." I squeeze my eyes shut as my mind goes back to that night in the closet. It was so much more than a simple kiss. It was two people totally into the moment, letting go of inhibitions. That's something that can't easily be faked, at least not by me. "Anyway, I think if we fake that part, it will be enough. We won't need the rest."

Mason clucks his teeth. "Do tell."

I bite my lip, revisiting the make-out session. I run my hand down the side of my neck. "Little feathery kisses on my chin and neck and back up again."

"Good to know." I roll my eyes as he flattens the paper and scribbles again.

Does he really have to take notes?

Hopping off the bed with the eagerness I bet he has on the first day of school, he holds his hands out to me. "Come on. Let's do this." He cracks his neck from side to side, like he's ready for combat.

I take a deep breath. "On second thought, I should go. Do you think you'll be able to make it look good?"

As he walks me to his bedroom door with eyes trained on the floor, he nods. "I'll do my homework."

I do not want to know what that involves.

"See ya tomorrow." I open the door to leave, but he shuts it and turns me around.

His eyes bore into me. In a flash, he grabs me around the waist, and a squeak escapes my lips. He kisses my chin, works his way down my neck and back up, then presses his lips to mine.

It's an amazing kiss, but I push his face away from mine. "You are a fast learner."

"Pfft. I'm an overachiever." He winks, and that genetic link to Samuel shines through.

I nudge him in the ribs. "I've created a make-out monster."

When he opens the front door, I point across the street to Rachel's house. "She has no idea what she's missing."

Mason blushes as he backs up, tripping over the throw rug. He waves as I skip to my car.

Homework has never been that fun.

Chapter Forty-Four

Samuel

I'm still not sure how I got roped into building a kissing booth so Samantha can find her mystery guy. That's the stupidest idea ever, especially since she already knows he's me.

"Argggh." If I hit my thumb with this frickin' hammer one more time, I'm going to throw it through the window.

Brody and Jason chuckle. "Stop bellyaching, bruiser," Brody says.

Rachel struts by us, acting like she's the foreman of the project. All that's missing is a hard hat. "It's for a good cause."

I growl. "That's up for debate."

She flicks me on the top of my head.

I rear back with the hammer. "Don't mess with me."

"What is your problem?"

That's a loaded question. First off, there are about a dozen things I'd rather be doing. Then, being bossed around by her is getting on my last nerve. On top of everything, I'm building a device to let my girl get slobbered all over, and that thought makes me angry.

"Can I help?" Mason asks, sauntering up wearing his "Pi never tasted so good" T-shirt.

"Nope." I slam the next nail into the wood with one swing of my hammer.

Paige tsks. "Why not? The more the merrier, right?"

Sometimes her perky attitude makes me want to scream. I glance over at Brody, and he bites his lip to keep from laughing.

"Take my place," I say, handing Mason the hammer. I stand up and stretch out my back. "I'm out of here."

I march past Samantha, who is carrying a basket full of snacks. She glances away when I pass her. I smell her fruity scent from across the room, and it's driving me crazy. I can't handle building this stupid booth with her in the room too.

Walking through the parking lot toward my truck, I retrieve my keys. As soon as I click the fob to unlock the driver's side door, I hear footsteps behind me. Not now.

"Samuel, stop right there."

I groan and peek around to see Rachel running toward me in heels. "I'm tired of taking orders from you. Go away."

I open the door, and she slams it closed.

"What's your problem?"

She crosses her arms. "What's *your* problem?"

My breath comes quickly. "This idea is stupid."

She gathers her long blond hair into a ponytail with the hair tie she has on her wrist. "Maybe, but it's not about you, is it?"

I stare at her silently, and her steel-gray eyes get huge.

"It *is* about you, isn't it?" She sneers at me, waiting on my reply.

"Out of my way. I have things to do."

Rachel grabs my keys out of my hands.

"Give them back."

"No." She walks away. "Get in my car. We need to talk." She turns around to face me and puts her hands on her hips. "Now."

Bossy lady, I think, but I follow her to that awesome convertible BMW and open the passenger door. "The least you could do is let me drive. This is a sweet ride."

She holds out her hand, her car keys dangling from her index finger. "Don't speed."

As we get settled in her car, she points to the right. "Go this way."

"Yes, ma'am. There's a reason we didn't keep dating."

"Because I have class."

Rachel stares out the side window, and after all this bossiness, she doesn't have much to say.

"Where are we going?" I ask.

"We're going to ride around until you get that stick out of your butt."

Glancing down at the gas gauge, I reply, "Good thing you've got a full tank."

"You like her, don't you?"

"Who?"

"Samantha," Rachel says with a laugh.

I shake my head, making her roll her eyes. "You know me. I don't like anybody except myself."

She switches the radio station to one playing an alternative rock song and bobs her head to the music. "I love this song. You may not know you like her, but you do. It's in your eyes." My pain-in-the-butt friend pokes at my face.

If I had a bratty sister, I'm sure she'd be exactly like Rachel.

"What is so wrong with liking Samantha?" Leave it to Rachel to cut right to the chase.

"Nothing. She's sweet, pretty, and adorable..." I cringe, forgetting what I'm doing. When I get the courage, I side-eye her. She smiles. "Why are you looking at me like that?"

Rachel shrugs. "And you can't stand the thought of someone else kissing her. Am I right?"

My knuckles are white from clenching the steering wheel. "I didn't say that."

"You didn't have to."

I drive into the parking lot of the mall and kill the engine then collapse my head on the steering wheel. After I take a long, drawn-out breath, I say, "I like her. A lot."

"I kind of figured that out a long time ago." Rachel does an obnoxious golf clap and adds, "I'm glad you finally decided to be honest with yourself because you deserve someone as great as Samantha."

My mouth drops open. "I don't know what you mean."

"Pfft. I know you're not this cocky player everyone says you are. You want Samantha. So what's the problem?"

"I don't know. I... uh. I've never felt this way before. And when we..."

She sucks in a huge lungful of air. "Oh my word. It *was* you!"

Son of a... "Of course not."

"Liar. You made out with her. Then you panicked and pretended it wasn't you. Why did you do that?"

I rest my head back on the headrest. "It's complicated."

"No, it's not."

"I've been spending a lot of time with her, that's true. Yes, I kissed her, and yes, it was awesome. I got a text from her brother telling me he'd kick my butt if I touched her, and he was a millimeter away from making good on that promise. I thought I was doing the right thing by pretending nothing happened, but it all blew up in my face."

She points at me. "You're afraid of Craig?"

That, and the fact that I want to make my mother proud, but I don't want to get into that right now. Rachel knows about Mom's illness and would understand my need not to stress her out, but I just don't have the emotional energy to tackle that conversation with her.

"Have you seen Craig lately? He's huge. Remember back in middle school when Freddie Templeton was crushing on Sam?"

"Yeah, Sam was so excited she was going to have her first boyfriend, even though I knew he was bad news."

"Ha. Craig knew he was a player and wasn't about to let him near his sister. I saw firsthand what his wrath is capable of. That poor dude transferred to another school because of Craig."

"That was a long time ago, but I guess now, he's only trying to protect her from your reputation. You must show him you're not like Freddie. Prove to him he's wrong, that there is a Southern gentleman inside you begging to show up." She nudges my side.

I scoff. "And you're going to be around to put a bag of frozen peas on my black eyes?"

"I think she's worth a few bruises. Don't you?"

"Yeah." She's totally worth whatever Craig throws my way. "In fact, Craig had a really good chance to whip my butt when he caught me sleeping with—"

"Excuse me?"

"Forget I said that."

Her eyes are as big as saucers. "No. Frickin'. Way."

"Nothing happened."

Through a round of giggles, she says, "Sure thing, buddy. Whatever you say. But I told her there's no way you kiss that good."

I cover my chest with my hands. "Hurtful. Maybe *you* were the problem."

She punches me on the arm. "Maybe we weren't meant to be."

I nod, letting her words of wisdom sink in. "What do I do now?"

"You yank up your big-girl panties, get in line at the booth, and blow her mind... again. And it wouldn't hurt if you'd go ahead and fess up to everyone, you big ole chicken."

"I'm more like a donkey than a chicken."

Rachel stares at me for a moment before she deadpans, "Truer words were never spoken."

"If I kiss her again, I don't know if I can stop." I blow out a breath. "This goes deeper than Craig's beef with my bad rep. About a month ago, I went to visit him at college. They were having this big frat party."

When I pause, Rachel motions for me to continue.

"Anyway, I got a text from my father telling me my mother re-lapsed. I was in a major funk, so Rocky, one of Craig's new college buddies, took it upon himself to shove liquor at me, thinking it would help me forget my problems. Then the jerk started talking about meeting Samantha when he visited their house one weekend."

She gasps as she clamps a hand over her mouth.

"Yeah, the things he said he did with her... Let's say I didn't han-dle it well. The campus police came and were about to arrest me when Craig stepped in. The cops let me go, and Rocky told him this lie about *me* wanting to take advantage of Samantha. Craig believed him because it sounded like something I would do. He decided I was no good and would never be allowed around his sister, even as a friend." I shake my head, still not believing it. "He completely be-lieved Rocky, and word got back to my parents about the fight and the near arrest."

"Wow. Just wow."

I snort. "No kidding."

Rachel nods as she stares out the window. "I think if you come clean to Samantha about why you've been so standoffish, I know she would understand, and she'd be able to tame Craig. And your par-ents..."

"Dad needs to focus on Mom right now. But you did make me realize something. I'm no longer afraid of Craig." After a moment of silence, I admit the real problem. "I'm afraid of Sam."

I feel like a weight has been lifted off me. Yes, part of my hesitan-cy was Craig, but most of it was my fear of Sam-Man not feeling the same way I do.

After a deep breath, I ask, "What if she doesn't see me as more than a pest, especially after everything that has happened?"

Covering my hand with hers, Rachel says, "I think you should at least try. If you need my help, let me know. As you are aware, I'm pretty good at planning things."

"It would never work. I'm no good for her. She deserves way better than me. She should be with someone who can be everything she needs."

"Hmm," Rachel says as she mulls over my words. "I think you don't give yourself or Samantha enough credit, but what do I know? Right now, we need to get back to school. With any luck, Brody and Jared have finished constructing the booth and the only thing left to do is paint it."

"Yeah, but remember Mason's helping too." I use air quotes around the word *helping* to emphasize how little he's probably able to contribute. "You've obviously never seen him with a hammer. He's much more comfortable with a protractor."

Through a round of giggles, she says, "Let's go."

I gun the engine and take off back toward the school. "This ride is sweet."

"Yeah, but don't get used to driving it."

Chapter Forty-Five

Samantha

Kissing lots of guys is supposed to be fun, but this mystery-guy plan sucks. And if I get sick from one of them, it's going to be Rachel's fault. The booth is built, and there is a line of guys wrapped around the room, waiting for us to start our charity kissing booth. But my heart pounds in my chest as I find it hard to breathe while I contemplate kissing a bunch of random guys. Kissing Mason was awkward enough in private. This will be unbearable.

The noise around me pounds in my ears until I can't take it anymore.

"Stop!"

The commotion in the room stills as all eyes stare at me. Rachel cocks her head to the side as she waits for me to continue. Out of the corner of my eye, I see Samuel and Mason walking toward us. Mason waves a dollar bill in front of his face. Samuel acts like he ate a bag of nails.

Me, too, Mule.

Samuel grabs his cousin's arm and whispers something in his ear. Mason shakes his head, then mouths "back off" to Samuel and yanks his arm from Mule's grip. Samuel storms away like a petulant child. Before he turns the corner, he glances back, and we stare at one another. He stuffs his hands into his pockets while he rests his back against a wall.

I stiffen my spine and focus on Mason, who has suddenly gone pale. Whatever Samuel said got him all messed up.

To Rachel, I say, "I can't... I mean, I don't want to do the kissing booth anymore."

Walking up to Mason, I gulp then blow out a breath. Before I can talk myself out of it, I say, "I know it was you. You kissed me at the dance. Right?"

My pleading expression must make it obvious that I don't want to go through with this. He's off the hook if he will just play along. He blinks, then as he rocks back and forth on his heels, he winks. "Yep, it was me."

A collective gasp travels through the room.

Paige bounces toward us as cheerfully as ever. "You two are perfect for each other."

Brody saunters up behind Mason and claps him on the back, sending him stumbling forward. "Dude, I didn't know you had it in you."

With a furrowed brow, Samuel does a slow, unenthusiastic clap like he's pretending to be happy even though he knows it's all for show. Even from where I'm standing, I can see his jaw muscles clench.

Mason gives me a gangly hug then a searing-hot kiss, making my lips burn, which results in the typical "aww" from Paige. "Call me later?" he asks, knowing good and well there will never be anything between us.

"Sure." I watch as he saunters back to Samuel, who acts like he could spit fire. Mason pops Samuel on the back in a playful way, but he shoves Mason aside. I hope I didn't cause a rift between them because I would feel awful if I messed up their relationship.

My guilt leaves me, and I sink onto the floor as I realize my plan didn't work. Mule didn't cave. What is wrong with him? I'm so disappointed with Samuel right now I could scream. He hasn't changed at all. Mule is as stubborn as his nickname.

Paige grabs her purse and walks away from us. "It's been fun, but I'm ready to have my own make-out party. See you tomorrow. Leave the booth, and I'll help tear it down this weekend."

Rachel turns in circles as she watches people disperse. Her expression changes from shocked to annoyed, and I guess it's because we didn't use the booth that she worked so hard on, not to mention make any money for charity. I make a mental note to figure out some way to get the school involved in a fundraiser this spring, maybe for the American Cancer Society in honor of Mule's mother.

She clears her throat, and a sputter escapes her throat, bringing me out of my thoughts. "Mason? Really?" She snorts like she doesn't believe me then motions with her head. "Let's get some food. I'm starving."

As I follow Rachel out of the building, tears threaten to spill down my cheeks. Mule watched me lie to my friends and say his cousin kissed me, and he did nothing to correct me. He did absolutely zilch to set the record straight. So much for my fairy-tale ending.

Chapter Forty-Six

Samuel

Mason and I slog through the school parking lot toward my truck. He whistles a Bruno Mars song, which makes me almost as angry as the fact he kissed Samantha and she seemed to like it. He might not be the guy she was seeking, but she liked his kiss anyway. The way she didn't push him away, I would think...Yeah, she was into it. *Please tell me I don't kiss like my cousin. Ick.*

Out of the blue, I break the silence. "Why'd you have to do that?"

"Why didn't you stop me?"

I grab his collar and sling him around to face me. "I'm serious. Leave her alone."

He tries to push me off, but I've got a good hold of his shirt. "Man, let me go. I can't help it that she and I connected."

I let go and give him a shove, sending him stumbling on his heels for a second. "Yeah, so?"

He rests against my truck, legs crossed at his ankles. "Aren't you forgetting something?"

"I don't think so."

"You lost the bet." Mason's eyes twinkle.

Kicking a rock out of the way, I try to act nonchalant. "I don't care about the bet anymore."

He chuckles. "Of course you don't because you lost."

"No, I didn't lose. I know it wasn't you at the dance."

"The bet was she would say it was me, and she did. Besides, you are being ridiculous."

I kick the tire so hard this time, I think I break a toe. "No, you are. And the bet was that your *kiss* would make her think you were the mystery man."

"Pfft. Details." Mason stares up at the darkening sky and lets out a groan. "I don't know if you've got this through your thick skull or not, so I'll use words at a third-grade reading level. You messed up, dude... again."

I press my eyes with the heels of my hands as a feeling of dread comes over me. I take a few breaths to calm my nerves. None of this is Mason's fault, and I'm a jerk for taking it out on my cousin. "I'm afraid."

"Of what?"

With one good jerking motion, I unhook the tailgate and sit on it, making the truck bounce from my weight. Mason sits beside me.

"I like her."

He snorts. "You said that already. There's got to be more."

With my feet dangling off the tailgate, I say, "I'm afraid of how I feel. I'm afraid Craig will beat me up. I'm afraid I'll disappoint my mom for getting in a fight, and... I'm terrified Samantha won't feel the same way."

He points at me. "You're *chicken*?"

"Pretty much. Her brother is about the size of my truck. I will sing soprano for the rest of my life if I make a move." I use air quotes to emphasize my words.

"You do have a valid point on that, but love hurts, man. And... Samantha likes you. Don't worry about her not sharing the same feelings. I promise you this. She. Likes. You."

Warmth washes over me. Other than my mother living fifty more years, nothing would make me happier than to know Samantha saw me as more than a friend or her tutor.

"She's worth being completely neutered for. You know that." He gives me a "don't lie to me, cuz" expression.

"Yeah." I smile at him.

Mason stares at the sky. The sun has begun to set, and it's the perfect combination of pinks, oranges, and yellows. Like a snapshot, my mind files the image away for future use.

"Dude, say goodbye to your balls."

"Ha ha. You should be a comedian."

Jared jogs up and plops on the tailgate next to Mason, his legs swinging so much, the entire truck rocks. "So, that was fun."

When we don't respond, he adds, "Is this the brooding hero bus, or what?"

I roll my eyes.

"Shut up, Jared," Mason says.

Thanks, cuz.

The door creaks open again as Rachel and Samantha come out of the school. They freeze when they see us in the parking lot. Mason waves. Rachel manages a semi wave and marches off to her car. Samantha and I share a moment before she breaks away to get inside her car. It's Tuesday. I know where she's going.

I jump off my tailgate. "If you guys don't mind, I need to use my truck as a vehicle."

"Is that a hint?" Jared asks Mason.

Samantha's car speeds out of the parking lot.

"Come on, guys."

To Mason, Jared asks, "Are you hungry?"

He shrugs. "I could eat."

"Can you have this conversation somewhere else?" I ask as I watch Samantha's taillights get fainter.

"Burger Heaven?" Jared always wants to eat there. He has no imagination.

"Naw. Sushi?"

She's getting away. "Guys..."

"I'm not a fan of sushi," Jared says to Mason.

"Barbeque?"

"Hey!"

Jared and Mason stare at me with disgust. How dare I interrupt their discussion about Nashville restaurants.

"Off my truck. I have to talk to Samantha."

They both stare at me like I'm speaking Mandarin.

"Now."

"Whatever, bruh. All you had to do was say something." Jared slides off the tailgate.

Mason hops off, giving me a one-arm hug and chest bump. "Don't do anything I wouldn't do."

Maybe if I hurry, I'll catch her before she goes inside the Nashville Youth Center because I would put money on the fact that she's headed there.

No such luck. By the time I arrive, she's already slipped inside the ratty gym. I park my truck next to her VW Bug and wait. Wait for Samantha to come out. Wait to tell her how I really feel. I exit my truck and prop my foot against the tire. To pass the time, I text Mason.

Me: *Gonna do it.*

Mason: *Proud of you, cuz.*

Me: *Any words of wisdom?*

Mason: *Hmm. Always be yourself. Unless you can be Batman. Then always be Batman.*

I laugh out loud at my dorky cousin. While I wait for Samantha, I get back in my truck and lean my head against the headrest to take a quick nap. The last few days have been crazy. Thank goodness Mom's doing better and the antibiotics are working. Crisis evaded, and I'm not going to stress her out ever again.

With clarity I haven't felt before, I'm ready to tell Samantha how I feel and apologize for being so stupid. I should never have been afraid of Craig in the first place.

An engine revs, jolting me back to reality. I must have fallen asleep. Samantha's car zooms away, and I slam my fist on my car door. Right when I get up the nerve, she jets away from me. That's my luck. She doesn't want to talk to me. That much is obvious. The next best thing is to follow her to her house.

In my rush to get out of the parking lot, I almost back up into another car. I hit the brakes, and my tires screech. In the distance, the taillights of the VW Bug shine. I ram the gas pedal to the floorboard to catch up to her. She drives through the streets of Nashville toward her home, with me tailing two cars behind. She passes the turnoff to her neighborhood.

Her turn signal blinks, and she drives her car into Green Hills Estates. She's probably going to Rachel's. Instead of turning into Rachel's driveway, however, she turns left into Mason's, and my heart sinks. I screech to a halt two houses down from his and watch her practically float up the sidewalk. She doesn't even have to knock before he opens the door. He plants one on her cheek, but it's not until Samantha wraps her arms around his neck and pulls him into a massive lip-lock that I lose it.

"Are you kidding me?"

No one hears my string of curse words, especially Mason and Samantha, because they've already scooted inside. When his bedroom light goes out, I punch the ceiling of my truck. If I don't have at least one broken bone in my hand, I'll be surprised.

He flat-out lied. Mason said she was into *me*, but then she shows up at *his* door, practically skipping the entire way. Now they are doing who knows what up there in his room. This cannot be happening. But it is.

Chapter Forty-Seven

Samantha

Mason and I sit on the floor of his room as we relive the night. It was a disaster, all because of Mule's pride. "He has some nerve following me all over the place."

Mason turns on the television, and we start one of his race car games. I don't care what it is as long as I'm able to drive fast without any consequences.

"Remind me, why are we doing this?" he asks as he starts the game.

"Your cousin can't have it both ways. I want him to suffer a little bit. It will be good for him. Thanks for going with the pivot in the plan. I could not deal with all those guys. Blech."

"I still don't like messing with his head." He runs my race car into the wall.

"How long do we need to sit here in the dark pretending to make out?"

I check the time on my phone. "I'd guess at least fifteen minutes."

"Oh, is that how long it takes to—"

My ears burn with embarrassment. "No! I mean, I don't know. It seems like a long enough time. Maybe he'll get bored and go away."

His phone buzzes, and he glances at the screen. "Not hardly. It's Samuel. He wants to know if he can come over." He crawls over to the window and peeks out. "He's pacing back and forth out front, and if he doesn't watch it, he's going to rip all his lovely locks out by the roots."

"Serves him right."

Mason turns off the game and turns on Netflix. "If you plan on hanging out here until he leaves, you better settle in because you're going to be here awhile."

"Ugh. How about one of the *Iron Man* movies?"

"You read my mind. We may have to watch them all before Cranky McCranky leaves. We could study if you want."

Eye roll. "No, I do not want to study."

Thirty minutes into the second movie, Mason is curled up in a ball on the floor, snoring. I sneak a peek out his window, and I don't see Samuel's truck anywhere, so I pick up my purse, tiptoe through the hallway, and go out to my car.

Samuel sits propped up against my car with his eyes closed. He has a godlike appearance, with the glow of the moon illuminating through his hair onto his face. A slight snore filters through the quiet night.

"What are you doing here?"

Samuel falls over at the sound of my voice.

Chapter Forty-Eight

Samuel

Her voice through the quiet night wakes me from my snoozing position against her car. I jump, my bones stiff from sitting on the hard driveway for hours. "Hey."

"Hey," Samantha says, walking toward me as she motions with her hand to shoo me away from her car. "Again, what are you doing here?"

"I had to talk to you. It couldn't wait."

Glancing around, she asks, "Where's your truck?"

I point down the street. "On the cul-de-sac. I figured if you saw my truck here, you'd never leave, and I *really* need to talk to you."

Sam-Man stares at me like she sees right through me. "So talk. Make it fast because I'm in a hurry. I have a Trig test in the morning, remember?"

"That didn't stop you from doing whatever with Mason."

Slow as molasses, she turns to stare at me. "Green isn't a good color on you. Go home."

As she continues toward the driver's side door, I catch her arm and rotate her to face me. "I've been a big idiot."

"I already know that. I'm not *that* dumb." Sam-Man tries to inch around me, but I hold her closer to me, pinning her against her car.

"You're not dumb."

As she dips her chin, her hair falls over her face. I sweep a lock of hair away and tuck it behind her ear. She swallows. It's now or never. I can't back out this time because if I do, I'll never get another chance. I'll lose her forever, and it's not because I think she's into my cousin. He wouldn't do that to me. I'm afraid I'll lose her to the next

235

idiot who shows her attention, and it will kill me to see her with anyone else when she should be with me. It's time to get rid of my fears and do something.

I trail feathery, light kisses over her neck, all the way to the other side, then work my way up to her ear. Her body trembles, and I hold her tighter, one hand behind her head, the other on her waist, drawing her toward me. She comes to me without hesitation.

Cheek to cheek, I whisper in her ear, "You're the one for me." I move my mouth to graze her jaw. We are nose to nose, and if I don't kiss her right now, I'm going to explode. Holding back the urge to crash into her with a massive lip-lock, I force myself to place a soft, gentle kiss on her lips. Another one. A third. That's as much restraint I have before I claim her mouth with mine, and our tongues dance together, like our bodies did on the dance floor. Her moans are going to be the death of me.

I hold on for dear life while she makes a mess of my hair. She can rip it out for all I care. We come up for air but dive right back in. *Yes! This is happening.* All my pent-up feelings for her from the last seven years are unleashed in two heavenly minutes, and I never want this to end.

She places a hand on either side of my face, and I could gaze into those eyes forever.

Chapter Forty-Nine

Samantha

Finally! That's more like it. If only he hadn't made me play this stupid game, we could have been doing this all the time. Our breaths mingle together as we stand in silence until a white four-door car drives by really slow, and Mule jumps back from me like my touch electrocuted him. He watches the car as it passes by.

Unbelievable.

He'll never change. Heat rises up my neck, and there's nothing he could say to make it better. Backpedaling to get away from him, I trip over the edge of the driveway. He grabs my arm and catches me before I tumble. His prickly contact infuriates me.

I shove his hands away. "Don't touch me."

He has the nerve to seem completely innocent, like he hasn't done anything wrong. He steps toward me again. "Sam-Man."

"You are still afraid to be seen with me."

Taking another step toward my car, I inhale one more deep breath before I turn to him. My lower lip trembles even though I'm trying my hardest to control the involuntary twitches by biting on it. He reaches for me, but I swat his hand away.

"It's not that."

I finally work up the nerve to glare at him. "It is." My stupid voice cracks.

"Sam-Man, I—"

"Shut up. I'm sick of this."

Trying to catch my breath, I lean over the hood of my car, my hair falling over my face. Through my hair, I notice he hasn't moved.

He's frozen in place, hands fisted at his sides. "I'm not good enough for you, am I?"

His mouth drops open. "That's not it at all."

He walks toward me but stops after I give him the death stare.

"You're embarrassed. That's why we've never been seen together in public. We study in private. We hardly talk at school, and you even wanted to kiss me in private, but that wasn't even private enough."

With a pained expression, he shakes his head. "You know the reasons for studying in secret, and none of them have to do with me being embarrassed of *you*."

I laugh a deep, evil cackle. "I know the *excuses*. I thought we were good together, but you know what?" I shove him out of my way to unlock my car door. "I'd rather fail Trig and lose my scholarship than have to spend one more second with you."

The hurt etched across his face nearly breaks my heart, but I'm dying inside too. I was a fool for thinking there could ever be anything between us.

"Please let me explain."

"Shut up!" I yell. "You know, you are the smartest and most talented person I've ever met. How is it you're also the dumbest when it comes to being comfortable in your own skin? I like who I am. If that's not good enough, then that's on you."

This time, he lets me open my car door. After I get in, I slam it, not caring if his hand is in the way. I rev the engine, and Mule scoots his feet back in time for me to screech out of the driveway.

Chapter Fifty

Samantha

There are more doodles on my notebook paper than trig problems. I don't care about the difference between a cosecant and a cotangent. At this point, I don't care about passing or about getting that scholarship because I don't care about anything anymore.

I slam my notebook closed and collapse onto my bed, wishing I could rewind and make different decisions, like not asking for Samuel's help in the first place.

My phone rings, and if it's Mule calling one more time, I am going to throw my phone out the window. It chimes again. Ugh! I snatch it out of my purse and answer it. "What do you want?"

"Is that any way to talk to the most awesome brother in the world?"

I sigh. "Sorry. It's been a bad week. Really bad."

"What's going on?"

Using all my athletic ability, I throw a pillow across the room. "I don't want to talk about it."

"Sis, you either tell me what's going on, or I'm coming home, and you'll have to say it to me in person. It's completely your choice."

I sniffle again and wipe my nose on my sleeve. "He says he likes me, but he doesn't really like me. He kissed me and denied it. Then he kissed me again tonight, but he's still—"

"Hold on. Back up. Who?"

I groan. "Mule."

A string of curse words fall out of his mouth. "I'll be there within the hour."

"No, please don't."

"Too late. I'm out the door."

Gah!

Craig punches his fist into the palm of his other hand as I spill my guts. He mumbles to himself. I can't tell if he's angry at me for falling for Samuel or if he's furious at Samuel—or both. It doesn't matter. I'm mad at both of us too.

"I don't want to have anything to do with him anymore. If I fail Trig, I fail."

He sits on the edge of my bed and scrubs his hands through his dark hair. "Sis, how did this happen?"

I draw my knees to my chin and rest my cheek on them. "I don't know. He's not the person you think he is."

He scoffs. "Or he's exactly like I thought he was. He doesn't do relationships, sis."

"I know. I guess I'm not pretty enough or smart enough to be seen with him."

"Stop with the pity party. You're fine and plenty smart." He points a finger at me. "You didn't do anything wrong. Well, maybe one thing. You fell for King, and don't forget the whole edibles incident."

I snort while I nudge him. "Do you think Mom and Dad would homeschool me for the rest of the year?"

"Nope. Besides, you'd miss softball season."

He has a very good point, but my shoulders slump anyway. It would be so much easier if I didn't have to deal with any more of Mule until I leave for college, wherever that may be.

His phone buzzes. When he reads the message, he smiles. "It's a message from Mom. She got a text from the neighborhood association saying they caught the guy who was breaking into houses the other night. Seems like he was snooping around, and someone called the police. Glad that's over."

I punch my fist in the air in elation. "Yes! It wasn't just a raccoon that I heard after all. I called that in."

His eyes widen. "You? Was this before or after you got stoned?"

If looks could kill...

He side hugs me. "I'm kidding. I guess you don't need King anymore."

My triumphant attitude fades when he brings up Mule's name. "Why did he do this?"

Craig stares at the ceiling then groans. "I don't know." He nibbles on his bottom lip, like he's pondering his next words. "Uh, after I caught you and Mule in your room, he sent me a video of Rocky saying some really bad things to you."

"What are you—" All of a sudden, a glimpse of me telling Mule about the FaceTime video zips through my mind. "Oh my gosh. I sent that to Mule because we were talking about how awful Rocky is. I remember now. That guy is terrible."

"I'm beginning to see that now. I should probably apologize to King at some point." He shivers then adds, "I can't believe I just said that. Sis, after all that's gone down with King, do you have even the slightest feelings for him?"

That's the million-dollar question. After everything, there's no way I should have the slightest feelings left for him. Of course I can't.

Possibly.

Maybe.

I gaze into my brother's eyes, and it's like I'm staring at myself. He will know if I'm lying. He'll feel it before I do. Covering my face with my hands, I answer his question with the truth. "I do."

Chapter Fifty-One

Samuel

Samantha avoids me like the plague as she walks the halls at school. Paige also avoids me. At least Rachel doesn't hate me... yet. She waves as I travel alone through the hallways. She gives me a pitying smile as she zips past me toward Paige and Samantha.

Things might be different if I wasn't so skittish about cop cars after the incident at the frat house, but when that white car drove by, I went into fight-or-flight mode and jumped away from Samantha. It looked way too much like the one the campus police drive, and I had a serious flashback of getting arrested. She didn't give me time to explain.

Samantha hangs her head low, and her hair falls over her face as she saunters down the hall with her friends. She nods at whatever Paige says in her ear. Rachel puts her arm around Samantha and gives her a big squeeze.

Brody whacks me on the back with his backpack. We watch the girls as they huddle together.

"Wish I had some news on the female side of things, but Paige's lips are tight... quite unusual for her," Brody says.

"Didn't know she could hold it in."

He flicks my nose and asks, "Have you thought of a way to fix this mess you've gotten yourself into with Samantha?"

"Nope. Nothing is going to change her mind about me, and I can't blame her."

"Not with that attitude." He motions for Paige to come to him, which she does, bouncing across the hallway to give him a big smooch on the lips. He leans over to me and says, "Glad those lips aren't too tight."

Gross.

I enter my classroom and walk past Samantha, who pores over her Trig notes before our exam starts. She knows this stuff, but if she crams at the last moment, she's going to panic. I know she doesn't want to hear anything from my mouth, but I need to give her one last tidbit of help, so I whisper, "Don't overthink this. You'll be fine."

She jumps at the sound of my voice. Eyes trained on her desk, she mumbles, "Thanks."

When I hold out a pencil, she snatches it, being careful not to touch my hand. At least she acknowledged my presence. That's something.

Way before everyone else, I'm finished with my test, as usual. Out of the corner of my eye, I watch Samantha as she goes over each question for the third time. Her knee bounces, and I'm pretty sure I saw a bead of sweat trickle down the side of her face. Sam-Man slams her pencil on her desk and lets out a big breath of air. As if she is trying to read my thoughts on what to do, she glances over at me, then back at her paper, and picks up her pencil again. It hovers over her paper.

No, Samantha. Don't change anything. Don't do it. You've got this. She shakes her head and lowers her pencil then clasps her hands on her desk. *Whew. That's my girl.*

"Time's up, class," Mr. Henderson says to the chagrin of most of the students. He smirks as he collects the exams. When he gets to Samantha's desk, he practically has to pry the test from her grasp. "I'm sure you did fine."

I know she did.

"I know all of you are dying to know how well you did, so I'll have them graded by the end of the day and posted on the outside of my door using your student ID."

The bell rings, and everyone except Samantha and me dart out of the room. She sits frozen in her seat.

Mr. Henderson stares at her. "Would you like me to grade yours right now?"

Samantha nods so vigorously, I think her head is going to fall off.

"Sit tight. It will only take me a few minutes. You and your tutor play nice while I work on this."

No one should be envious of the evil stare she gives me.

I wave. "Hi, Sam-Man."

"Ugh, go away."

"I want to see how well you did."

She swings back around in her seat and crosses her arms over her chest. "Mr. Henderson, please make him leave."

He glances over his glasses. "The longer I take dealing with you two, the longer it's going to take me to grade your paper. So, if you can't be friendly, please at least ignore one another."

Peering behind herself, toward me, she replies, "I can ignore."

For the next five minutes, we sit at our desks, waiting as Henderson has a field day with his red pen. The more marks he makes on her paper, the more she squirms in her desk. While he grades her paper, I busy myself with a pencil drawing of her beautiful face. Finally, he writes something at the top of her paper and draws a big circle around it. He clears his throat.

She sits taller in her seat. I can't pry my gaze from her face. Please, let her pass. She deserves this more than anyone. He turns her paper around and shows her a big eighty-one in red at the top. With a squeal, she punches a fist in the air.

"Woo-hoo!" I jump out of my seat, knocking the chair over in the process, and before she has a chance to shove me away, I grab her in a bear hug to squeeze her tight. The warmth of her body pressed against mine sends a surge of energy through my spine.

On autopilot, I kiss her forehead. "I knew you could do it." I take a step back and gaze at her shocked expression. "I'm so proud of you."

She smiles then blinks before she pushes away from me and bounces up to Mr. Henderson.

He taps on his keyboard. "Let's see what your GPA is now."

"It's 3.1." If he didn't realize I had already calculated it, he seriously underestimates my math skills. He stares a hole through me. Sometimes I can't make my brain stop.

"Keep up the good work," he says, beaming like a proud pop.

She gives him a side hug then runs out of class.

Henderson looks at me and laughs. "I don't know what you did, but you're good. Want to tutor again next semester?"

"Nope. I mean, no, sir." I never want to tutor anyone ever again—unless it's Samantha, of course. I'd teach her how to paint if she asked me to.

I float through the hallway on a high from her grade. When I approach Mason standing by his locker, I say, "Hey, cuz."

He gulps as if he's afraid I am going to throw a punch at him.

"Mace, I'm sorry about everything that's happened. You're the closest thing I have to a brother, and I don't ever want to mess that up."

Mason drops his books on my foot, and we both laugh. He holds out a fist for me to bump, and I gladly do it. A huge weight lifts off me because I hate how I treated my cousin.

While I help him retrieve his books, he says, "I heard Aunt Amie is doing better."

"She's so much better. Thanks for asking."

We stand and stare at each other. "What about Samantha?"

I scratch the back of my head. "Not good, but I sure could use your assistance winning her back. Want to help your dumb cousin?"

With a wide grin, he says, "It would be my pleasure." He punctuates his words with a low bow. He is so dorky.

When he straightens from bending, I wrap an arm around my cousin. "Let's see if Rachel will help too. Oh, and Mr. Henderson likes you more than me, so perhaps you could ask him for a tiny favor."

"Pfft. I've got this. All you need to do is keep calm and divide like terms."

We fist-bump as I let out a huge belly laugh. Now that the stress of Samantha's test is over, it's time to win her back.

Chapter Fifty-Two

Samantha

This is crazy, but I don't even dread being in Trig class today. I'm still riding a high from passing my last exam and having a GPA good enough to keep my scholarship, but no matter how hard I wish things were different, I still care for Samuel. I hate myself for feeling this way, but it's the truth.

I have to get over him. And he had the nerve to hug me when I passed the test. *Stop sending me mixed signals!* He cares enough to keep me pining for him, and it makes me so angry, I could spit nails. I feel him staring at me, and that irritates me so much I can't see straight.

Mr. Henderson places the dry erase marker on the tray and clears his throat. "It has come to my attention that there is some unfinished business between two classmates."

Uh-oh.

He motions to Samuel. "Go ahead. It's the least I can do since you held up your end of the bargain."

Samuel walks to the front of the class. He opens the door, and Brody, Jared, and Mason enter with Rachel and Paige behind them.

I mouth, "*What is going on?*" to Paige, and all she does is wink.

Rachel stands, holding a large poster board in her hands. "Hey, y'all, remember the kissing booth we were going to do?"

A few grumbles filter through the room. I sink into my chair, knowing I was the culprit who ruined their fun.

"There is one person who really wanted to participate." She motions to Samuel.

The guys in the room groan, but the girls squeal when Samuel peels out of his hoodie, revealing a T-shirt that says, "Fibonacci, as easy as 1.1.2.3." *I can't believe I know what that means.*

"You all know me as the player who gets the girls," Samuel says.

The guys whoop it up, and the girls let out woo-hoos. Mr. Henderson shakes his head like he can't believe he's letting this happen. And why *is* he letting this happen?

"Or the go-to guy when you need... party supplies."

The room goes wild, except Mr. Henderson, who scowls.

"Or the guy whose mom has cancer."

It's now completely silent other than a few whispered words. Not many people know about his mother, but they do now. His honesty about his mother's health makes my anger toward him melt. For him to bare his soul about that is humbling and atypical for him.

"Yeah, surprise. I have some secrets." He glances around the class. "The last few weeks have been a bit strange for me, but I'm ready to come clean on some things."

He points to Rachel, and she walks around like one of those girls who shows everyone the boxing round. She holds a sign with the number one hundred forty-two on it. "That's my IQ."

A collective gasp goes through the room, including from me. I never thought he would admit how high his IQ is to anyone, let alone a room full of classmates, some of whom are filming this to post on their social media accounts.

Rachel throws that sign onto the floor, and the sign behind it shows the number eighteen. "That's the number of college credits I've already earned."

"No way," a guy yells from the back of the room, causing a roar of laughter. It even gets a chuckle out of Mr. Henderson.

Samuel grins and holds his hands up in defense. "I know. I'm a geek. It's part of who I am. And I scored a thirty-six on the ACT."

A massive groan comes from Mr. Henderson.

Mason raises his hand. "I did, too, for that matter."

Rachel smacks him in the chest with the sign as she raises a new sign with the number four on it.

After Samuel clears his throat, he adds, "That's the number of paintings I've won awards for."

I don't hear anyone gasp louder than myself. Rachel holds up a fourth sign with a number two on it. "That is the number of times I've kissed the girl of my dreams."

Oh my gosh.

"It's me!" a cheerleader yells. *Not on your life, girl.*

"I made a huge mistake. At first, I thought I was too cool to be smart and creative and in love with the most wonderful person I have ever known. She's athletic and funny and smarter than she realizes. But really, I was terrified she wouldn't feel the same way. I guess I still am."

I cover my face with my hands as I sink down in my chair in hopes people don't see my freak out.

"If Samantha Baughman would come up here, I think I owe her a dollar for a kiss."

My ears ring from all the hands pounding on the desks. Even Mr. Henderson laughs and claps.

Glancing over at Paige, Rachel motions with her head for me to go forward. And in typical fashion, tears stream down her face. "Go," she yells. "Go get him before someone else does." She drags me out of my desk chair and shoves me toward the front of the class.

"Sam-Man, Sam-Man, Sam-Man," the class cheers as sweat tickles my back, and my ears are on fire.

Mule gets the biggest grin on his face. I wish I could smile back, but I'm too embarrassed to have any other emotion. When I get close to him, he grabs me around the waist until our bodies are squished together. Tons of catcalls surround us.

"Kiss, kiss, kiss."

Oh, for crying out loud. Mule is holding me in front of the entire class and Mr. Henderson. I'm sure my teacher's going to tell my father. I gaze into Mule's eyes.

"I'm so sorry. I'll never hurt you again." He's being so honest in front of everyone. This is a huge step for him.

While I appreciate all the truth bombs, I'm not going to let him off that easy. "Yeah, yeah. Until the next time you are embarrassed of me."

"Burn," Brody and Jared say at the same time.

"Ooo." I love how the crowd doesn't let him off easy either.

His pretty face turns an unusual shade of pink, and I swear I see a piece of his soul drop to the floor because I didn't immediately rush to forgive him on the spot. It's time Mr. Know-It-All gets schooled.

The bell rings, and Mule's mouth turns down into a pathetic pout. If I don't put him out of his misery soon, he might cry in front of the entire class.

Mr. Henderson points to the door. "All right, fun time is over. Get out of here before I assign you homework."

Everyone jumps up and scoots past us. Mr. Henderson clears his throat. "I'm going to lunch. Mr. King, you owe me for the rest of your life."

"Yes, sir."

As soon as he leaves and only Mule and I are left in the classroom, I cross my arms over my chest. "You thought you could embarrass me in front of the whole class and I would forget how much you hurt me?"

He swallows hard and stares at his shoes, his expression like a five-year-old's who dropped an ice cream cone. "Sam, I didn't know how else to make it up to you. You said I was embarrassed of you, and I wanted to show you I wasn't. I never meant to make things worse."

I chew on my lip while he bends down and picks up the posters Rachel left on the floor. As much as he deserves for me to push him away, even I can't take the wait anymore.

When he stands back up, I hold out my hand. "Where's my dollar?"

He freezes with his mouth hanging open then closes his eyes before he blows out a breath. With a belt of laughter, he shoves a hand in his jeans front pocket to retrieve a dollar bill. "I guess I deserve that."

"And more." I grin and give him a quick peck on the cheek. I snatch the dollar from him. He cradles my face with his hands, and when our lips meet, nothing else matters.

The kiss is awesome, even if it is a lot more PG than our first one. With a twinkle in his eyes, he pecks my nose. "I have one more surprise."

I shake my head. "No more, please."

"Guess who is going to Auburn with you?"

I'm sure my eyes are bugging out of their sockets. "Really?"

He nods. "Yep."

"You assume I upped my SAT scores enough."

"I know you did."

Two cheerleaders standing in the doorway groan as they catch sight of us. Samuel wraps an arm around me, like he couldn't care less who is watching. *Finally!* And to think he was afraid of me. That's the funniest part of it all.

I wrap my arms around his neck and squeeze the life out of him. His arms encircle my waist, and I could stay like this forever, but we're both going to be late for our next class. So we toss the posters in the trash then dash out into the hallway. After one more quick peck on the lips, we head in opposite directions.

From the other end of the hallway, Samuel yells, "I really do think you are sec-c."

"You're such a dork, but I think you are cute as pi. And I love you too."

He punches a fist in the air as he turns the corner.

Best day ever.

Chapter Fifty-Three

Samuel

My heart is about to beat out of my chest. I got her back. I made a complete fool of myself in the process, but I don't care. I love her, and nothing else matters. As we walk hand in hand toward my truck after school, I think I can fly.

"How does it feel to come out of the closet, so to speak?" She smiles at me.

"It's amazing." I help her in my truck and drive her home, never letting go of her hand the entire way. Nothing could wipe the grin off my face.

She leads me inside her house, and I'm reminded of the last time I was here. That was fun until it wasn't.

In the kitchen, Samantha turns to me, and with a slight grin, she asks, "So, you were afraid of me?"

Right when I open my mouth to answer, Craig saunters toward us, making my confidence shrink. I'm still a little intimidated by her huge brother, if I'm being completely honest.

He puts his arm around Samantha and scuffs the floor with his boot before he says to me, "I want you to know you were right about Rocky. I am sorry."

Sam-Man pops her brother on the back. "See? That wasn't so hard now, was it?"

Craig grunts as he sticks out his hand for me to shake. We do the bro-hug, back-slap combo, and I'm glad we can be friends again.

Sam-Man pulls us both close. "Aw... this is so sweet." To me, she adds, "You know he cries at Hallmark movies, right?"

Craig's mouth drops open, and he sputters before he says, "I thought that was our little secret."

She giggles. "You deserve it."

"I guess I do."

"You think?" I ask, shaking my head. "We've known each other forever, dude. You *should* trust me a little more than some guy who is only interested in partying."

Staring at the floor, he says in a muffled tone, "I know."

I sneak a peek at Samantha, and she's as shocked as I am. But if I have learned anything from the last few weeks, it's that holding a grudge sucks.

To test my theory that Craig is really going to stay out of Samantha's business, I give her a hard kiss on the lips then glance over at Craig, who has ten emotions running across his face, but none are anger.

"I'll still kick your butt if you hurt my sister."

I nod because I know *he* would, and I also know *I* won't give him the opportunity. She wraps her arms around me, and I feel like the luckiest guy in the world.

"To make it crystal clear, I think you are the sec-c-est guy to ever wear a dorky T-shirt."

I chuckle. "I guess I deserve that one."

"And more."

I hold up a finger. "It's a loaner from Mason for losing a bet."

"I don't even want to know what that means." She shakes her head and gives me another kiss. "Are you really into me?"

"I'm not being obtuse. You are really *acute* girl. I'm totally into you, Sam-Man."

"Aww. You are as sweet as 3.1415926."

Craig groans and gives his sister a side hug. "I'm out of here. You two dorks disgust me." He snaps his fingers. "Before I forget." He picks up an envelope from the kitchen counter. "This came for you today."

Samantha backs away from her brother, but I stop her with a hand on her back. I whisper, "Is that what I think it is?"

She nods. "I didn't want the bad news to come by email this time."

Craig waves the envelope in front of her face, and with shaking hands, she snatches it. He laughs at her hesitancy and says, "Open it."

In her ear, I whisper, "No matter what the score is, I'm... I'm so proud of you."

Sam takes a huge breath, staring at the envelope. From behind, I wrap my arms around her waist and kiss her cheek. She blows out a raspberry and rips into the envelope.

Please let it be at least eleven eighty.

She gasps and swings around to face me.

"Well?" Craig asks.

She shoves the notice into my hands. As fast as my brain can process, I read her scores then scoop her up into a big hug.

"You got six fifty in math, twelve hundred total."

"Woo-hoo!" Craig yells.

I knew she could do it. She slides her arms around my neck and holds me tight. "Thank you so much."

"*You* did this, so own it."

She plants her lips on mine, and much to the chagrin of her brother, I kiss her back. If Samantha likes me for who I am, I couldn't care less about the rest of the world. I don't need to be Einstein to realize I just made the smartest move of my life. Even an idiot genius like me can solve that equation.

Epilogue

Samantha
Nine Months Later

Sweat covers my palms and trickles down the back of my blue Tigers uniform while I stand at the free throw line. The Lady Vols wave their hands in the air to distract me, but I am laser focused on adding two more points to Auburn's score. The ref throws me the ball, and I twirl it around in my hands, once to calm my nerves, another time for good luck. I flick my gaze to the scoreboard. The sounds of the cheering crowd and my teammates fade away. I take a breath and blow it out as I calm my nerves.

I can do this.

Of course I can. I'm playing ball for my dream school and doing well in my classes, both achievements I never thought would happen a year ago. I'm living the dream I never thought I would.

Bounce, bounce. Bend knees. Arms over head. Release, and... swoosh. All net. *Oh yeah.* One more. *I can do this.* The second one hits the rim and teeters on the edge before it falls into the basket, and even through the cheers of nine thousand screaming fans, I hear one specific sec-c voice.

"Sam-Man!"

I find him in the stands where he always is and smile as I run to my position. He returns my grin, and I look away, getting my head back in the game. He'll be there for me when the game is over, like he always has been, like he always will be. Mule is everything I knew he could be, and so am I. Together, we can solve any problem that comes our way.

Acknowledgements

To the entire Red Adept Family, especially Lynn, Erica, and Darlene. I really appreciate all your help with this project.

To Kelly Ann and Jymie for always being there for me. I trust you to give me honest feedback, and you've never let me down.

To Mark and Maddie for being my entire world. Thanks for believing in me—and for the she-shed.

About the Author

After several decades of writing medical research documents, Cindy Dorminy decided to switch gears and become an author. She wanted to write stories where the chances of happy endings are 100% and the side effects include satisfied sighs, permanent smiles, and a chuckle or two.

Cindy was born in Texas and raised in Georgia. She enjoys gardening, reading, and bodybuilding. She can often be overheard quoting lines from her favorite movies. But her favorite pastime is spending time with Mark, her bass-playing husband, and Maddie Rose, the coolest girl on the planet. She also loves her fur child, Daisy Mae. She currently resides in Nashville, TN, where live music can be heard everywhere, even at the grocery store.

Read more at www.cindydwrites.com.

About the Publisher

Dear Reader,

We hope you enjoyed this book. Please consider leaving a review on your favorite book site.

Visit our site to find more quality books!

Read more at https://RedAdeptPublishing.com.